THE PARADOX OF HEROES

Volume I

Nicholas Hanna

PROLOGUE

The crowd stands on the platform at Grand Central Terminal, waiting for the Six Train to arrive. They're going uptown, and the board says five minutes. It's midautumn now; and the cool October chill can be felt, even down here. There are women in high-heeled boots chatting near the stairwell, and a mother trying to corral her children, who are playing too close to the edge. Businessmen in suits talk finance as they pass by. "M&M's!... Skittles!...One dollar!" shouts a kid selling candy, as he weaves in and out of the tightly packed commuters.

Everyone is immersed in their own little world. Some alone, staring at their phones; others in pairs, talking about work, or life, or love. They don't notice that there's one man who isn't doing anything. The man who is dressed in all black. The man who stands alone, making no sound, thinking only of the task at hand. As the train arrives, and they all pile inside — no one notices the assassin.

He stands in the middle of the subway car; staring straight ahead, and loosely holding on to the metal pole. As the train clatters through the dark tunnel, he takes no notice of the pretty redhead to his right. She sees him, though: a dark, brooding man, probably in his late-twenties. He's slighter taller than average, with broad shoul-

1

ders; his jet-black hair is buzzed low, and he has a close-cropped beard. Everything about him looks foreboding — except his grey eyes, they have a mystery to them that she can't quite understand. But those eyes never blink. They never move. He sees only one thing — the target.

As the train progresses through its stops, it finally reaches hers — 77th Street — and she gets off. She'll never see him again, and that's OK. *That's New York.* she figures; an endless stream of what-ifs and near misses. The small, fleeting loneliness she feels will pass in a block or two — it always does, she knows that. As she walks, she fixes her long, red hair into a messy bun; then, she climbs up the dirty metal stairs to the street. An icy blast of air hits her as she emerges from the dark subway tunnel — she shivers, and pulls her navy-blue peacoat tight around her — then she walks on, smiling to herself, thinking how much she loves New York in the fall.

ΔΔΔ

Back on the train, the target gets off at the next stop — 86th Street. He's an elderly man: bald on top, with long, wiry grey hair around the sides of his head. He carries a brown leather briefcase in his left hand, and adjusts his round glasses with the right. It's twilight now, and the street lamps are on. He crosses Madison Avenue, towards the park; he turns left on Fifth Ave, then goes down past the Met. He looks around, and sees no one else, so he ducks behind its high walls on the south side.

Now in the park, he opens his briefcase and removes the item that has caused him so much worry throughout the day: a small, red flash drive. He smiles, relieved that he's done it. As he puts it away, he turns the corner and bumps into someone: "Oh, sorry...excuse me..." He adjusts his glasses and looks up — that's when he sees him. His face goes pale, and he feels chills all over — he knows what will happen next.

△△△

After it's done, the assassin wipes the blood from his hands. There's a lot on his shirt, though — too much in fact — he got carried away again. He picks up his black leather jacket off the ground, and puts it on — he knows now to remove it first. As he walks back to the street, he puts the red flash drive in his pocket and continues south. But he can feel something wrong within him: even after the job's done, he doesn't feel...the way he used to.

He turns off, into the park, and finds a quiet spot to be alone: there, he sits on the ground and buries his head between his knees. He doesn't know how to make this feeling go away — and lately, it's been eating at him more and more. He thought that after this job was done, he'd feel better — but he doesn't. About an hour goes by, and he knows he must go; he's covered in blood, with a knife up his sleeve — he's being reckless, and he can't afford to do that.

As he walks back to the street, he sees a girl standing alone, staring at the bronze Alice in Wonderland statue. She's beautiful, with loosely-tied red hair, and in that moment he knows only she can help him. He walks over to her and smiles. She sees him, and smiles back. "I... I saw you on the train..." she says, blushing, "you looked like you were having a bad day." He looks around, then back at her, as his smile fades. "Do you wanna talk about it?" she asks, cheerfully, "Maybe I can help?"

He nods his head, but doesn't speak; then, he brushes a wayward red curl from her face. He leans in close, as though he has a secret to tell her: she trembles with anticipation — in her romantic heart, these are the moments she'd always imagined could happen. Then he kisses her, softly, on the lips; and all at once, everything stops. That's when she feels it — the sting of the knife. She looks down and sees the cold, bloody, steel blade as it's slowly pulled out. Her lip quivers as she falls to the ground, unable to speak. Through her tear-filled eyes, she sees him walk away — he only looks forward, as her world fades to black.

ONE

Boom! Danny woke with a shock! His heart was pounding. Straining his eyes to see, he looked around; but there was nothing except a dark, endless void. Was it the room? Was something wrong with him? Was he even awake? All of these things ran through his mind, as he frantically moved his eyes in all directions — he could see nothing, however, but the total blackness that enveloped him.

Where am I? he thought to himself, *I must be in my room...no, wait, I'm not home...or am I?...Where was I last night?* He struggled to decipher his surroundings, trying to get a glimpse of something familiar to him. Suddenly, there was a large flash of light, and another giant *boom*, as loud as a gunshot. "What was that?!" he yelled. Now, fully awake, his head pounded like a drum — but he still couldn't see. His heart began to race, as an anxious feeling took hold of him.

Flash! Boom! The flash was bigger this time. "Oh!" he cried, painfully, "Lightning!...It's lightning!...There's a window open!" His burning eyes were scanning all around, trying to make sense of this place. Another *flash,* as the room flooded with light. "There it is!" he exclaimed. There was a window, right above him. *I don't have a window over my bed?!* His mind was racing now.

Why can't I remember where I am?! The roaring thunder made him cringe in agony, as if a bomb went off beside his head.

His eyes slowly came into focus, as they adjusted to the darkness that surrounded him. He could faintly make out a dark-grey wall on his right side, parallel to him, with the cutout of the window directly above. He struggled to turn his head to the left, but could see nothing else. Suddenly, a more disturbing realization — he couldn't move his body!

"Hello?!" he shouted. Another blast of thunder caused him to recoil in agony: "Is anyone here?!" His screams were becoming more desperate: "I-I need help!... I can't move!" There was no reply: "Can anyone hear me?! ...I need help!" No one came: "Please!...Help me!" After several more unanswered cries, Danny realized he was alone. *What the hell is this place?!* His stomach was twisting in knots. *How'd I end up here?!*

△△△

More time passed; maybe five minutes, maybe twenty, he couldn't tell. It seemed like time had slowed down, or stopped altogether; but at last, he started to regain control of his body. He moved his fingers first, making sure each one was responsive; then his toes, they were coming back to him. Now he realized that something must have happened, and he was slowly recovering — but what could it be? *Was I in an accident?...Maybe I'm in the hospital?* His incoherent mind was trying to make sense of this strange situation. "I can do this..." he whispered to himself, "I can figure this out."

Danny was always very intelligent — and he knew

it. Growing up, he was usually the smartest kid in his class; he may not have been the most committed student, but when he tried, he easily bested his peers. Now, in his first semester at Carrington College — a small, private school in Upstate New York — he finally found a place where he felt challenged, motivated, a real desire to prove himself around others who were just as bright as he was. It also didn't hurt that his new roommate, Maverick Wright, was really cool. Danny wasn't exactly the type to make new friends easily — or at all, if he were being honest — but Mav was, and they quickly became best friends. The two were practically inseparable, but where was Mav now? *Is he looking for me?* Danny didn't know. All he knew was that right now, in this room, he was alone.

ΔΔΔ

Eventually, his elbows started to regain their mobility. Then his knees began to bend. It was happening, albeit slowly — he was starting to move again. Looking around, he saw more grey; but this time, he could faintly make out large stones in the walls, almost as if he were in a Medieval castle. No, that couldn't be it, that was stupid — he was just in his room, wasn't he? "Dammit!" he shouted, "Why can't I remember?!"

He tried to reassure himself: "OK, one thing at a time...I just need to stand up, and look around...then, it'll come back to me." Easier said than done, though. At least the lightning and thunder weren't troubling him as much as before; whatever had happened to him, the effects were wearing off.

Now, the real test. *Try to sit up.* He twisted and

turned, struggling to get onto his left side. *First step done.* Then he pulled his knees up to his chest, which seemed even harder. *Now the big one.* He stuck his legs out over the bed, and pushed up with his arms. "Yes!" he rejoiced, finally sitting upright. His back was facing the window; and although he desperately wanted to look outside, he decided that for now, this was good enough. His head was spinning and his vision was blurry: he needed to get his bearings *inside* first — whatever was out *there* could wait.

Waiting wasn't bad, though, it gave him time to think. *Where was I last?...How did I end up here?* Around him were four, solid stone walls, with the window to his back. "Wait, I must be missing something..." he muttered, "where's the door?" He tried looking more carefully, but it was hard to focus in the dark. Then another flash of lightning and he saw it, ever so briefly: the entire room lit up before him — no door. *How could there not be a door?...I got in here, somehow.* His mind was trying to put the pieces together: "So if there's no door, I musta come in through...the window?" He turned slowly on the narrow bed, being very careful not to fall off — if he did, he wasn't sure he could pull himself back up. "I can do this... I can do this..." he kept repeating, trying to calm his nerves.

One hand on the window sill: "Yes!...OK, I have it." He reached across and turned his body — two hands now: "Got it!" He pulled himself up, on his knees. The window was large: a rectangular cutout in the wall, with long, vertical iron bars — almost like a prison cell would be, or so he imagined. Grabbing the bars to steady himself, he looked outside: to his horror, he realized he couldn't have come in that way — he was at least five stories high!

To make things worse, he had a serious fear of

heights. Looking down through the bars, he felt light-headed, and his knees began to shake. His breathing became heavy, as he tried to find some explanation other than the one staring him in the face: he couldn't move, he couldn't remember anything, he was trapped in a room with no door, high up, in a strange place — he had been kidnapped! Taken! Abducted! He must have been — someone had put him here!

"Why me?!" he panicked, "What would anyone want with me?!" His breathing got heavier, as his whole body shook violently with fear. Then his knee slipped — *crash!* He fell backwards off the bed, onto the cold, hard floor. He cried out in agony as he landed on his right shoulder: "Aaahhh!...Why is this happening to me?!" He tried to steady his breathing. "Just stay calm..." he told himself, "you can get outta here...you can do this!"

Never one to wallow in defeat, he pulled himself up. He could stand now; shakily, yes, but it was still standing. For once, he thought being short might actually be a blessing: standing 5'6" never felt so great before, but in here, he was glad he didn't have to support a taller frame with these unsteady legs.

"First thing to do is check the walls...maybe the door is hidden." Each flash of light would illuminate the room, and help him on his search. He also got a rough idea of the area: "About twenty feet wide by...ten deep." This was the analytic Danny taking over.

Another sudden realization: the clothes he was wearing were his own. He wore a grey hoodie over a white T-shirt, and dark skinny jeans. His shoes were black-and-white Converse All Stars — he always wore Converse. These were his clothes alright, so he felt the pockets: no phone, no wallet, no keys. They must have been stolen by whoever brought him here. When he pulled back his left sleeve, however, he saw that his watch was still in place. *How could they've left this?* Danny's watch — his father's watch, actually — was his most prized possession. Why didn't they take it? After all, it was valuable — a black Rolex Submariner — it read '11:57' and it was still on his wrist, but why? *Maybe they didn't check?...Maybe they just got what they could and left?* He inspected the timepiece, trying to find a reason as to why it was still there. *No, they musta checked...they brought me here, after all.*

Nothing about this made sense; he searched everywhere, but there was still no way out. Whenever there was a brief flash of light, he would check the floor and ceiling for trap doors — but there weren't any. He moved the bed and checked under it — still nothing. As he tried to remember where he was last, and what he was doing, he heard a switch, and a green light turned on in the corner of the room. *It's a clock.* He checked his watch again: midnight. "A clock that turns on at midnight?" he puzzled, "No, it's not a clock, it's counting down...it's a timer." The timer started at fifteen minutes: "OK, this must be a prank...in fifteen minutes the door will open, then they'll all come in and say it was a joke." But, who were 'they' anyway? He decided to retrace his steps: if he could move now, then he should be able to remember, too. He sat on the edge of the bed and started thinking. *What's the last thing I remember?*

"I know, it's a school trip!" he yelled, "Yes, that's it!...Something about history, or culture...I remember now!" It was starting to come together: "OK, but *why* am I on this trip?" He probed his memory, trying to deter-mine his reason for being there. "Forget that for now..."

he told himself, "who else came along?...Was Mav here?... Yes, I remember, he was late!" Was it coming back to him? "But, he's always late...was he late here, or for something else?"

He struggled to think of anyone else he could remember seeing: "Wait...Mister Bell, he planned this thing...that must be why I'm here!" Professor Ignatius Bell was Danny's favorite teacher at Carrington — although they'd just met a few months ago, they became fast friends. Danny excelled in his advanced calculus class, but why wouldn't he? When it came to puzzles, or anything else that needed solving, there were few better. When Mr. Bell first told Danny of the upcoming cultural excursion, he wasn't really interested — but that soon changed when he found out who else would be going.

Ashara Jones — or Ash, as she liked to be called — sat next to Danny in class; though she'd hardly know it, he was always too scared to talk to her. He almost did once, when she asked to borrow a pencil; but he just sat there, frozen, with his mouth half-open, trying to remember words — any words — but none came out. Needless to say, she wasn't exactly swept off her feet.

Danny sat thinking about where Mav was, where Mr. Bell was, where Ash was — her, most of all — when his attention was brought back to the timer. It was in the final minute now, so he stood up and brushed himself off. He was ready to walk out and face everyone, who he was sure would all be lined up, waiting to laugh at him.

Final ten seconds now. "OK, guys, very funny!" he shouted, "You got me this time!" Five...four...three... *I hope Ash didn't see this...*two...*here it comes...*one...*click!* The timer hit zero, but to Danny's shock, no door revealed itself. Even worse, the walls on either side of him began to move...in...towards him — he was going to be crushed!

TWO

Theodore 'Teddy' Logan was at home, preparing to clean out his storage closet. "You've put this off far too long." he said, as he nervously opened the door: to his relief, the contents didn't all come crashing down on top of him. He surveyed the jumbled mess, contemplating the task at hand: "Right, top first." He reached for the bags and boxes on the top shelf, and began sorting through them. The pile to the left was garbage, useless stuff that nobody would want, while the pile on the right was for donations; in the middle were those things that he could not be parted from. There was nothing in that pile, not yet anyway — he would leave *that* box for last.

One hour went by, then two, and he managed to get everything else in the closet sorted and packed away. Now there was just one box left — the box in the back — the one he hadn't opened in...how long was it? He didn't remember; he didn't want to remember. In fact, he probably hadn't seen it since he put it back there eighteen years ago. He stared at that box, the one with 'MILES + STELLA' written in bold, black marker across the side. "This is good for now..." he muttered, as if he were trying to convince someone else, "I'll take the garbage out, box up the donation pile, then get some dinner."

Teddy never married; not that he didn't have the

chance, but every time things got serious, he ran. He wouldn't allow himself to get too close to anyone. His life wasn't his own; even the house he was living in wasn't really his — after Miles died, Teddy had basically assumed his life. He stepped into the void that was once occupied by his older brother, and in so doing, he went from a kid trying to figure it out, to a full-fledged adult, all in the blink of an eye. His entire life, all he ever wanted was to be like Miles. *Be careful what you wish for.* he thought now.

He took out the trash, and put everything else in a box by the front door marked 'DONATIONS', then he grabbed his keys and started outside; he paused briefly in the doorway and looked back, before closing it behind him. He climbed into his car — a blue Subaru STi — and set out to get some food. While driving, his thoughts were on that last box in the closet; then on to his brother, and the day that changed everything...

ΔΔΔ

What a day that was. Teddy was just twenty-two then, living in Miles' and Stella's spare room. It was a typical Thursday; nothing out of the ordinary. He was playing Playstation and Stella was buzzing around the house, when she decided to surprise Miles at work — he had been acting strange the past few weeks. It was probably just stress, she thought; but with all the changes lately, who could blame him? They hadn't been out in months, and she decided that a picnic at their old spot in the park would cheer him up — that always did the trick.

"I'll be back later, Teddy!" she announced, as she walked to the door, "You sure you can manage without me?"

"I got this." he smirked.

"OK…" she giggled, "good luck!"

Luck? Like he'd need any of that! *She clearly doesn't know who she's dealing with.* he thought, with all the confidence of a man in his early-twenties — guys that age always think they have it figured out.

A few hours passed by, and he realized she'd been gone a while. *They're probly just enjoying some alone time.* he assured himself. After all, they hadn't been 'alone' in months. Besides, Teddy had other things to worry about: he was newly graduated with a degree in mechanical engineering, and he was on the job hunt. OK, so maybe today he was playing Gran Turismo; but tomorrow, for sure, he would start 'adulting'. Anyway, what was the rush? He had just finished school, and had the rest of his life to figure things out.

But as more time passed without word from either of them, he got worried. He tried calling, but both of their cell phones went straight to voicemail — there was no answer at Miles' office, either. Something was wrong, he could feel it. It was just past nine o'clock, when there was a knock on the front door: he opened it, and saw two police officers standing on the other side — one man, tall and thin, probably mid-forties; and another who was slightly overweight, around Teddy's age.

"Are you…" the older one looked at his notes, "Theodore Logan?"

"Y-Yes…" he answered, nervously, "i-is everything alright?"

"It's about your brother…"

He didn't remember the rest of what was said, just the sinking desperation he felt while hearing it. They needed him to come down to the station and identify the bodies. Hit-and-run, they told him — a truck had lost control and ran into them as they crossed the street to Central Park. That was when Teddy knew his life would never be the same.

Coming back to reality, he looked up and saw red lights — he slammed on the brakes! The car skidded to a stop, halfway into the empty intersection. "Come on!" he screamed, "Get it together!...You're too old to act this dumb!" He swallowed the lump in his throat, and carried on when the lights turned green.

△△△

Later that night, after he'd finished eating, he went back to the closet: "Time to do this." He pulled the box out, opened it, and stared down onto a pile of old clothes, shoes, and DVDs: "This isn't so bad." As he sorted through the box, he put the clothes and shoes to the side and began fishing through the rest. "Nintendo 64!" he exclaimed, "And these games...Mario Kart, Goldeneye, Super Smash Brothers...all the classics!" His face turned red; he felt stupid for being so scared. "I can't believe I was afraid of all *this*..." he chuckled, "if I'd just grown a pair sooner, I coulda been playing with these years ago!" With a big smile and calm nerves, he continued exploring the newly found treasure chest.

The last thing in there was a Nike shoebox; when he opened it, he saw Miles' old work ID. It was a white badge with the words 'Millennium Technologies' written in blue lettering above the picture. "I guess you'll always be twenty-eight..." he sighed, as he looked at the mirror behind the door, "but not me." At forty, there was some grey in his thick, dark-brown hair, and a little more in the stubble around his chin — but he could easily pass for a man in his early-thirties.

There was an old cell phone in there too: a blue Nokia 3310. *Miles' phone.* He picked it up, and instinctively began pressing buttons: to his surprise, a red light started blinking at the top. "Wow..." he marveled, "these things really *are* indestructible." He put it down on top of the clothes, and continued his exploration.

After he'd reached the bottom of the box, he packed everything back inside, neatly — except the Nintendo, that he planned to set up on the big screen in the morning — but the phone made him curious: "Didn't I see an old charger, somewhere?" He tried to prod his memory: "Oh, crap!...I threw it out!"

Teddy flew down the stairs and out the front door: he went straight for the bag of junk that he'd tossed out so casually, earlier that night — he ripped it open so fast, he almost fell in! "Come on!" he yelled, as he frantically dug through the trash, "Where is it?!" Then he found it: "Yes!" But the feeling quickly vanished, when he noticed his now-awake neighbors giving him angry looks from their windows. "Sorry!...Sorry!" he shouted, "Lost my charger!" He held the cord high in the air as proof.

Once back inside, he plugged it into the wall and connected the other end to the phone — the red light stopped blinking and became solid: "This is crazy...what am I doing?" He felt anxious and scared — but mostly excited — he loved a good mystery as much as anyone. Just then, he caught a look at himself in the hallway mirror: he was covered in dirt and grime. "I need a shower..." he told his reflection, "I'll leave this to charge in the meantime." As he walked up the staircase, towards the bathroom, he just missed the light on the phone as it changed from red to green.

ΔΔΔ

The small, confined shower, combined with the severe, almost scalding-hot water, caused the bathroom to fill with steam. It was hard to see, and even harder to breathe; but Teddy didn't mind — he just relaxed in the heat. "*Ahhh...*" he turned off the tap, "*that* was what I needed." He got dressed, and stumbled towards the bedroom, half-asleep.

The phone! He quickly turned back as the thought popped into his head — he'd forgotten all about it! He rushed down the stairs and picked it up, but then he hesitated for a moment. *Is this an invasion of privacy?* He felt weird; he knew what he was doing wasn't right. What if he found something he didn't want to see? What if Miles was having an affair when the accident happened, and that's why he was acting strange? What if he found something that would tarnish the idyllic memory he had of his older brother?

Teddy felt nervous, like a kid who knew he was breaking the rules — but he couldn't put it down. He went through the recent calls — nothing out of place: "I'm just being stupid." Next, he went through the messages; but again, everything looked normal. The last thing he did was check the drafts — there was an unfinished message! 'It's hidden, Safe in'

His eyes began welling up, as he realized these must have been the words Miles was typing when it happened — but he wiped away the tears when he noticed something odd about the text: the word 'safe' was capitalized. Did he mean something *was* safe? Or was something *in* a safe? Did Miles even have a safe?

$$\triangle\triangle\triangle$$

He struggled with these thoughts as he lay in bed, unable to sleep. He looked at the clock: 2:02am. "There'll be no sleep tonight!" He leapt to his feet and started looking around: inside the closets and the kitchen cabinets, behind the pictures on the walls, in the A/C vents, even behind the washing machine — nothing. He had seen every square inch of that house over the years; one thing or another had gone wrong eventually, and he'd fixed them all — but he didn't remember ever finding a safe. *Maybe at the bank?* No, Miles wasn't the type to keep important things far from him — and Teddy *knew* this was important.

But now, he was exhausted, and he had to give up. "I'm dying..." he admitted, "I've gotta get to bed." As he started walking up the stairs, it hit him: "The bed!...I've never moved the bed!...It's too big!" He ran up the stairs two-at-a-time — a renewed vigor had taken hold of him — he pushed the bed out of the way with a strength he didn't know he had!

But there was no safe. *Stop getting your hopes up, Teddy!* His enthusiasm popped like a balloon; he felt deflated. Then, as he was walking over to push the bed back into place — the floorboards sank beneath him! His foot almost fell through! "What?!" He moved them out of the way, and there it was: a floor safe, just as he knew it would be — he was right! Now, how to open it?

THREE

The walls were closing in! Danny's mind was blank; he couldn't think — he couldn't move! The feeling of absolute helplessness had consumed him, but then, suddenly — they stopped! His legs were like rubber; he wobbled and stumbled backwards onto the crude, narrow bed. His nerves were shot; all he could do was breathe heavily, in and out, over and over again. His panic had reached its peak; and as he looked over at the timer, he saw that it was back on — only now the light was yellow. It displayed '09:21' and was counting down: "I hafta get out!"

He stood up and swallowed his fear, then he wiped away the liquid that had pooled in his eyes. Why he was in this room, and how he got here, were no longer important: the only thing that mattered now was getting out — the only option left to him was survival.

The shock and fear that had gripped him so tightly were now gone, replaced instead by resolve and determination — he *would* get out of here. "There's a way out!" he declared, "Now I just hafta find it!" He began searching again, near the timer: it was a digital screen that didn't match with the walls. They were very old, but the timer wasn't — it didn't fit in with anything else around him.

Underneath it was a keypad: "So, if the door is hidden...and there's a digital timer, with a keypad under it... there must be a code, a password!" Now he was starting to get it: "I just hafta figure out what it is." The timer was down to seven minutes.

He pulled the sheets off the bed and searched them thoroughly. "Nothing here." he said, as he tossed them away. Next, he searched along the sides of the mattress for holes or stitches — just anything to make itself obvious — but, still nothing. "Aaahh!" he screamed. Frustration was starting to take over now: his mind was clouded, and he was running more on emotion than logic. "I need to calm down." His breathing was still heavy — too heavy to think straight. He knew he wasn't helping himself by losing hold of his emotions, but at a certain point human nature kicks in — and he's only human, after all.

"What am I missing here?" he asked himself, "I searched the room, the bed, the walls...there must be something left that I haven't checked." Then it hit him — he hadn't checked himself! He reached into his pockets, front and back; then his hoodie — still nothing. "Come on!" His frustration was boiling over: the air was cold, and he could see his breath — but inside, he was burning up. He took the hoodie off and threw it at the timer; then he dropped back onto the bed, and buried his head between his knees. He knew there was a way out. He knew he just needed the code and he'd be free. But he didn't notice the timer was running down — he didn't see when it went to zero. There was another *click*, and the walls began to move again: "No...no...nooo!"

He kicked the metal-framed bed into the center of the room, hoping it would stop the walls from crushing him. His panic was reaching a fever pitch as he scrambled, trying to find a way to prevent his impending doom.

The walls reached the ends of the bed and seemed to stop. *Come on, hold it!* The metal creaked and clanged; each metallic squeal caused waves of terror to pass through him, until finally — it surrendered. The bed frame bent and twisted, screeching as it slowly folded inwards, as if taunting him. But then, like before — it stopped.

Danny took a deep breath — he could now touch both walls at the same time. The room, still about ten feet deep, was now no more than five feet wide. A new timer began; this light was red, and it started at five minutes. He knew there would be no more chances: this was it — it was now or never.

He stumbled to the window and grabbed the bars; steadying himself, he pushed his head through as far as it would go. He relished the cold air blowing on his face — it helped to calm his nerves. The claustrophobia he was feeling, in the tight confines of the room, made it impossible to think. He inhaled deeply as he slowly pulled back, filling his tight lungs with fresh air. "It stopped raining..." he realized, in a moment of calm, "and the moon is full." Glancing down at his hands, the moonlight revealed what he'd been so desperate to find: "What the..." It wasn't on him, it was *on* him — words, written on his left forearm:

> To leave this room, you need only one thing.
>
> If it is lost, you will die. _ _ _ _ Good luck.

"A riddle?" he puzzled, "I hafta solve a riddle or I'll *die*?!" He felt the rage burning inside him. Who could be so careless with someone's life? With *his* life? This still didn't make sense, but he was closer now than he was before. What did it mean? "Four numbers, or letters..." What could it be? What did he need to leave this room? "A door!...I need a door!...That's four letters!" He started to hope. *If it is lost, you will die?* What if his answer was wrong? How many chances did he get? How do you lose a door, anyway? *Well, there isn't a door...so maybe it's lost?* He made up his mind: 'door' was better than nothing — and without that, he had nothing.

He climbed over the mangled bed frame to the far side of the room: the screen read '02:39' and kept counting down. He nervously entered the four-digit password: D O O R. The timer stopped; the light went out, but nothing happened as painful seconds went by. Then it turned back on, now reading '01:30' — he was wrong, and he'd lost a full minute because of it! "Shit!" Now he knew the consequence for wrong answers — he couldn't afford any more!

He positioned his arm under the timer, and tried to read the words again: right at the end, it said 'Good luck'. Was it 'luck'? *Is that the answer?* His hands were shaking; he had to take his time — if he pressed one wrong key, that could be it! The timer was at '01:15' when he finished typing the letters: L U C K. The light went out again. Danny looked around: the walls weren't moving, but there was no door, either.

Then it came back on: '00:15' — wrong again! "Fifteen seconds?!...No!...This can't be happening!" He started to lose it; he was in full panic mode now: "I-I can't do this!...I need more time!" His anxiety crescendoed: "Wait, that's it!...Time!" The countdown was almost over — five seconds!

He hit the keys: four...T...three...I...two...M... one...E. The lights on the timer disappeared. Was he right? Did he get it before the end? Then the noise began; the same noise he'd heard twice before — the walls were moving!

This was it! This was the end! He was going to die! The sound of the walls slowly grinding over the stone floor was agonizing — was this the last sound he would ever hear?!

But they never came — he was still alive. He slowly opened his eyes, and saw the walls moving *back*. He looked at the timer; it flashed with green letters: 'T I M E' — he was right! When the walls reached their starting position, there was a *click*, then a *clang*, and a hidden door opened in front of him — he was free!

He picked up his hoodie and put it back on; then, he stepped towards the door, and slowly pushed it open. What would he find out there? *Who* would he find? The corridor was dark and narrow, but he nervously inched his way forward; he couldn't see, so he felt the walls with his hands. As he rounded a corner, he saw a flicker of yellow light on the floor — he was getting close to the end now. The mystery of who put him in that room, and why, would soon be answered.

He could see a large, open space at the end of the hallway — it was lit by torches. He paused when he reached the end of the tight corridor: this room was circular, with several passages leading in and out — like they were arteries, and this was the heart.

He looked around, and saw someone standing on the far side, with their back to him: it was a girl, dressed all in black. "H-Hello?" he managed to push out, almost choking on the words. In the dim yellow light, he could make out boots, tight jeans, and a jacket. Her long, dark hair cascaded down her back. As she turned, he knew immediately — it was Ash.

FOUR

The assassin tossed his blood-soaked clothes onto the bathroom floor, leaving red streaks on the pristine white marble. The glass of the shower enclosure was starting to fog; he climbed inside, letting the hot water wash over him. As he looked down, he saw pink and red swirls circling the drain. He sighed: "It happened again." He felt ashamed of what he'd done; for being unable to control his urges. It's his job to kill, he was trained to do it — but now, he can't seem to get enough. Is he even a man? Men have normal jobs; normal lives. Men have names — he doesn't, not a real one at least. He has a number, that's what they call him. The stylized tattoo on his left forearm gives it away: Seven — the only name he's ever known.

He had no home, no family, no past, and no future — he doesn't remember any other life than this. They trained him, they gave him purpose — he was *chosen*. What he does is for the greater good, that's all he knows. It's not that he wants to kill — frankly, he's never enjoyed it — but he's good at it; and lately, he feels the need for more.

Am I an addict? he wondered, *Can someone be addicted to killing?* Surely, drug addicts know what they're doing is bad for them — meth-heads don't *enjoy* their insatiable hunger, do they? No, of course not — how could anyone? They just can't stop. They've been doing it so long, it's conditioned now — they just keep the cycle going.

As he stepped out of the shower, he grabbed a towel and wrapped it around his waist: he wiped the fog from the mirror as he stared blankly at his reflection. Who is that staring back at him? This isn't who he used to be — that person was long gone — but it isn't who he wants to be, either. It's the man he is though, for better or worse, and he knows he can't change now — he's done too much to go back.

He exited the bathroom and looked around: his apartment is nicer than most in New York City, but not nearly as nice as he could afford. They pay him well to do bad things — so he became the bad guy. The apartment reflects the man: at a glance, it seems impressive; but inside, the spartan furnishings and half-unpacked boxes bely the fact that it's been lived in for years. There are no pictures of loved ones or treasured memories to be found anywhere — he has neither — and the barren walls are painted the same virgin-white as the day he moved in.

The only indication that this place is inhabited, is the meticulously organized walk-in closet. It's large, not just by New York standards, and there are clothes for every occasion: suits and tuxedos, T-shirts and jackets, pants and shorts, shoes of every type — this is a man who can blend in anywhere. That's what he has to do, after all: in his line of work, he must appear to be all things, to all people, at all times.

After he got dressed, he picked up his phone: '5 Missed Calls'. *Something's wrong.* He checked the numbers, and they're all the same: 'Unknown' — he knew what that meant. *They never call.* He gets his orders sent by encrypted message, and he's paid via wire transfer from a private Swiss bank account. Since the day of his first job, almost eight years ago, he hasn't interacted with anyone over there. *Do they know what I've done?...Could they know?*

Not one to speculate, he walked to the back of the closet and opened a hidden compartment — he grabbed a card, on which there was printed a single phone number and nothing else. He called the number, and as expected no one picked up. He let it ring exactly six times, then he hung up, and put the phone down beside him. After thirty seconds, there's another call: 'Unknown' — he hit the green button to answer.

"Did you retrieve the item?" spoke a distorted, robotic voice.

"Yes." he replied, calmly.

"You will be sent delivery instructions." the voice continued, "Do not attempt to access the device."

"Is that all?"

Click. The line went dead.

Is that why they broke protocol?...Just to tell me not to access the device? This is a man who doesn't need to be told — they know that. *What do they think I'll find?* He walked over to his jacket, hung on the back of a chair, and pulled out the flash drive. "What secrets are you hiding?" he asked the tiny red object, as if expecting a reply. His eyes then moved down to the silver MacBook on the table: "I've broken the rules once today..."

FIVE

Danny was rooted to the ground, staring wide-eyed at Ash as she moved towards him. He had just barely escaped with his life, and who should he find waiting for him in this strange, dark place but his dream girl? Her pace was slow at first, but then it quickened. As she approached him, he tried to speak — but words just couldn't form in his mouth. *Is she involved in this?* he wondered, *Did she escape, too?* His mind overflowed with possibilities as she drew nearer.

She walked right up to him with her arm outstretched; he instinctively raised his hand to meet hers, but he was taken by surprise — she grabbed him by the neck and pushed him up against the wall! "What is this?!" she demanded, "What's going on?!" Danny, who couldn't speak to her in the best of times, was stunned into silence: "Answer me!...What're you doing here?!"

"Uhh-hh...I-I..." He grabbed at her wrist, trying to loosen her surprisingly strong grip; it wasn't until he was gasping for air, that she finally relented.

"Speak!" she ordered, "Where are we?!"

"I don't...*cough*...I don't know..." he replied, "I-I was in this room, and...*cough*..."

She sighed: "And you're stuck here too."

"Yeah..." he confirmed, "I just made it out...

29

barely."

Ash seemed to be on the verge of tears. She inhaled sharply and held it in, trying to suppress the anxiousness within her — then she slammed her right boot into the floor, and turned away. Danny didn't know what to do; he had no words of comfort. She walked to the middle of the room, pressing her head down into her hands.

"Were you..." he began, cautiously, "how long have you been out here?"

She swallowed hard, then turned to face him. "I dunno..." she said, trying to collect herself, "half an hour, I guess...maybe more."

"Is...is there anyone else?" he stuttered, "Are there...m-more rooms?"

"I don't know, OK!"

Danny was taken aback by her sharpness: "Sorry... I'm just tryna—"

"No..." she stopped him, "*I'm* sorry...it's just, after that..." she motioned to one of the tunnels, "now I feel trapped again."

Danny never thought of Ash as the vulnerable type — but under the circumstances, who could blame her? She was average height, about 5'3", but she had a commanding presence about her that just couldn't be ex-plained. Everywhere she went, eyes would gravitate to her: maybe it was her poise, her breezy confidence, that aura of enigma which she seemed to radiate. She had a special brand of cool, which no one else seemed cap-able of possessing; and what's more, she made it look so effortless. Danny was hypnotized from the moment he first laid eyes on her.

But he wasn't the only one, Ash always had a trail of hopeless would-be suitors. Beauty and intellect rarely go hand in hand, but she made it look so simple, so natural, that you'd be forgiven for thinking she was the source. Not that she noticed — or cared, for that matter — and she was rarely seen in the company of others. She just didn't relate to them — and she wasn't sorry about it, either. She'd always had more in common with Galadriel, and Jane Eyre, and Hermione Granger than any *real* people.

She was like a secret world unto herself — but a world that others were desperate to explore. She averaged about seven date requests in a given week, and she could usually count on at least one desperate attempt per day to win her affections. Sometimes it was a note, slipped discreetly under her door; or roses, sent to her in class — one boy even wrote her a song, thinking it would make him 'different'. Nothing worked, though, and the saying around campus was 'no one is worthy'.

Danny approached her again: "What about these other tunnels...did you see where they lead?"

"No..." she responded, finally regaining her composure, "I was waiting to see what would happen...if anyone..." The way she looked at him made Danny feel as though his very existence disappointed her. *She was hoping for a savior,* he thought, *but instead, she got me.*

"Umm, well...maybe we should check them out?"

"OK." she nodded, as she wiped her eyes.

"Should I—"

"Follow me."

She walked past him, towards one of the openings; he trailed close behind, trying not to lose her. The hallway was dark and winding, like the one he went through when he escaped the crushing room; it began wider, but tapered in the further along they got. "Wait up!" he called, "We should stay together!"

"Here..." she grabbed his hand, "try to keep up." He couldn't believe it — they were actually holding hands! Most guys would probably have loftier goals, but for Danny, this was heaven. Just one problem, though — he was so nervous that his palms were sweating! *Does she realize?* he worried, *What if she thinks I'm weird?...Don't be stupid, just relax!* His heart began to race; only this time from excitement, not terror.

"This is it..." she stopped abruptly, "a dead end." She let go of his hand and felt the walls: there was no sign of a door, or hidden passage; the space was narrow, and there was almost no light. Danny stood behind her as she put her ear to the wall: "Something's happening back there!" She turned her body and pulled his arm, wedging him in next to her: they were now face-to-face, squeezed tightly together at the end of the cramped hallway. "Put your ear to the wall and listen." she instructed.

He leaned his head, and pressed it against the cold, stone wall; but it was hard to focus with Ash's face just inches away — and her body pressed so close to his. The air around her was sweet and sugary; like molten caramel, and vanilla, and fresh cotton candy. Was it the perfume she wore? Maybe her shampoo? Whatever it was, it was intoxicating, and he imagined it as liquid candy bubbling up all around them — he was slipping into a trance.

"Well?" she asked, snapping him out of his delusions, "Did you hear it?"

"Umm...no, not...not really...what'd it sound like?"

"Ugh, it's gone now!...Were you even listening?!" The frustration in her voice deflated him. For once, he was happy for the darkness — at least she couldn't see his face turning red.

"Wait…" he pressed his ear further, "I know that sound." How could he forget? That was the sound that had terrified him just minutes earlier — the sound of walls grinding across the stone floor.

Then they heard it: painful, terrifying, agonizing screams, followed by…silence. Above them, a red light turned on: it flashed '0:00'. They both knew what it meant — someone had timed out.

"Let's go." she whispered; then she turned and went back the way they came — he reached down to grab her hand again, but she was already gone. She moved quickly through the tunnel, and once they made it back to the large circle room, she turned to face him: "You know what that was, don't you?" Danny nodded, and she looked him in the eyes: "We hafta get outta here."

"But…how?" He was still in shock from what they'd just heard.

"We'll find a way." she told him, as she brushed back her long, raven hair. Her confidence boosted him; after all, they were the ones who escaped. *They* got out — who knows how many more weren't so lucky?

"Should we search the other tunnels?" he proposed, half in hope of getting close to her again.

"No, let's check this room out first." She pointed to the section of the outer wall, nearest to them: "Let's start on this side…you go that way, and I'll go the other."

"Alright…" he agreed, "and we'll meet over there."

They both started off in opposite directions, feeling the walls for clues, or seams, or hidden locks — really, just anything that could help them escape. Danny still had no idea where he was, or why he was there; but being with Ash, finally talking to her — it wasn't all bad.

"Nothing." he reported, as they reached the end.

"Same..." she sighed, "there must be something we're missing."

"Wait!" He had an idea: "When you made it out, how much time was left on your clock?"

Ash was puzzled: "Why does it matter?"

"Just tell me..." he insisted, "how much time?"

"A minute, I guess...around that...I dunno." She didn't see the importance of the question.

"What color was the timer?" he pressed, "Was it red?"

"No..." she replied, "it was yellow...what's your point?"

"The red timer came on *after* the yellow one..." he explained, "it started at five minutes, and I didn't get out until the very last second."

"So?" she mused, still not seeing the connection.

"My point is, you shoulda only been waiting six or seven minutes before I showed up...but you said you'd been here at least thirty, right?"

She finally got it: "The timers...they're staggered!"

"Yes!" he exclaimed, "That's why we just heard..." he glanced towards the recently explored tunnel, "well... y'know."

"OK, so...we wait?"

"We wait..." he confirmed, "until they're all done."

"But, how'll we know?...I can't listen to another one like *that*."

"Neither can I, but—"

"*ooo*..." Both of their heads snapped around!

"Did you hear that?!" She grabbed his wrist, but Danny could only nod.

"*llooo*..." There it was again! Louder this time!

34

"It's coming from that tunnel!" She darted across the room, towards the sound.

"Wait!" he tried to whisper and shout at the same time — but it was no use, she kept going.

"*Hellooo?*" the voice called — it was loud and clear now.

"Someone got out!" she yelled.

Danny caught up to her: they both stood still, watching the dark opening for a sign of life.

Then, finally — a girl appeared.

SIX

Ash and Danny stared in wonder at the girl who emerged from the tunnel. She was about the same height as Ash, with shoulder-length hair — but that hair was dyed in many shades of purple. The roots were a deep violet that progressively got lighter, culminating in a pale lavender at the tips. She wore a black 'Nirvana' T-shirt under a denim jacket, black leggings, and checkered black-and-white Vans sneakers.

"What's going on here?" she asked them. They looked to each other, then back at her; both waiting for the other to speak. "Hello?" the girl tried again, "Are you gonna tell me?"

"W-Who...who are you?" Danny stuttered.

"Seriously?...We have AdCalc together." His mind was drawing blank. "Zelda!" she snapped, "Zelda Barnes!"

"Oh, right..." he feigned recognition, "yeah... Zelda...exactly."

"Whatever..." she snarked, "I wouldn't expect *you* to remember, all you do in class is stare at her."

Ash's eyebrow went up, as she looked over at him — this time, he couldn't hide his embarrassment. "So..." she started, turning back to Zelda, "you just made it out?"

"Well, I wasn't hanging out in there if *that's* what

you mean."

"Cool it with the sarcasm..." she warned, "we're all in the same boat here."

"Yeah..." Zelda smirked, pushing her way past them, "the love boat."

Zelda had an attitude — there was no denying that. Growing up, she wasn't exactly the most popular girl in school; and with a name like 'Zelda', you can just imagine the Nintendo jokes. Her closest friends included exactly zero females, and she was generally thought of as 'one of the guys'. She used to be self-conscious; but eventually, she realized that she didn't care what anyone thought: she was who she was — too bad if they don't like it. Besides, she knew she was special — *they* were all the same.

If Ash — with her long, dark hair, full, pouty lips, and big eyes — was the perfect fantasy-dream-girl come to life, then Zelda was the total opposite. That's not to say she wasn't pretty — she was — but just a different type that you needed to be close-up to appreciate. She was the 'ugly duckling' most of her life, and that's how she still saw herself; but since she started college, there was definitely a change in the way people looked at her. No longer was she the 'nerdy tomboy', she was now the 'cool punk rock chick', and she struggled to come to terms with all the new attention she was receiving — especially from guys.

"This is serious!" Ash insisted, trying to impress on her the gravity of the situation.

"We just heard someone get crushed down there!" Danny yelled, "Didn't you freak out when the walls moved in?!"

"Walls?" she scoffed, "Nothing was moving."

Ash looked at her with confusion: "Whaddaya mean?...How'd you get out?"

"Easy..." she shrugged, "when I woke up, there was a model of the solar system on the floor, and a note that said I had to find the object that didn't belong."

"So, you found it?" Danny asked.

"*Obvi*..." she rolled her eyes, "how else would I be here?" Both Ash and Danny looked skeptical, so she continued: "Jupiter has seventy-nine moons, not eighty...I just found the one that didn't fit, and there was a code written on it...then I typed the code into a keypad, and... voilá."

"Was there a timer?!" Danny pressed, "What color was it?!...How much time was left?!"

"Relax, dude, I don't know about any timer...I was out pretty quick...now, what do you guys mean about moving walls, and people getting crushed?"

Danny was about to explain, when Ash beat him to it. "The rooms we woke up in..." she began, "the walls close in when the timers expire."

"What?...That's crazy, that'd be dangerous."

"This *is* dangerous!" she screamed, "Don't you get it?!...We're in danger!"

Zelda turned to Danny: "You gotta help your girlfriend chill, man...she's losing it."

"Uhh, she's not my—"

"Listen!" Ash exclaimed, "We need to get outta here...now!"

Zelda examined them carefully — she could tell they were anxious — they really *believed* they were in trouble: "OK, guys, just relax...don't you know what's going on here?" They both looked lost, so she went on: "Don't you remember what Mister Bell told us?" Mr. Bell?

He *was* here!

"No, what'd he say?!" Danny begged, "We don't remember anything!"

"Wow, OK...well, he said that we were chosen for this 'special assignment'." She paused, thinking that would jog their memories — but their blank stares said it all: "A secret club, or something?" Still no reaction: "Anyway, this whole trip is supposed to be a test...to see if we have what it takes."

"What it takes?" he questioned, "What it takes for what?"

"To join!" she replied, "Isn't it obvious?...Why else do you think we're here?"

"Look..." Ash chimed in, "that may be true, but it doesn't change what we heard." She pointed to the tunnel that they just explored: "Someone *died* in there."

Zelda wasn't convinced, but she could tell they were rattled: "OK, then why don't we see where the rest of them lead?...That way, we can know for sure what's going on."

"I don't think that's a good idea." Danny objected.

"Come on..." she urged, "it's not like there's much left to see."

"Whaddya mean?" Ash wondered.

"You each came out of a tunnel..." she explained, "I came out of a tunnel...and, you checked one more, right?"

"Yeah." They replied in unison.

"Well then, count 'em up..." Zelda counted the number of passages out loud: "...seven, eight, nine, ten... there's ten, and we know for sure where four lead...so, if we each take two, we can figure this out in no time."

"I-I dunno..." Danny stammered, "what if something happens while we're in there?...What if we get separated?"

"What's wrong?" she taunted him, "Afraid you'll lose your *girlfriend*?"

"She's not my...it's just, I think we should stick together, that's all."

He turned to Ash, expecting her to back him up: "No, she's right."

"Huh?...But—"

"We checked this room already, and there was nothing...maybe one of these is a way out."

"Glad you see it my way!" Zelda beamed, "Now, which one of you got out first?"

"I did." Ash answered, pointing to the opening on her left, "I came through this one."

Danny gestured towards his hallway: "That was mine."

There were two passages in-between, and Ash started towards them: "I'll take the one on the left."

"I got the other one!" Zelda volunteered, "Wouldn't want *him* getting lost in the dark."

He narrowed his gaze at her: "Just shout if you guys need help...I'll be right here."

"That's reassuringgg..." her voice echoed, as they both disappeared into the tunnels.

Danny stood alone in the large circle room: now that he had a moment to himself, his mind began to wonder. Where was Mav? Was he the one they heard getting crushed? The thought made him sick; his knees felt weak again, and he could feel the fear start to build up inside him.

ΔΔΔ

It was only a couple of minutes that the girls were gone, but it felt like a lifetime — he started to worry if they would ever return. *I never shoulda let them go alone.* But they did return.

"Dead end." Zelda announced, as she emerged from the dark hallway.

"Did you see a red light?" Ash inquired.

"Yeah, triple zeros."

Ash looked at Danny: "Same." They knew that whoever was in those rooms had timed out.

There was another tunnel — between Danny's, and the one they explored earlier — and he knew it was his turn: "I'll...c-check this one."

"Try not to get lost!" Zelda shouted.

He felt his way through, but he already knew what he'd find — he had figured out the sequence. As he moved further along, he could see faint traces of red light on the walls; sure enough, the familiar flashing '0:00' signaled the end. *Where's Mav?* His stomach twisted and turned, as he hurried back out to rejoin the girls; his thoughts were only on his roommate, and what had become of him.

When he finally made it back to the big room, he saw both of them standing together, staring at the tunnel between Zelda's and the one they checked before. "What's going on?!" he called to them.

"Come quick!" she yelled, "We hear something!" He rushed over: he hoped desperately to see his best friend emerge from the darkness.

They could hear a voice calling out; it was getting closer — and this time, it wasn't a girl.

SEVEN

It had been three days since Teddy discovered the hidden safe under the bedroom floor. He tried desperately to open it, using every possible combination he could think of: every birthday, anniversary, or significant date that could have been important to his late brother — but nothing worked; nothing could get it open.

Now he was at work, staring out the window of his cramped office. He hadn't gotten much done this week, except weigh and ponder any significant numbers that he might have overlooked. *Maybe the month he was born... plus Mom's...then mine?* No, that didn't make sense. *How about Stella's birthday, and...their anniversary?* It was getting hopeless, but he wrote them all down anyway.

Just then, there was a knock on the door and someone called to him: "Hey, Teddy!" He was jolted back to reality — it was Tony, one of his co-workers: "You still with us, buddy?"

"Yeah..." he replied, "sorry, just something on my mind...what's up?"

"It's cool..." Tony assured him, "I know how it is... just checking if you're coming tonight."

"Tonight?"

"Yeah, my birthday."

"Oh, right!...Sorry...yes, of course I'm coming."

THE PARADOX OF HEROES

"No pressure, just need a rough headcount for the wife."

"No, for sure…" Teddy promised, "I'll be there… umm, what time is it again?"

"Just be at my place around eight…oh, and by the way…" he looked around, making sure the coast was clear, "I invited the new girl, just in case." He gave Teddy a wink, then headed for the door.

"The new girl?…Emma?…Uh, well—"

"Don't worry…" Tony said, "you don't hafta get married or anything."

"No, it's not that—"

"Relax, Ted, see you at eight!" With that, he was gone, and Teddy now had *two* things on his mind. *Why not?* he thought, *It could be fun.*

ΔΔΔ

The next few hours seemed like weeks, as they slowly inched by. A couple of times he checked his watch, and he could have sworn that the minute hand was moving *backwards*. When five o'clock finally came, Teddy rushed out the door and ran to the elevator; there were already a lot of people waiting, though, so he took the stairs — more jumping than stepping, really — some two-at-a-time, all the way from the fifteenth floor to the first.

Once he made it outside, he stopped to catch his breath; but with the thought of the safe waiting for him at home, he started running again. He ran all the way to the subway station, and just managed to catch his train to Brooklyn.

The subway car was tightly packed; everyone

squished together like sardines—but Teddy didn't mind. The entire ride to his stop, he thought only of cracking the safe; he had a whole new list of possibilities to try, and he was sure that with one of them, he'd finally do it.

There were still several blocks to home once he got out to the street; he didn't run this time, but he walked as fast as he could. He knew that to some of the people he passed, he must have looked very suspicious— like he'd just done something bad, and was trying to get away quickly. He didn't care, though — he had a mission to complete.

When he finally made it home, he fumbled around in his pocket, trying to get his keys out; he had to step back, and take a deep breath to calm himself, before pushing the key into the lock. Once he got the door open, he barreled inside. He slammed it shut behind him, and tossed his soft leather briefcase haphazardly onto the floor — then he ran up the stairs, and through the hallway, towards the bedroom.

The safe was small—roughly a foot in each dimension — and when he pulled it out three nights ago, he'd rested it on the floor, next to the dresser, with the combination lock facing up, just like he found it. Still, Teddy wasn't a man to take liberties; so every time he left the house, he would place things around and on top of it: clothes, shoes, pillows — it didn't matter, just as long as it wasn't readily visible. This particular morning, he'd taken the sheets off the bed and piled them on top.

He checked the clock on the nightstand: it read '5:48pm'. "I've got time." he told himself—then he got to work.

ΔΔΔ

Minutes went by, then hours: he crossed the wrong combinations off his list as he cycled through them. He was an engineer, a scientist, a logical man who did things slowly — but even he was getting frustrated by this tedious process. "Aaahh!" he screamed, "What the hell do I hafta do?!" He threw his notepad across the room, then he collapsed onto the floor and pushed his back against the wall: he pulled his knees in, and rested his head on them. "This is stupid..." he mocked himself, "you don't even know if there's anything in there."

He exhaled, slowly, and as he brought his head back up, the clock on the nightstand caught his eye: "Oh, crap!...The party!" He jumped to his feet and scrambled to get ready: quick shower, shave, underwear, pants, shirt, jacket, socks, shoes, done! It was already eight-thirty by the time he was out the door, *and* he still had to get to Queens.

He jumped in his car and headed off; even after he got there, it took him fifteen minutes just to park.

Ding-dong! He looked down at his watch: '9:23'. *I'm late.*

Tony opened the door: "Better late than never, Ted!"

"Sorry, I was—"

"Just come in and grab a drink...there's tons of food in the other room."

"Thanks."

He stepped inside and greeted some of his co-workers, then he headed straight for the food — with all his investigative work lately, he hadn't done much eating. He grabbed some chips and pretzels, and was in the middle of stuffing buffalo wings down his throat, when he felt a tap on the shoulder — he turned around to see

Emma, standing right behind him: "Hey, leave some for the rest of us."

His eyes opened wide, and his face turned a bright shade of red — he almost choked, as he quickly wiped his face and tried to swallow at the same time. There was still food in his mouth, so he covered it to speak. "Hey..." he began, "sorry...yeah...missed lunch today." He tried his best to laugh it off.

Emma smiled, and brushed back her blonde hair. "I'm just teasing." she said. Teddy had run into her a few times at the office, but other than the customary 'hellos' and 'goodbyes', they didn't really have much of a rapport. Tonight, though, she wasn't dressed for work: she wore a tight-fitting red dress, with black stockings; and the heels she was wearing brought her crystal-blue eyes level with his. For the first time in the last few days, his mind wasn't on cracking the safe.

ΔΔΔ

For the next few hours, Teddy and Emma talked, they laughed, they told stories from their past — including a few bad dates they'd both been on — they even shared a dance, once some of the more nosy people from the office had gone. By the time they both realized, it was already two o'clock in the morning. The few people that remained were all inside, finishing the last bottles of wine; but they sat together outside, alone in the small backyard.

"I've gotta be honest..." he confessed, "I only came here tonight because I was hoping to see you."

Emma smiled, and looked away. "Really?" she blushed.

"Really."

"Well, I was hoping to see you too." she revealed, "I mean, you never talk to me at work...I was starting to wonder if you even noticed me."

"Of course I notice you!...I notice you all the time! ...Or, what I mean to say is...I see you, but not in a weird way." She could tell he was embarrassed, and she started to laugh; he laughed too, diffusing the tension.

"Hey, lovebirds!" Tony called from the back door, "I'm not throwing you out or anything, *but...*"

"Don't worry!" Teddy shouted back, "We were just leaving!" Tony gave him a thumbs-up, as he dropped a bag into the trash bin; then, he turned back inside.

Teddy and Emma stood up, and walked back to the house. When they went in, she called an Uber — it arrived quickly, and they both thanked Tony and his wife; then they said a few more goodbyes, and headed out.

"You sure I can't give you a ride?" he offered.

"No thanks..." she replied, "it's late, and we're going in opposite directions." Emma stepped closer to him, while playing with her ring: "Well, goodnight..."

"Goodnight."

Teddy leaned in and kissed her on the lips — it wasn't a particularly long kiss, just a couple of seconds. They both smiled, bashfully, then she opened the door and began to climb in.

"Wait!" he stopped her. He looked down, and saw that her ring had fallen off; so he picked it up, and handed it back to her: "You dropped this."

"Thank you!" she exclaimed, "It was my mother's, and it's *always* falling off...I guess that's what happens when you have things that aren't yours."

"Do you wanna go out this weekend?" Even *he* was

shocked by his bluntness.

"Of course!" she cheered, "What'd you have in mind?"

"We'll figure something out."

The Uber driver was getting impatient, and he started blowing the horn: "Guess I'd better go." She climbed inside, and Teddy waved her off. He turned and began walking to his car, but with each step he took, his smile grew wider. Then, suddenly, his brain clicked — it was what she said about the ring. *Things that aren't yours...*

"That's it!" he yelled. He ran back to his car and jumped inside. He raced home, breaking every posted speed limit and running three red lights along the way — it didn't matter, this was a breakthrough! A revelation! He almost crashed into his house as he swung the car into the driveway — then he ran inside and up the stairs, gunning straight for the bedroom. He flicked on the lights and dropped to the ground, beside the safe: he picked it up, and started turning it over — up and down, left and right — he looked everywhere.

Then he found it — carved roughly into a corner on the bottom were three tiny letters: 'DRZ'. "That's why I couldn't crack it!" That's why Miles' last message was to tell someone else it was hidden. That's why none of the combinations he'd tried had worked. He grabbed the picture of Miles and Stella off the dresser, and spoke to his brother: "The safe isn't yours!"

EIGHT

Danny stepped back, away from the girls; he was still watching to see who would come out of the hallway, but if this wasn't Mav, if it was someone else — anyone else — he didn't know if he could handle it. The voice got louder, and Zelda called to them, letting whoever-it-was know that the tunnel had an end. Ash remained silent.

Eventually, they saw him emerge from the passage: he was tall and lanky, with shaggy brown hair and a slightly reddish, unkempt beard. He was wearing a grey T-shirt under a faded-green track jacket, and ripped jeans. It was Sam Jacobs — he was a junior, and the oldest of the students on the trip. Clearly shaken, he stumbled out into the open space; his oversized boots made it appear as though he had weights around his ankles.

Danny lowered his head and shut his eyes: his heart was pounding out of his chest. *Get it together!* he told himself, *This guy's alive, and you're mad about it?!* He felt ashamed for wishing it was Mav, but still, there were only two rooms left and four that had timed out — the chances of his friend being safe kept dropping.

"Sam!" Zelda shouted, "You're Sam!"

"Yeah?" he said, hazily.

"Are you OK?...What happened in there?"

"What?" They could clearly see that he was disoriented: "Who-o...t-the walls...I...I coulda..."

"Oh, God..." she rolled her eyes, "not you too." Sam stared at her, bewildered; his eyes then moved to Ash, and on to Danny, who was dropping further away.

"We tried to tell you." Ash remarked.

"Tell you?" Sam puzzled, "W-What's going on?" His face was pale white, and his hands were shaking.

"I'll fill him in..." Zelda offered, "you deal with the drama queen back there." She grabbed Sam by the arm, and pulled him with her to the other side of the room: "Listen, here's what we know..."

Danny had stepped back, all the way to the outer wall — he was now right up against it, and he slid to the floor. With all the adrenaline pumping through him, he had forgotten how cold it was; but now that he had time to settle, he felt it again. He drew his sleeves over his almost-numb hands, and wrapped his arms around his legs, pulling them into his body. Ash walked over and sat next to him; she hesitated for a moment, before speaking.

"Look..." she began, "I dunno what's happening... *she* thinks it's all for show, but—" He turned his head towards her: his stone-like expression caused her to abandon her words. Under normal circumstances, he would have given anything to be this close to her, and now he was — but, at what price? He might have lost his best friend. Ash put her hand on his knee: "Hey...we're gonna get outta here."

"It's not that..." he told her, "it's Mav, my roommate...I think he was here...I don't remember exactly, but I think—"

"The tall one?" she cut him off, "Who flirts with all the girls?"

"Yeah!" he confirmed, "Did you see him?!"

"I think…I think I saw him on the bus…" she struggled, trying to remember, "when we left school…I don't know for sure, but I kinda remember him being late."

"That's him!…He's always late!" Danny felt a rush of excitement — but it quickly faded — he didn't know how he should feel: would it be good or bad if Mav were here?

Ash read him again; she could tell that his mind was racing, so she tried to reassure him: "We don't know what room he's in, or if he's in one at all…but there's still two more, so…I'm just saying…we have hope." Those words meant a lot: 'we have hope'. She could have said '*you* have hope', or 'there *is* hope', but instead, she said 'we'. Danny felt like they were really a team now — they were in this together. He didn't know what it was, but something about her soothed his nerves. "OK?" she smiled, trying to coax him along.

"OK." he agreed.

She stood up, and offered him a hand; he took it, and she pulled him to his feet. "Two more." she resolved; then she led him to the remaining 'unknown' tunnels, and they sat down between them.

ΔΔΔ

After a few more minutes went by, Zelda came over to update them on Sam: "He's still a little shaken, but he'll be OK."

"Do you believe us now?" Danny asked her.

She still wasn't buying it: "Listen, even *if* the walls were moving, it doesn't mean you were gonna die…it might've felt that way, but it didn't happen, so we don't know for sure."

"We heard someone get crushed!" he screamed, "Don't you get it?!...This is real!"

Ash put her hand on his chest and eased him back; she saw how emotional he was getting, and she knew that fighting amongst themselves would only make things worse. "We know what we heard." she repeated, narrowing her gaze at Zelda.

"I'm not saying you're lying, but you didn't actually *see* anyone get crushed, did you?"

Ash and Danny looked at each other. "Well, no..." she answered, "we didn't *see*, but—"

"Exactly!" Zelda claimed, "That's all I'm saying... this whole thing could be a test, designed to scare us... push us to the breaking point...we don't know where we are, so I say, unless we see it with our own eyes, we shouldn't take anything as fact."

There was a brief pause, then Ash turned back to Danny: "Maybe she's right?"

"Maybe." he mumbled. Her explanation made sense, no one could deny that; but still, he and Ash heard the screams — she didn't — and whoever made them sounded *very* real.

"Besides..." Zelda added, "you don't even know if someone was in that room...maybe you just heard what they wanted you to hear?...This whole place is probly rigged with hidden cameras and stuff." With that, she turned and walked back to Sam, who was slowly starting to get his bearings.

'They', Danny thought, *what does she mean by that?* "She seems to remember a lot..." he whispered, "doesn't she?"

"Relax..." Ash advised him, "let's not start turning on each other." He knew she was right, but he wasn't thinking straight; his friend was missing and might be... well, he didn't want to think about what he might be.

△△△

More time passed without any activity; it was much longer than the time interval between when Zelda and Sam got out, and everyone was starting to get anxious. Sam, meanwhile, had calmed down and started to regain his composure; he asked the others if they knew anything about Katie, his younger cousin, and where she might be. Ash and Danny hadn't seen her, but Zelda — whose memory seemed to be the best — said she remembered seeing Katie on the bus, and also at dinner the night before.

She had filled Sam in on everything up to that point: Ash had been the first out, followed by Danny, and the other winding corridors in-between had all been checked. Then, Sam asked the question that no one had thought to ask before: "How do you guys know that Ash's room was the first?" The other three looked around at each other — it hadn't occurred to them that the remaining two rooms may have already timed out.

"No, that can't be..." Ash insisted, "if they're done, then why are we still stuck here?...Why hasn't anything happened?"

"What if this is it?" he proposed, "What if we're trapped in here?"

"Guys, stop..." Zelda cautioned them, "this is all part of the test."

"How do you know so much about it?!" Danny charged, "Why are *you* the only one who remembers?!"

"Hey!" she began her defense, "I dunno what you're

tryna say—"

"Cool it!" Ash intervened, "We need to stick to-gether!...Let's just check the other two and see for our-selves, OK?"

They all agreed, and Zelda went straight into the second tunnel — the last one in the sequence. Ash checked the other passage, while the boys waited out-side. Neither spoke; they were both looking for someone, and they knew that relief for one of them could mean dis-aster for the other.

Ash was the first out; judging by her quick return, and the grave expression that she wore, Danny already knew what she would report. She looked at him and shook her head. Sam and Danny exchanged glances; they knew now that at least one of them would be disap-pointed — possibly both.

ΔΔΔ

Minutes ticked by, and Zelda still hadn't returned. *Maybe she got out?* Danny wondered, *Or, maybe she found someone?* Sam was just about to go in after her, when he heard a voice — then another. "There's two of them!" he exclaimed, "There's someone with her!"

Danny felt a rush of adrenaline — could this be his friend? Ash stood beside him: she could feel his tension. His eyes were pressed shut, and he was muttering to him-self: "...please be Mav...please be Mav...please be Mav..." He kept repeating it under his breath.

"Katie!" Sam cried. Danny's right leg buckled, and he dropped to the floor — but then, he heard Sam scream again: "Nooo!" This time, it was an agonizing wail.

He looked up, to see Zelda coming into the light:

following close behind her was Mav — he made it out! Danny didn't stand up properly before he began running to his friend: "I can't believe it!" he cheered, "You're alive!"

Mav was much calmer; he seemed more relieved than excited. "Barely, bro..." he coolly replied, "barely." Danny looked to Sam: Ash and Zelda were trying their best to comfort him, but he had broken down. Just then, Danny realized that Katie was gone — maybe dead, who knew? But she didn't make it out of her room, that much was certain. His happiness at finding Mav was sharply diminished by that thought, and he knew that he could easily be the one that needed consoling, not Sam.

Mav was tall and broad-shouldered; his muscular frame was covered by a brown leather bomber jacket, grey jeans, and desert boots. Underneath, he wore a white T-shirt on which was printed a drawing of a seductively-posed woman, with angel wings on her back.

On the face of it, Mav and Danny made unlikely friends: while Danny was quiet and introverted, Mav was anything but. He was born in Virginia; the son of Trinidadian immigrants, and the first in his family to go to college. When he was a child, his family was poor and they moved around quite a lot; because of this, he was constantly having to make new friends — a skill that would pay off later in life.

He was always very popular wherever he went. The gym rats, the geeks, the frat guys (and girls), the soccer players, the party chicks, even the foreign students that barely spoke English — everyone knew him, and everyone liked him. But that wasn't all he had to offer: Maverick Wright was a mechanical genius! He knew how things worked, and how to make them work.

He could also operate just about anything with a motor: cars, boats, motorcycles — even planes! If it had gears, switches, or any other type of moving parts, it fell under his domain.

On his first day at Carrington, he arrived to find his randomly assigned roommate — Danny — sitting alone on his bed, reading a comic book: The Death of Superman. While all the other newly-liberated students were getting to know one another, after their parents had left, Danny was avoiding them — like he always did. He might even have written Mav off as just another attention-seeking, drama-addicted teenager, but Mav surprised him by immediately pulling out his own graphic novel — The Dark Knight Returns — and dropping it in Danny's lap. That first day together was a four-hour-long version of the classic debate: Batman vs. Superman.

Over the next few months, they would spend hours together talking superheroes and playing video games. Mav got Danny to go to a few parties, and engage with others outside of classes and group projects; while Danny gave him an anchor, one constant in an otherwise transient life. Mav knew many people, yes, but there wasn't anyone that he actually considered a true friend until now.

"Man, that rocker chick thinks this is all some game..." he pointed out, "but I dunno."

"Her name is Zelda..." Danny informed him, "and I wouldn't put too much into what she says."

Mav looked over at her again. "We'll see..." he shrugged, "but she's cute as hell."

Danny chuckled, and elbowed him in the ribs; he then proceeded to tell him everything up to that point: his own nightmarish experience in the starter room, and what sounded like another person being crushed to death. As he was finishing up the story, Ash walked over to brief them on Sam. "He's not holding up well..." she reported, "his cousin's still missing, and honestly, I don't know how helpful he'll be."

"That's OK..." Danny told her, "that could easily be me." She touched his arm and nodded, then she returned to Sam and Zelda.

"Guess it wasn't all bad, huh?" Mav implied, nudging his shoulder.

Danny smiled, and glanced at him sideways: "Not now, Mav, not now."

The girls got Sam to his feet; they assured him that they'd find Katie eventually. After all, they were students on a school trip — they couldn't be in any *real* danger, could they?

Once they were up, they started over to Mav and Danny. "Look!" Zelda noticed, "What's that?!"

With all the recent activity, no one had realized that a small, green light was illuminated on the floor — in the exact center of the room. All five of them gathered around it, and Danny crouched down to get a closer look: "It...it looks like...a button." He looked up at the others — the green light shrouded them in a sinister glow. His gaze instinctively went to Ash, almost as if he were waiting for her approval — she nodded, and he pushed down on it.

Instantly, they felt the ground start to shake — the stones under their feet began to fall away! Danny fell backwards, and the others scattered to the outer edges: one brick fell away, then another, then another, until finally — it stopped. There was now a circular void in the center of the room, about two feet in diameter. "It's OK!"

Danny shouted to them, "It's over!" A flat object of some kind rose up and filled the void.

"What *is* that?" Zelda marveled.

Mav could see glints of light reflecting off of it, and he tried his best to answer: "It looks like a metal plate... or something metallic, anyway."

Danny ran his hands over it, cautiously: "It's got ridges, or grooves...there's something carved into it." It was hard to tell for sure; while the walls of the room had the torches to light them, the center was still very dark.

Ash knelt down and felt it for herself: "Quick!" she signaled Mav, "Bring me a torch!"

"Alright!" He rushed to the wall and pulled one from its holder.

"What is it?!" Zelda asked her.

She looked up and replied: "Words."

NINE

Beep! Beep! Beep! Beep! The sound of the blaring alarm jolted Seven awake. He rolled over, groggily, and after a few swings of his hand, it stopped. He looked at the time: it was five o'clock. He sat up in bed and rubbed his eyes, then he touched his feet down on the cold, wood floor.

He stood up, walked over to the far side of the room, and flipped a switch: the blackout shades slowly retracted, revealing a view of Lower Manhattan from high up in his Chelsea apartment. The sun hadn't yet risen, but this was his usual wake-up time and he liked routine. Besides, he's never needed much sleep — four or five hours usually did the trick.

Through the large, floor-to-ceiling windows in his bedroom, he soaked in the idyllic view: the artificial lights from the surrounding buildings cast a dim glow in the space around him. *This is perfect.* he thought, as a hint of a smile began to form on his mouth. This was his favorite time to run: no one on the street, and darkness all around.

He threw on a black sweatshirt, pants, and running shoes, then headed for the door; but as he went to open it, his mind was flooded with memories of the previous day: the job he'd finished, the girl in the park, and

the mysterious phone call. Just then, another thought —
the red flash drive. He had left his decryption program
running through the night; the organization didn't want
him to look inside — but for that reason, he had to.

He went to the laptop and checked the status:
'94% Complete — 38 Minutes Remaining'. *Just enough
time.* he figured; then he went out the door, through the
hall, and down the elevator. Once he reached the ground
floor, he exited through the building's lobby, paying no
mind to the attendant who tried halfheartedly to greet
him.

As he stepped out, onto the sidewalk, he was met
by a frigid gust of wind — he shivered, put the hood over
his head, and pulled the drawstring tight around his face
— then he set off, heading south.

ΔΔΔ

His mind was clear now; this was the most enjoy-
able part of his day. He could just be by himself, completely unplugged: no cares or worries, no jobs, just free.
Running made him forget who he was and what he'd
done. He also didn't feel *those* urges — the ones he could
neither explain nor control.

As he approached his usual point to turn east, he
noticed someone behind him: not too close, but not too
far, either — that was how *he* would trail a target. *Did they
send someone?* he worried, *Do they know what I'm doing?* A
normal person would just dismiss this as paranoia — but
he isn't a normal person, so he had to find out. He veered
west, then south, and eventually east again, rejoining his
normal route. But sure enough, the tail was still there —
through it all, still following him.

He knew what to do: he slowed down at first, seeing if they would approach — but they didn't — then, he picked up speed. Once he reached the small jumble of intersecting streets in the West Village, it was easy for him to lose his marker. He crisscrossed in and out of the narrow lanes; then, as he rounded a corner, he ducked into a dark gap between two buildings — it was just wide enough to conceal him — and there, he waited.

Finally, he saw the man: middle-aged and slightly built, wearing blue shorts and a grey hoodie — he had stopped jogging and was looking around. This didn't look like a company man, but he couldn't afford any chances — so none were taken. Seven stepped out from his hiding place and grabbed him from behind: he threw him up against the building, and jammed his left forearm under the man's jaw! "What do you want?!" he demanded. The man was shocked — his face, plastered with fear. "Why are you following me?!" he screamed again, pressing his elbow into the man's throat.

"K-K-Keys!" he choked out.

"What?!"

"You...dropped...keys!" Seven released his hold, and the man collapsed, coughing violently. As he slowly got back to his feet, he looked up — he was shaking, and wiping his eyes. "I'm s-sorry..." he stuttered, "you... *cough*...you dropped your keys back there." He reached out with his trembling hand and offered them back.

"Oh..." Seven replied. The man dropped the keys into his palm and stumbled backwards; once he was a few feet away, he turned and ran down the street. Seven put them in his pocket and continued on his route — but walking now, not running. Eventually, he decided that this time, he wouldn't finish; so he turned around, and went back the way he came. As he walked home, his thoughts were only on the flash drive and what he'd find inside. What was it that they wanted to keep secret? Did it have to do with him?

△△△

When he got back to the building, he walked through the lobby and into the elevator. *Am I just being paranoid?...Like with the man on the street?* He was told to be paranoid, though; taught to be suspicious — that's what he did, that's who he was.

Ding! The elevator arrived at the twelfth floor: he stepped out and walked through the hallway, down to the end — apartment 12D. He opened the door and went straight to the computer. He took off his sweatshirt, tossing it casually over his keys which he dropped on the table; then, he read the status, silently. *Less than one minute left.* He used this time to go into the bedroom and check his phone — no missed calls, no messages. "If this material is so sensitive..." he asked out loud, "then why haven't they sent instructions yet?"

He went back to the dining table and sat down. The decryption was done: '100% Complete'. He didn't know what he was looking for, so he went slowly, sifting through small bits at a time. It was mostly scans of technical documents, reports of experiments, and scientific data — he also saw what looked like scans and outlines of human bodies. Out of context, this didn't make sense to him; however, there was one page that looked different from the rest. Everything else was typed out, long-form, but one page was a simple table — it looked like it was written by hand. There was also a logo stamped on the top: 'S.H.O.T.'

"What is this?" he wondered, "SHOT?" He printed the table to get a better look, but as he tried to open the next file, the screen began to flicker — just a quick pulse at first, but then it started flashing rapidly. "Stop that!" he told the laptop, as he swatted his hand down on the case. But the metal was hot — *very* hot. The fan went into overdrive trying to cool it, but to no avail. The whole thing began to smoke, and sparks shot from the vent in the back — he watched, helpless, as the screen burned itself out!

He sat still, completely stunned by what was happening. Suddenly, he realized the flash drive was still plugged in! He tried to pull it out, but he couldn't hold it. "Shit!" he exclaimed, recoiling his hand from the scalding heat. It was too late — the small device had melted and twisted into a deformed blob of molten metal and red plastic.

"What the hell is this?!" he yelled. Was it the device? Maybe it had a self-destruct built in? Then it dawned on him: he grabbed his sweatshirt and threw it off the table. Underneath, he saw his keys — attached to them was a tiny, dark-grey object, with a red blinking light. *That jogger...he wasn't a civilian!*

"They knew I would access the device!...That's why they didn't send instructions!" He jumped to his feet, and ran to the bedroom closet: he got dressed quickly, grabbing what cash he could from the safe. Then the weapons: two guns and four knives. The last thing he did, before heading to the door, was put on his black leather jacket — but then, he remembered the page he'd printed.

He ran to the printer, picked it up, folded it, and

slipped it into his back pocket. He was about to leave, when he heard something outside — noises, coming from the hallway — there was some kind of movement. He realized now it was too late — they had come for him.

TEN

Mav brought the torch to the center of the room. Now with the light, Ash could see the words carved into the metal plate. "'You have completed the first trial'..." she read, "'in this labyrinth, you will be tested...prove yourselves worthy, and at the end, you shall be greatly rewarded...follow the sign'." Below the carved text was a symbol:

"What's that?" Mav wondered, "An eight?"

"No..." Zelda countered, "that's the symbol for infinity."

"She's right..." Ash concurred, "it means infinite, or always."

"Like 'always watching'." Danny remarked.

"So, what now?" Mav posed, "It says 'follow the sign'...what sign?...That?"

"It has to be." Zelda insisted. The others agreed, and Ash instructed each of them to grab a torch and start looking.

"But, look where?" Danny asked her.

"The walls..." she replied, "every brick, every inch

of this place." They each picked up a torch, and began inspecting every crease and crevice of the large circle room. All but Sam — he still seemed shell-shocked at the prospect of losing his cousin.

Brick by brick they searched; the four of them each separating to a quadrant of the room. "Any luck?!" Danny called in hope — but a round of 'no's' were all he received.

ΔΔΔ

Time passed, and they continued to look — but the symbol was still nowhere to be found. "Maybe there's something else?" Mav suggested, "Some other sign we should be looking for?"

"Like what?" Zelda quipped, "An 'exit' sign?"

"Ha. Ha. Ha." he mocked, widening his gaze at her.

"There's nothing on the walls..." Danny pointed out, "but, the button was on the floor...and the plate is on the floor..."

"You're right..." Ash acknowledged, "that's a good call." She knelt down, and began checking around her feet.

Danny looked to Mav: he was holding up his index fingers in their directions. Then he started bumping them together, wearing his wide, trademark smile, and raising his eyebrows suggestively. Danny's heart sank; he gestured his hand in a swatting motion, trying to get him to stop — but to his horror, Ash looked up and saw this silent argument playing out across the room.

"What are you two doing?" she smirked.

"No, uh..." Danny panicked, "nothing...just, uh..."

Mav burst into a roaring laughter, and fell over onto the

floor; his loud, joyous cries echoed off the walls and enveloped the room. Zelda, who had also been watching things unfold, covered her mouth as she giggled. Eventually, though, she had to let it out — she fell back against the wall, clutching her ribs. Ash looked up at Danny: she, too, was unable to contain her amusement, but to spare his blushes, she pulled her jacket over her face. Then, Danny caved — even *he* couldn't help but laugh. With all the stress and fear that had gripped them so tightly that night, this was a welcomed release — it was just what they needed to ease the tension.

Everyone but Sam, however; sitting alone in the shadows, they had forgotten he was there. While the laughter was slowly dying down, he stood up: he was sitting under one of the empty torch-holders, and he noticed something underneath. "Hey, guys?" he said. They didn't respond, so he cleared his throat and tried again: "Hey, everyone!" This time, they heard.

"What is it?" Zelda walked over to him, "What'd you find?"

"Look." he showed her, pointing to the bottom of the wrought iron bracket.

She raised her torch and ran her fingers over it: "It's an arrow!"

"Where does it point?" Ash inquired.

"Straight ahead..." she responded, "but that doesn't make sense, this room is a circle."

"Mav!" Danny shouted, "Check the one behind you!"

Mav quickly looked under the nearest torch-holder: "Yep, an arrow!...This one points the same way!"

Danny checked the one closest to him, then he looked to Ash — she was standing at the next one in line.

He gestured with his eyes, and she could tell that they'd both found the same thing. "These point the *other* way!" she announced.

Each torch-holder was checked in succession, until they all met at the same point. "This is it!" Danny exclaimed, touching his finger on the symbol, "Infinity!"

"Whaddowe do now?" Sam threw out. They all looked around, waiting for someone else to make the next move.

"Here." Zelda handed her torch to him, as she reached up and grabbed hold of the fixture — then she pulled it down. As soon as it reached the bottom, the floor began to shake! This time, it wasn't falling away: it was moving up, like an elevator, about two feet in from the walls — everyone was thrown off balance! They fell over onto the rising floor, but Zelda was right on the edge where it split — her legs were hanging off the side! "Aaah!" she screamed, "Help!"

Without hesitation, Mav threw himself over and grabbed her! "Don't let go!" he yelled; then with one big heave, he pulled her back up! He landed hard, on his back, with Zelda on top of him. In her shock, she wrapped her arms around his neck and held on tight. He reciprocated as he spoke in her ear: "I gotchu, I gotchu!"

Ash and Danny lay side by side: looking straight up, they watched in awe as the ceiling opened from the center — it spiraled away, seemingly into the walls. They kept rising further up, until the floor they were on had reached the level of the old ceiling, and became whole again — then it stopped. Now, they had advanced further. Now, the next trial would begin.

ELEVEN

In a small, cramped room, a large bank of monitors is set up — but only one showed signs of activity. Just below that screen, there's a white label with black lettering: 'Level 2'. The display is colored green, due to the infrared camera that feeds it.

Two men, wearing minimalistic black uniforms, are silently watching the events unfold. One man, in his fifties — average height and build, with short, grey-and-white hair — is on his feet, pressing down on the back of a chair. The second man — early-thirties, slightly shorter and thicker — is sitting to his left.

The younger man took off his black baseball cap, revealing a military-style buzz cut, and placed it down in front of him. "Time to check in." he announced, as he picked up the phone. The older one looked at the time, then gave him a nod.

Ring...Ring... "Yes, I'm calling from the control room..." There was a pause, as someone else came on the line. "Hello..." he said, sitting upright in his chair, "yes, sir, they have..." The voice on the other end, clearly his superior, asked him questions: "...yes, sir, five of them... yes, sir, they did...I will...thank you, sir." With that, the line went dead.

There was another long silence, before the

younger man spoke again: "Do you think they'll make it?"

"Not a chance." the older one replied, "I've been here a long time, and I haven't seen *anyone* make it to the end."

"Yeah, but...five?...That's a lot for this level, isn't it?"

"I guess we'll see." he shrugged, then he sat down. The conversation was over, and they sat in silence once again: they went back to their duty — watching.

TWELVE

Mav loosened his hold on Zelda; once she realized it was safe, she did the same. Still laying on top of him, she slowly raised her head and opened her eyes — what she saw was his face, just inches from her own. "Enjoying yourself?" he beamed.

"Ugh..." she scoffed, "don't flatter yourself." She buried her knee in his abdomen and pushed up — he coughed and gasped, as she pressed down on him with all her weight.

When she let off, he stood up and extended a hand to Sam; with his large grin still in place, he knocked him on the shoulder: "Well played, old boy!"

"Thanks." Sam replied, rubbing the back of his head.

Ash and Danny were up, too — they had already started to look around. The room was empty and almost completely dark, except for a single torch that provided light. Right next to that torch, there was a small opening in the wall. "That looks like the way." Danny ventured.

"Well?" Zelda posed, "What're we waiting for?"

The five of them approached the opening, and started filing through — Ash was the first, with Danny behind her. Mav stopped just short; he stepped to the side, and using his hand, gestured for Zelda to go ahead: "After you." She rolled her eyes and walked past him; he proceeded to follow, as his smile grew even wider.

Just as Sam, the last of them, had walked through the doorway; there was a loud, booming *thunk!* The shock pulsed through the room — they all snapped around towards it! An iron plate had slammed shut behind them, sealing the opening they'd just gone through — there was no going back now. "OK..." Ash said, trying to calm the others, "it's OK...at least we're moving forward."

"Look at that!" Danny yelled. There was a window, similar to the one he saw earlier — it wasn't very tall, but it was long, extending almost the full length of the room. It was mostly open, except for three vertical iron bars on the side closer to them. But that wasn't what he was pointing to — next to the window was a computer screen! It was black, but with the faint glow of static to indicate it was on.

The group approached it, cautiously: on the screen, an outline of a handprint appeared. Danny hesitated at first, then he reached up and placed his hand on it, matching the outline exactly — it flashed to life! He was startled, and quickly recoiled from it.

A small dot was blinking in the upper-left-hand corner. Then words began to appear — red letters on the dark background — as if they were being typed in real time:

To leave this room, you need to pull the lever. But watch where you step, and don't crack under pressure.

They looked around: with the moonlight that came in through the window, they were able to get a rough estimate of the area — it wasn't as big as the circle room, but still large. "About...thirty feet by fifty?" Danny guessed.

"Yeah…" Ash agreed, "that seems about right…and look!" She pointed to the middle of the wall, on the other side of the room: "There's the lever!"

"So…" Mav alleged, "all we hafta do is go over there, and pull down on it?" There was a brief moment of silence, as they all contemplated the simplicity of the task.

"I guess so." Danny shrugged.

"That's too easy…" he argued, "I don't trust it."

"Wait!" Zelda exclaimed, "Look at that!" She was pointing down at the floor: it was divided into a grid, with strange symbols carved into each square-cut stone.

7	♧	Θ	Π	℮	5	F	∞	★	P
N	Δ	✚	O	~	∞	♏	η	8	♖
0	C	♀	δ	♎	J	↑	G	←	♠
K	♛	X	T	∞	♡	◈	Ψ	♌	U
Φ	M	∞	1	✦	6	Y	◊	☾	3
S	♍	Σ	♓	B	➡	τ	♑	↑	σ
A	Ɔ	W	∞	◇	I	♒	L	♂	E
♈	➡	♔	↑	↗	∞	π	?	♀	≈
Ω	−	♉	2	D	♋	Z	4	β	V
H	↑	Ξ	Q	α	9	∞	♟	R	◉

It ran the width of the room: from the wall with the window, to the other side. But there were blank areas too, before and after the grid — where they were standing, and also on the side with the lever.

"What does this mean?" Danny wondered.

"Nothing good." Ash remarked.

Zelda walked over to the screen: "Look at this...'but watch where you step'?"

"Yeah, so?" Mav prodded.

She looked around, and saw only blank faces: "Don't you remember what just happened?...When the bricks fell outta the floor?"

"You think that's what this is?" Danny questioned.

"I think so." she confirmed, "I think that's what these symbols are for...we hafta find the right pattern to get across."

"So, if we step on the wrong box..." Mav worked out, "we'll fall through?"

"Well, that's what I think it means, anyway."

"OK..." he nodded, as he took off his jacket, "there's only one way to know for sure." He looked around at the others, who were standing still: "What're you waiting for?...Take off your jackets and tie them together."

"Oh, God." Ash sighed, "What're you doing?"

"Look, we can stand here and debate this, or we can just find out...but, I don't feel like falling through the floor if she's right...so, come on...let's light this candle!"

Danny took off his jacket; so did Sam, who had been silent since they entered the room. Ash sighed again and rolled her eyes; but eventually, she caved. She removed her jacket and handed it to Danny, who tied one of the sleeves to his own — as he did, he noticed she was wearing a loose-fitting white tank top.

"Are we really doing this?" Zelda protested.

"*We're* not doing anything..." Mav asserted, "*I* am."

She reluctantly agreed, and handed off her jacket. Once the makeshift rope was completed, Sam tied one end to the iron bars, while Mav did the other end around his waist — then he stepped forward, towards the grid. He stood in front of the first tile, marked with the 'H' — it was the closest to the wall, directly under the bars. Danny held on to the harness, and Sam grabbed hold of the anchored end — just in case.

Mav took a deep breath; he held it briefly, before slowly exhaling through his nose. He grabbed hold of one of the window bars with his left hand, then he slowly extended his right leg out — over the 'H' tile — and stepped down on it.

"Anything?" Danny asked him.

"Nothing." he replied, turning sideways to face the wall. He grabbed another bar with his right hand, then slid his left leg over, onto the tile. With all his weight on it, they heard *crack!* The tile broke away from under him! Mav heard gasps and screams from the others, and he felt Danny's hands grab hold of him — but he was OK! He didn't fall through!

He reached his left foot up, onto the solid floor, and pulled himself back in; Sam and Danny checked him out, making sure he wasn't hurt. Then, he looked over at the girls — they were both pale, like all the blood had drained from their faces. "Well..." he said, panting heavily and looking at Zelda, "I guess you're right."

"You're insane!" she declared, before turning away in a huff.

"What now?" Ash prompted, "Any ideas?"

"Umm..." Danny sounded, "I'm not sure, but maybe...there's infinity signs on some of the tiles." He pointed them out to the others: "There's one in the first row...that could be the starting point."

"Yeah, but..." Mav contended, "that first one is too far to reach with the jackets...if we're wrong, it's game over."

"There's something else..." Sam observed, "look at the arrows."

"Hmm...you might be onto something." Zelda claimed.

"No..." Ash countered, "look at the rest...the arrows are too far apart." She then walked over to the first infinity sign, and began counting the tiles between them: "I think Danny's right, these are closer together."

"The infinity sign was right last time." Mav conceded.

"Exactly!" Zelda charged, "*Last time*...why would they give us the same thing twice?...It doesn't make sense, it's probly just a trick."

"Only one way to find out." He lined up in front of the arrow tile.

"Wait!" she stopped him, "Are you crazy?!...You just fell through!"

"Worried you'll lose me?" he smirked.

"Oh, my God!" she cried, turning to Danny, "Does he *ever* stop?!"

"No, he doesn't...but still, she has a point...maybe we should wait before trying any more."

Mav shook his head: "Dude, I'm over waiting...we need to take back control."

"I hate to say it..." Ash admitted, "but he's right...

eventually, we all hafta get across."

"Thank you!" Mav exclaimed, clasping his hands together, "At least *someone* gets it." He positioned himself in front of the arrow: this time, he couldn't hold on to the bars, so he relied on Sam and Danny to hold the line in case he fell through. He looked at Sam first, who was standing by the window — he tugged on the knot, and gave a thumbs-up. Then Danny, directly behind him, checked the bonds on the other jackets and let Mav know he was clear. Finally, he made sure the improvised harness was tight around his waist — then he stepped forward. Right foot first, then the other: one second...two... *crack!* The tile broke under his weight! He stuck his arms out and twisted his body in midair, just barely managing to grab the ledge!

"Hold on!" Danny yelled.

Mav swung his other hand up. "I have it!" he called to them, "Pull me in!" Sam and Danny pulled on the jackets, as Mav hoisted himself back up onto the stable ground. Once he made it up, he crawled to the wall and sat on the floor, with his back against it — he was breathing heavily, and checking his arms.

"Are you OK?!" Danny panicked, "Did you break anything?!"

"I'm good." he assured them, trying his best to sound calm, "It's just my arms...I scraped them, but it's fine."

"You need anything?!"

"No..." he repeated, "I'll be fine."

The whole room fell into silence; it was only a few moments, but it seemed like an eternity. Finally, it was broken by Sam: "Now what?" No one answered; slowly, they each turned towards the infinity tile in the first row.

Mav was right, the jackets couldn't reach if they were tied to the window — it would be a *big* risk if they were to try that one.

"It can't be Mav this time." Danny told them, "He's the strongest, he needs to hold the rope."

"I'll do it then..." Ash volunteered, "I'm the lightest."

"No!" he objected, "Not you!" The others all stared at him: "Umm, what I mean is...I'll do it."

"I can handle it!" she screamed, "I don't need you to protect me!"

Mav stood up, and placed a hand on each of their shoulders: "He's right, let Danny make the step...Sam and I will hold him."

"*Fine.*" Ash pouted; she went to join Zelda, who had drifted over to the window and was staring outside.

Danny was tying the harness around his waist, when Mav approached him: "You sure about this, bro?"

"No, but I hafta do it."

"OK...I get it."

Danny walked over to the infinity square and stood in front of it. He looked back at Mav and Sam, who both told him they were ready — then he took a deep breath, and stepped out with his right foot. He pressed it down gently, and lingered a while, making sure it was stable. He looked back at the others with a half-smile — was he right? He took another breath, then slid his left foot onto the tile — still nothing. This was looking good. "Hey..." he started, "I think this—" *Crack!* The floor shattered beneath him!

THIRTEEN

Books, papers, clothes, shoes, cables — all the things that Teddy had spent hours packing away so meticulously, only days earlier, were now littered on the hallway floor. *Crash!...Bang!...Rip!* He threw them all around, haphazardly — he just needed them out of the way. "Aaaahhh!" he screamed. His frustration was boiling over — he hadn't slept all night. How could he? He'd just found letters carved into the back of the safe! But now, with daylight outside, he was exhausted, he was hungry, and he was in desperate need of a shower. This had to stop: there was nothing more to be found in the closet.

He let out a long sigh, as he walked down the stairs and into the kitchen. He looked at the clock on the microwave: 8:19am. He needed sleep, but he was just *so* hungry. He checked the fridge, then the cabinets, and found some old Pop-Tarts. "'Best by'..." he read, "...well that wasn't *too* long ago." He dropped them in the toaster and set the timer. He couldn't think of anything now — his mind was completely blank. Standing in his cramped kitchen, he looked straight out across the living room and through the window: outside was cold — but the sun was shining, and the sky was clear. For a moment, he stood mesmerized by the calmness of it all: the outside world seemed in stark contrast to his cluttered, restless mind.

Ding! The toaster snapped him out of his trance. "I've gotta get some sleep." he muttered, as he cautiously picked up the burning-hot Pop-Tarts. He blew on them, being careful not to hold on for more than a second or two. Once the crusts felt cool enough, he bit in. "Oh!" he cried, painfully, "Ah!" The hot, molten filling burned his tongue and the roof of his mouth — but that wasn't going to stop him — he inhaled them, sucking in a few deep breaths as he did to cool the burning.

Once he was finished, he quickly downed a glass of cold water, then headed for the bathroom. Another hot shower followed, but he didn't linger in this one — it was quick. Then he meandered towards the bedroom, bumping off the walls a few times along the way. Finally, he reached the bed and collapsed into it, passing out instantly.

△△△

Before he'd realized it, there was something wet on his face; he shifted and squirmed, but he couldn't get away from it, so he lifted his head off the pillow to see what it was — a large puddle of drool had formed underneath him. *What?* he thought, *I just lay down.* He looked over at the clock: 3:58pm. *I don't believe it.* Teddy rolled over, onto his back, and stared at the ceiling. *I slept the whole day.*

He lay in bed a few more minutes, before he got up — he had slept for almost eight hours, but to him, it felt like eight minutes. He was still exhausted; the last week had taken its toll: organizing the closet, finding the safe under the bed, tearing through the closet — undoing all his previous work — plus, there was almost a full work-week *and* the party in-between.

He looked on the nightstand, then to the dresser for his phone — but it wasn't on either. He went downstairs and saw his jacket on the couch: he checked the pockets — there it was. "Wow." he remarked, looking at all the missed calls and messages — most of them were from people he didn't want to talk to. There was a missed call from Tony, then a message received soon after, thanking him for attending the party the night before. Teddy responded, thanking Tony again and adding that it was a great night — but there was really only one message that interested him: 'Hey! I had a great time last night. Can't wait to see you again! XOXO — Emma'. Teddy couldn't help but smile — a big, wide, teeth-baring grin — just reading those words caused a wave of euphoria to wash over him. He wasted no time — he called her right away!

Ring...Ring... "Hey..." he said, as she answered, "yeah, sorry...I didn't really sleep last night, and this morning I passed out...yeah, just woke up, actually..." Even though they'd spent so much time together the previous night, he still felt nervous. "So, I was thinking..." he proceeded, "about that date...I'm free tonight, if you're up for it?" As he spoke the words, his heart was beating out of his chest. He didn't have to wait long, though, Emma couldn't contain her excitement — she agreed almost before he'd finished speaking! "Great!...Let's meet at Grand Central...umm, how's six?...OK...OK...great!... I'll meet you there!" He hung up the phone, then collapsed backwards, onto the couch. His nerves had gone: now, all he felt was a mixture of joy and relief — he was cool; he was relaxed; he was confident.

∆∆∆

He lay on the couch a little while longer, before getting up; then, he got ready and left the house — he knew it was early, but he didn't want to be late. Everything on the way was routine, and he arrived at the meeting point with thirty minutes to spare — that was OK, though, he didn't mind waiting. He sat for a while, watching the people as they passed — to him, they were all just empty faces. He felt like he was in the Matrix, watching one mindless drone after the other — all unaware of what they didn't know.

His mind was brought back to reality, when he saw Emma emerge from the escalator: she was wearing a grey peacoat, dark jeans, and dark-brown boots. He watched her as she walked towards him: it seemed like her feet weren't even touching the ground — she just floated, effortlessly, through the crowd.

"Hi..." she blushed, as they greeted each other with a semi-hug.

"Uh, hey..." he stuttered, "so...you hungry?"

"Starving." she replied.

From there, they went out to the street and walked to a nearby Mexican restaurant. They sat down, ordered drinks — and lots of tacos — and began eating the tortilla chips that were placed on the table. Teddy then realized that they hadn't spoken a word to each other since they sat down. "I don't know why this is so weird..." he admitted, "we just spent the whole night talking, after all."

Emma smiled, and blushed again: "Maybe it was the wine?"

"Yeah, or all the other people buzzing around." Finally, things were getting back on track. After they'd both acknowledged the elephant in the room, they were able to relax — they picked up right where they left off the night before.

ΔΔΔ

After dinner, they decided to take a walk; it was still early, and there was no work in the morning. The conversation became more personal the further along they got, and they began to divulge more intimate details to each other: crazy things from their college days, their hopes and dreams for the future, and, without realizing it was happening, Teddy started telling her about his most private subject — he only caught what he was saying when he uttered the name of his late brother.

"Oh, my God!" she exclaimed, "I'm so sorry!...I didn't know!"

"Please..." he assured her, "it's fine, it was a long time ago...besides, I don't really tell people about it."

Emma smiled to herself; she was glad to be entrusted with this, the deepest of secrets. "Does anyone at work know?" she asked.

"No." he answered, "I like to keep my work life and private life separate." He looked down at his hand, which was entwined with hers: "Well, mostly separate anyway." They both laughed, making him feel better about his accidental confession.

"So..." she continued, "how's everything been going now?"

"Well, actually—" he started, before cutting himself off— he let go of her hand and stopped in his tracks.

"What is it?...Come on, you can tell me."

Teddy thought hard; he knew that he probably shouldn't tell her about his latest discoveries, but something about her was just so reassuring — and he desperately wanted to tell someone. He wanted to say the words out loud that he'd only been saying to himself; he wanted to know that he wasn't just being stupid: "OK, but you're gonna think I'm crazy."

"That's fine..." she insisted, as she sat on a bench, "I'm good with crazy."

He sat down next to her and began his story: "So, the other night I was cleaning out my storage closet...and in this box, I found my brother's old phone." She nodded as he spoke, letting him know she was paying attention: "I don't know why, but I plugged it in...there was an unfinished message he was sending when—" Teddy stopped himself, realizing he was about to describe the moment of his brother's death.

"It's OK." she said, taking his hand — she knew what came next. "So, what was the message?"

"Umm...well, he was telling someone...an unknown number...that something was safe...but, there was something odd about the text."

"What was it?"

"The word 'safe'..." he told her, "it was capitalized."

"So?" she mused, "It coulda just been a mistake."

"Yeah, I thought so too at first...but it wasn't...it meant something."

"How do you know?"

"Because..." he smirked, "there was a hidden safe in the floor under my bed."

Emma's eyes widened; her jaw dropped: "Are you

serious?!" He nodded, letting his words sink in as he savored the feeling of vindication: "So, what was in it?!"

"Well, that's the thing..." he went on; his tone much less enthusiastic.

"You didn't open it?"

"I did...I mean, I tried...it's complicated."

"So, what's the problem?" She sensed that there was more to the story; something that Teddy was holding back.

"I tried everything!" he declared, "Every possible combination I could think of!... Birthdays, anniversaries, important dates...I tried them all, but it just wouldn't open."

"Was there anything else in the phone?...Any other messages?"

"No..." he sighed, "that was it."

"So what's your plan?"

"Well, last night you said something...about your mom's ring."

"My ring?" She instinctively touched it, fidgeting nervously as she waited for him to speak: "What about it?"

"You said something about 'things that aren't yours'..." he reminded her, "and that got me thinking... what if the safe wasn't his?"

For the second time that night, she was floored: "Oh, my God!...This is a full-blown mystery!"

Teddy was relieved — at last, it wasn't just him. There was someone else — at least one someone — who thought this was important. "Oh, please!" she begged, "You hafta let me help you!"

"I-I dunno..." he stammered, "this is kinda personal, and—"

"Teddy!" she cut him off, "I can help!" He stared at her, then turned his eyes downward. "Look, if you could do this on your own, you woulda cracked it already."

"Well...maybe..."

He looked back up: Emma's hands were clasped together like she was praying, and she was purposely quivering her bottom lip. "Pleeease?" she stared at him, batting her big, blue eyes.

"Fine." he chuckled.

"Yes!...Thank you! Thank you! Thank you!...I promise you won't regret this!" Then she leaned in and gave him a kiss.

"Yeah..." he smiled, "I think this can work."

FOURTEEN

Danny's head whipped backwards! The harness slid up, catching him under the arms! "I gotchu!" Mav yelled. He didn't reply; he was shocked into silence by yet another near miss.

He started to inch back up, as Mav and Sam pulled on the rope; once he reached the top, he shakily took hold of the ledge and pulled himself back onto the solid floor. They grabbed him and helped him to his feet — but his knees were weak, and he couldn't yet stand on his own. Mav guided him to the wall and leaned him up against it; when he let go, Danny slid to the floor. His face was pale white: the momentary feeling of free fall had rendered him all but useless, at least for the time being.

He could hear the others talking, but he wasn't listening to their words. He looked around for Ash, and found her standing by the window — she was staring beyond him, though, to the other side of the room. *Why didn't she come to me?* he wondered, *Doesn't she care?* It slowly dawned on him that he may have just been imagining the closeness between them. Were they really working together all this time? Or was he just following behind her? After all, they were the first two out — she could easily have had the same connection with Mav or Sam, had one of them been out second. He was in overanalyze mode now. *Am I making too much of this?*

His mind was brought back to the present by Mav, who placed a hand on his shoulder: "You still with us, buddy?"

"Oh, umm...yeah." he stuttered.

"He's alright..." Mav told the others, "just a little shell-shocked."

Danny wobbled to his feet, using the wall as support: "So, what're we gonna do now?"

"Weren't you listening?!" Zelda scolded him.

"Uhh..."

"Yo!" Mav rushed to his defense, "Give him a break! ...*You* didn't just fall through the floor."

"Ugh, *fine*." she scoffed, "Well, go on then...fill him in."

Mav explained what they had just discussed. "Since the infinity tile broke..." he started, "they're probly all like that, so—"

"I told you that wasn't it!" Zelda cut in, directing her ire at Danny.

Mav flashed her an annoyed look, then he continued: "Anyway, we think it might be the 'bullseye' symbol over there." He pointed to the tile at the end of the first row.

"What?" Danny puzzled, "Why that one?"

"It's the furthest from the window..." Zelda explained, "plus, it's literally a target."

"No..." Ash spoke from behind them, "that's not it."

"Nice to have you back..." Zelda snarked, "but that's the most likely option."

"No..." she repeated, "it's not."

The two girls were staring each other down; Sam

and Danny looked on, unsure of what to do. Then Mav stepped in: "OK, relax...I'm going on the next one, so don't worry about it."

"No, I'll do it." Sam volunteered, "It's my turn."

"It has to be me!" Danny declared, "You two need to hold the rope!" The three of them began arguing about who should make the next try — Zelda eventually joined in, but mostly just to tell them again that she was right.

Ash watched them: her arms were crossed, and her brow furrowed — she pressed her lips together as she observed the squabbling foursome. "Enough!" she screamed. Her voice rang off the walls and silenced the room — everyone turned to her and stared, with their eyes wide open. They had seen her stressed and annoyed so far that night, but anger was a new one. "What if there's no pattern?" she proposed, "What if the symbols don't mean anything?"

"No way!" Zelda argued, "We already *had* a symbol in the last room, there's a precedent."

"In that room, the clue *told* us to follow the sign... read this one again, it doesn't mention anything like that."

"Then, why put them there?" Danny questioned.

"Like she said..." Ash replied, "to trick us."

"So, lemme get this straight..." Mav asserted, "you're saying there's no pattern?...That we just hafta *guess* which tiles will hold?"

"No..." she responded, "none of them will hold... not if we try to stand on them, anyway."

"You're not making any sense!" Zelda raved.

"The clue..." she pointed out, "it says 'don't crack under pressure'...don't you get it?"

The others stared at her, confused: "Look, the

symbols are there to mislead us...the reason the floor held with one foot, but not two, is pressure."

"So, what?" Mav asked her, "We should hop across on one foot?"

"No!" she fumed, "We need to *crawl* across."

"Crawl?!" The others shouted.

"You're crazy." Zelda sneered.

"Seriously..." Mav agreed, "you're making *her* sound normal...oof!"

Zelda elbowed him in the ribs: "Watch it!"

"So, crawl?" Danny pondered, "That might work."

"Thank you!" Ash exclaimed. She looked at him with a bright, glowing smile that made his knees even weaker.

Mav was shocked: "You can't seriously be co-signing this, Danny?"

"It makes sense..." he insisted, "the pressure is less if we crawl, because the weight is distributed over a wider area...and, I think she's right about the clue."

"You think she's right about *everything*." Zelda taunted him.

"Eff it." Mav shrugged, "Whaddowe have to lose, right?"

"Glad you see it my way!" Ash beamed. She walked over to Danny and grabbed the harness out of his hand: "My turn!" He tried to stop her, but he was too late — she skipped over to the far side wall, right by the edge of the grid. "Don't come any closer!" she warned, freezing him in his tracks.

"Alright...alright." Mav cautioned them. He placed his hand on Danny's shoulder, and eased him back; then, he stepped to her, slowly, and picked up the free end of the harness: "You do the crawl...we'll hold you." Sam and Danny grabbed hold of it too, as Ash got down on the floor. She lay flat on her stomach, being very careful to contact the ground with as much of her body as possible — then she reached her arms out, and began pulling herself forward.

She advanced in inches, at an almost snail-like pace: no one spoke a word as they watched her make slow, but steady progress. Time seemed to stop altogether; but finally, she made it onto the tiles with her whole body — and they didn't break. She let out a sigh, and a hint of a smile began to form on her face — but she shook it off and kept going; she wasn't clear yet.

There were no creaks or cracks to be heard, but by the time she was halfway across, the harness had reached its full length. "We hafta let go." Mav said to the others.

"No!" Danny objected.

"Trust me...at this point, we're just holding her back."

Danny's eyes darted around; his stomach twisted, as he tried to think of anything else they could do. Eventually, though, he had to relent — they couldn't leave her waiting out there any longer. All three of them let go of the jackets, and Ash continued forward — without a safety net.

Danny watched her intensely — he didn't blink; he didn't move. It wasn't until her fingers had reached the other side — and his face turned blue — that he finally exhaled.

Ash made it all the way over, and stood up: she turned, triumphantly, with her arms in the air. "Yes!" she cheered, "I told you!" She bent over and placed her hands on her knees; breathing deeply, and smiling ear-to-ear.

The three boys stood on the other side applauding, with Zelda begrudgingly joining in, after a not-so-subtle nudge from Mav. "OK!" he called out, "Throw us back the rope!...We'll do this one by one!" Ash tossed it over, and they repeated the process: Zelda was the next to cross, then Danny, but the remaining two were left with a dilemma — who would go last?

Mav insisted that Sam be next, and held the rope for him; letting go only once he'd made it halfway. Then Sam made another move, and their hearts sank — *crack*. It wasn't especially loud, but it echoed through the room like a gunshot. "It's OK..." Mav assured him, "keep going, *slowly*." Sam inched his way forward: he was almost there — *crack*. Fear gripped them, and they stood frozen in place. Sam, whose heart was pounding through the floor, summoned the courage to continue. When he was close enough, Danny reached down and grabbed his right hand — then Ash grabbed the left — together, they pulled him in.

Once he was safe, they all turned and looked at Mav: he weighed the most, the floor was compromised, and there was no one left to hold the rope. In typical fashion, though, he didn't wait for them to speak: he lay down on the ground, reached his arms out in front of him, and began pulling himself along — he dragged his body onto the fractured floor.

FIFTEEN

Seven pulled his guns out and loaded them: one in each hand. He extended the one in his right to the light switch, and flicked it off with the barrel; then he stood — back against the wall, with the door to his left — waiting. He calmed his heart rate with long, steady breaths. As the movement in the hallway got closer, he looked down to the space at the bottom of the door — there was a small, horizontal slit that allowed some light to seep through. The bright yellow light made it seem as though there was a raging fire just outside. He crouched down, behind some boxes that were stacked next to the kitchen cabinets: from this position, he could stay hidden for a while, and maybe find out more about his 'guests'.

Sharp, metallic sounds from the door broke the silence — they were picking the lock. He heard a *click*, then the gentle sliding of the bolt, as it was slowly eased back into its socket. From his hiding place, he could see the light grow brighter as the door crept open. A man entered, dressed all in black, and holding an assault rifle with both hands; he had blacked-out goggles, and a gas mask over his mouth. This was 'them' alright: standard issue 'soldier' uniform — one that Seven himself had worn many times. Another man followed soon after: dressed the same, and also carrying a weapon. In the doorway, a third man appeared — unlike the first two, he wasn't holding a gun, but a phone. His face was also covered, but he had no special goggles or breathing devices — it was clear that this man didn't expect to fight. He wasn't a soldier, he was the man in charge — the leader.

The three men made no sounds; not even with their feet, which seemed to absorb the impact of their steps. The first man disappeared into the bedroom, and the second to the bathroom; the third man — the leader — waited by the door. Seven didn't move — this wasn't the time, so he continued to observe. The first man came out of the bedroom and flashed the 'all clear' sign, then he moved through the living room, towards the large windows. The second man exited the bathroom and made his way to the kitchen — surely, now, Seven would be found.

He couldn't take the chance, so he moved his left hand to the crack in the door, and aimed it at the leader — then he raised his right. As the second soldier stepped in front of him, he pulled the trigger — one bullet, to the head. Due to the silencer, the other men heard nothing but a screeching sound, as the dead soldier collapsed into one of the chairs, knocking it across the floor.

The first soldier turned and fired! He released a barrage of bullets in Seven's direction; also silenced. The only sounds were those of the bullets hitting the wall, and the boxes around his head: they got close — *very* close — but they didn't hit him.

He didn't flinch — this was his life — he was used to it, and *no one* was better than him. He didn't shoot back, though, leading the soldier to think he was dead. As he walked over to check, Seven again turned his right hand upward — he waited for the intruder to draw closer. *Not yet...not yet...not yet...now.*

All the man in the doorway heard, was the sound of the dining table turning over, and crashing into the floor. He realized now there was no one left; except himself, and the most deadly assassin the company had — the very man he was sent to kill.

He turned and ran down the hall, towards the elevator: once there, he began frantically pressing the down button. His head swiveled back and forth; from the elevator, to the dark void left by the open door — he'd made a grave mistake bringing only two men. Beads of sweat ran down his face; he just couldn't wait anymore, so he gave up and ran to the stairs. He threw the door open and jumped over them: two-at-a-time, three-at-a-time — he had to hurry!

Several flights down, the creak of a door opening above caused him to freeze — he knew what it meant. With his panic getting greater, he picked up the pace — but the stairs seemed to go on forever. Lines after lines of jagged, grey, concrete steps — they mocked him. He felt as though no matter how many he put behind him, he was getting further and further from the end.

He kept running, he kept jumping; then, suddenly, as he looked back — he tripped! *Crash! Bang! Crunch!* The sharp, concrete ridges cut into his ribs, as he tumbled over them. He kept falling, end over end, as his pain-filled cries echoed off the walls and filled the stairwell.

Finally, the fall ended: he crashed down on the landing, and flopped over, onto his back. Above him was a sign for the second floor — he was close. He rolled over and began to cough — it hurt to breathe — and as he opened his eyes, he saw thick globs of blood. He knew that he had some broken ribs, and was bleeding internally — but he was still alive — he had to get away now, or that wouldn't be the case for much longer.

He staggered to his feet, using the wall to help him; then, out of nowhere, his face smashed into the floor! He didn't trip, or fall — he was pushed. His cries of agony once again rang off the walls. His pounding forehead was split open, soaking the mask in blood.

He felt a foot reach under his battered chest: it rolled him over, onto his back. Then his black ski mask was pulled off, revealing his face — it was the jogger from the street! The same man who handed Seven the keys!

The blow to the head, combined with the bright fluorescent lights above, made it difficult to see; but through his blurred vision, he saw someone step over him. As he slowly slipped out of consciousness, he knew the worst was about to begin.

SIXTEEN

"Stop!" Danny cried, "We'll find another way!" It was no use, though, his friend wasn't listening.

Their eyes were fixed on Mav, as he slid his way across the now-breaking floor — breathlessly listening for sounds of doom with each movement. But when he reached the halfway point, there were no signs of trouble — maybe he did know what he was doing? "It's OK..." Danny said, trying to reassure himself more than the others, "he's OK." The words had no sooner left his mouth, when they heard it — *crack!* Mav froze: he looked up at them — *crack!* That one was louder! *Crack! Crack!* The floor was breaking apart!

"Sam!" Zelda urged, "Throw him the rope!" He was halfway across: it should be able to reach him now. Danny held onto the harness, as Sam tossed it to Mav: it landed right in front of him, and he extended his arm — but it was *just* too far.

"Again!" he shouted. Sam reeled in the rope, then he threw it back out — *crack!* Mav's fingertips were touching the end of Zelda's jacket, but he couldn't quite take hold of it. *Crack! Crack! Crack!* The floor was failing! Sam tossed the harness one last time, as Mav pushed up and lunged towards it — the others watched in horror, as the floor completely broke away!

He hung in the air, flailing his arms in desperation — he had almost dropped below it when he threw his hands up one last time, and caught the jackets! Sam and Danny held the other end and pulled it with all their strength! He swung on the rope, almost dragging them down with him — but Ash and Zelda grabbed them and held them back. Mav was suspended in the air, swinging back and forth like a pendulum; they didn't try to pull him in, and he didn't try to climb up, either — they all just let it settle.

"Mav!" Danny called out, "You OK?!"

"I've been better!"

"We're gonna pull you up!"

"No, just hold it like this!...I'll pull myself up!"

Danny looked to the others, before responding: "OK!" Then Mav began pulling on the rope. They could feel his tugs; his uneven weight moving and shifting as he climbed higher. Nobody dared to speak; they just watched the ledge in silence, waiting for a hand to appear.

Finally, it did! Then another! Mav grabbed the ledge and pulled himself onto it! Once he had fully let go of the rope, Sam and Danny knelt down and helped him up. He didn't seem as shocked as he should be — he was actually smiling! As the boys were praising his heroics, Zelda stormed over and slapped him across the face: "You pull that shit again, and I'll kill you!" Mav didn't reply; he just smiled, and rubbed his cheek.

The other three stood in an awkward silence, until Danny finally broke it: "So...the lever?" The task was done: they had crossed the grid. The next challenge, whatever it may be, was waiting for them on the other side. The mixture of relief and jubilation that they felt, from conquering this room, suddenly faded: they remembered that they were still trapped, and the only way out was to go further in — through the unknown.

Danny and Sam untied the jackets, as Ash walked over to the lever and pulled it down — a section of the wall broke away, revealing another hidden passage. "Only one way forward." she told them.

"You don't need to tell *me* twice." Mav announced. He took his jacket from Danny, and put it back on — then, he walked through the doorway. He was followed soon after by Sam and Zelda.

Danny handed Ash her jacket; but as he was walking past her, she put a hand on his shoulder and held him back. "Hey, listen..." she began, "I'm sorry I snapped at you back there."

"Oh...no, uh..." he stuttered, "it's...it's fine."

"No..." she continued, "I know you were just tryna...anyway, I'm sorry." With that, she turned and stepped into the darkness, disappearing briefly from his sight.

ΔΔΔ

He followed after her, into another tight, winding corridor — it twisted and weaved, like the tunnels that led from the circle room. Eventually, a flickering yellow light began to creep in. *At least this next room has torches.* he thought. Once he reached the end, and stepped out, there was another loud *thunk*, as the passageway sealed itself behind him. This time, they weren't as startled — they were slowly getting used to this strange place.

The windowless room was a perfect square: the light was provided by eight lit torches — two per wall.

They stood in place, with their backs to the now-sealed doorway; to their left was a table, with small, wooden boxes, neatly aligned in a row — the boxes were numbered '1' to '10', and each contained three keys. Just above that table, there was another electronic screen: they approached it, and like before, a handprint appeared.

This time, it was Ash who unlocked it, and they each read the words in silence:

> This room is sealed with a tri-lock. It can only be opened with the right combination of keys, which must all be used together. Time is against you.

"OK..." Mav sighed, "at least we aren't falling through the floor, or getting crushed."

"Haven't you learned anything?" Zelda scoffed, "'Time is against you'?...Clearly, there's a consequence to every challenge."

"Wait..." Danny noticed, "do you guys hear that?"

"Hear what?" Mav asked him.

"I hear it too." Ash confirmed — it was the sound of air blowing through a vent.

"It's coming from above us." He grabbed a torch off the wall, and held it high above his head as he moved around, staring at the ceiling. Eventually, he ended up in the center of the room — above him was a small, circular air vent: "Look at this!"

The others walked over, to get a closer look. "OK, so there's an AC vent." Mav noted, "Does it matter?"

"Look around you." Ash insisted, "Does that look like it belongs here?"

"I wonder what it's for?" Zelda questioned.

"Umm, how bout ventilation?" he remarked.

"No..." Danny countered, "the vent isn't blowing

air." He raised the torch higher; his eyes grew wide, as he realized its true purpose: "It's pulling air *in*...it's sucking it outta the room!"

SEVENTEEN

"Call it in." the older guard instructed.

The younger of the two men picked up the phone, and dialed. *Ring...Ring...* "Oh, yes, hello..." he spoke, to the person on the other line, "I'm calling to update the Director." There was a pause, as the attendant transferred the call: "Hello, sir...yes, sir...yes, they have, sir...that's correct, sir, all five in fact...we are too, sir...I will...thank you, sir." *Click.* The line went dead.

"What did he say?" the older man asked.

"Not much..." the younger one replied, "just wanted to know where they were, and how many were left."

"That's it?"

"Yeah, should there've been something else?"

"It's just strange..." the older man stated, "they've never wanted updates like this before."

"Well, actually, he did ask...never mind, it's probly nothing."

"What is it?"

"Well, he asked about this one." The younger guard touched his finger to the monitor.

"What?!...He asked about a specific person?!" The older man was stunned. Why did they want to know about one of the kids? Were they playing favorites? Was this one special in some way?

"Yeah..." the younger guard confirmed, "does it matter?...I figured this was normal."

The older man looked him in the eye; his face wore an intensity that his partner hadn't seen before: "*Everything* matters with these people...*everything*."

EIGHTEEN

"Relax..." Mav cautioned them, "if the air's going out through there, it must be coming in somewhere else."

"What're you not getting about this?" Ash scoffed, "There *are* no rules." Danny opened his mouth to defend his friend, but the way she looked at him — with daggers in her eyes — caused him to think again.

"I think she's right." Sam chimed in, breaking from his customary silence, "That must be the 'time' factor in the clue...we hafta solve the puzzle before all the air is gone."

"Danny, you look over there..." Mav instructed, pointing to the wall they entered through, "and I'll check the other side." They each picked up a torch, and began inspecting the seams of the walls. "Make sure you feel in the corners!" he called out, "And the joints between the stones!" Together, they checked every crease and space they could find, feeling with their hands to see if air was coming in — but they found nothing. Next, they moved the table and inspected the wall with the screen — again, there was nothing. It was the same story with the last wall, too. Although that one had the keyholes, they were very small; even if air was coming in through them, it wouldn't make much of a difference.

They moved around the room, holding the

torches high above their heads to light the ceiling. They searched for another vent, or anything else that would allow air in; but once they met in the center, they realized there were none.

"You're wasting time!" Ash berated them, "We need to solve the puzzle!"

Mav knocked Danny on the shoulder, and gestured to her: "Go help her, Dan." He complied, walking over to the table with Ash and Sam. Zelda turned to go with them, but Mav grabbed her arm and held her back: "Not you...I need you to help me."

"You need all kinds of help..." she quipped, "but I'm not qualified."

"Oh, yes you are!" He crouched down and grabbed her legs, then he pushed up, raising her high in the air!

"What're you doing?!" she screamed; she slapped her hands down on his face, "Put me down!"

The other three stared in amazement. "What the hell is he doing?" Danny muttered—he was overheard by a stunned Sam, who was wondering the same.

"Let her go!" Ash yelled, "What's wrong with you?!"

"Relax!...Relax!" Mav pleaded, "Stop hitting me!"

"Then put me down!"

"I just need you to check the vent!...Whaddaya think I'm doing?!"

"What?!"

"The vent!" he repeated, "Check the vent!...See how much air it's pulling in!" Zelda stopped her beating, and stared down at him. "Go on..." he urged, "just put your hand to it."

She looked over at the others: they were all standing still, watching this bizarre scene play out with a mix of shock and amusement. "Just do it..." Ash sighed; she folded her arms and leaned back against the table, "if nothing else, it'll shut him up."

Zelda hesitated for a moment, then she slowly raised her right hand and pressed it to the air vent: "I can feel it!...It's not strong, but I can definitely feel air goin-aaah!"

Mav dropped her! He caught her again, just as her feet touched the ground: "That was for hitting me." Then he let go, and made his way towards the others, leaving the shocked Zelda frozen in place behind him: "So, we have some time then?"

"*Some* time..." Ash confirmed, "but the more air that's sucked out, the worse it'll get."

"Alright..." he noted, sounding rather subdued, "then let's get to it."

Zelda didn't rejoin the group; instead, she inspected the wall opposite the table — the one with the keyholes. It wasn't like the other three, which were similar to the walls they'd seen throughout the night: large, grey, stone blocks; not symmetrical, and very, very old. This wall, however, looked like one solid piece from end to end: it was flatter, smoother, and more uniform than the stone used in the other walls. As she ran her fingertips over the surface, she could tell immediately that it was machine-finished.

Next, she examined the keyholes: they were out of alignment, and each one had a different orientation — one was positioned normally, one was turned sideways, and the third was at an angle. She knew there must be a purpose behind it, but what?

She was so focused on them, that she didn't hear Sam approaching from behind — as he reached out and touched her on the shoulder, she screamed!

"I'm sorry! I'm sorry!"

"What is it?!" Danny cried.

"It's fine!" Zelda shouted back, "I'm fine...Sam just startled me."

"Did you find something?" Ash inquired.

"I dunno..." she used her hand to call them over, "come take a look at this."

Ash put down the keys she was holding, and walked across the room. Danny was also curious; but as he turned to Mav, he was shocked by his appearance: "Mav!...What's wrong?!" The others turned to see him leaning over the table: his eyelids were drooping, and he looked like he was about to faint. "What's wrong with you?!" Danny pressed again. Mav looked at him: he tried to speak, but couldn't.

"It's the vacuum!" Ash exclaimed, "He overexerted himself before, and now his muscles are low on oxygen."

"I...I'm...fine..." he stuttered, "I just need...to catch...my breath."

"You're not gonna catch it in here..." Zelda told him, now using a much softer tone, "you need to rest."

"*Relax*..." Danny insisted; he put a hand on his shoulder, and eased him to the ground, "just chill, we'll take care of this one...you've done enough for us already."

Mav slid to the floor, taking long, steady breaths. The others realized that if he was already feeling the effects, it wouldn't be long until they were too.

"So, Zelda..." Ash resumed, "show us what you found." She walked them back over to Sam, and began pointing out the differences between that wall and the others — including the odd arrangement of the keyholes.

"It could be nothing." Danny threw out.

"Has anything so far been nothing?"

"Well, the symbols on the floor back there—"

"Those *had* a meaning..." she asserted, "to mislead us."

"So..." Ash wondered, "why set the keyholes this way?"

"That's what I was working on, when Sam startled me."

"I'm sorry!" he begged again.

"It's fine..." she assured him, "let's just figure this out." She looked back at Mav — he was laying on the floor, with his jacket rolled-up under his head: "We need to hurry."

Danny knew she was right. He looked at Ash, who was running her fingers over the keyholes: then she crouched down, like she was trying to look through them and into the wall. He caught on to her intentions, and brought over a torch. "Thanks." she said, taking it from him. For a moment, his thoughts were once again on her. *Does she feel it too?...Is there a chance?* He only snapped out of it when she stood up, and handed it back to him: "Here, take a look." He bent down, and held the light to the keyholes: he adjusted it with his hand, as he moved his head around, trying to look inside with the best angle.

"What's in there?" Zelda asked him.

"It's like...it looks like...like the inside of a *machine*." She looked to Ash, who nodded in agreement; then, Danny stood up and handed her the torch: "See for yourself." She knelt down and looked through: inside, she saw joints and cogs, pulleys and levers — the lock wasn't *in* the wall, it *was* the wall.

Zelda stood up, and turned to the others: "What *is* that?"

"I'm not sure." Danny responded.

"Me neither..." Ash shrugged, "but that might be why they're set this way."

"Whaddya mean?"

"I think it probly has to do with what's inside the wall..." she explained, "something with the internal mechanism."

Then, they all turned to Sam — he'd been quiet for a while — not unusual for him, but they wanted his opinion. When they saw him, though, his condition was shocking: his long, lanky frame wobbled as if it were being blown in the wind; his eyes sagged, and his shoulders were slumped over. After Mav, he was the biggest in the group, and it was clear now that the low oxygen level was getting to him.

"Sam!" Zelda gasped.

"Huh?" he sounded.

The three of them now felt a heightened sense of urgency — one by one, they were going down. They helped him over to the table, and laid him on the floor next to Mav, who was barely still conscious.

"We gotta get outta here!" Danny panicked, "Now!"

"Just calm down..." Ash pleaded, "the more

worked up we get, the more it'll affect us." She placed one hand on his chest, and the other on his back: "Close your eyes and breathe." He did as she said — but with her hands pressed against him, it wasn't easy to slow his heart rate.

Sure enough, Zelda stated as much. "That's probly not the best way to calm him down." she remarked. This time, she was the recipient of Ash's death stare — she threw her hands up in deference, and walked back to the keyholes.

Danny did calm down though, surprising even himself — once again, Ash seemed to have the magic touch. "Better?" she asked, as he opened his eyes.

"Much." he breathed; then they rejoined Zelda, and got to work on solving the puzzle.

"Well, it's three numbers..." she pointed out, "let's start there."

"Their symbol is infinity..." he reminded them, "why don't we try eight-eight-eight?" Ash and Zelda both agreed, and he took all three keys out of the '8' box: he gave one to each girl, keeping one for himself, then they put the keys into the locks — Zelda on the left, Ash to the right, and Danny in the middle.

"Turn on 'three'..." Ash instructed, "one...two... *three*." They turned and twisted the keys: pushing them, pulling them, struggling to make them move — but it was no use; they were wrong.

"OK..." Zelda gave up, "any more ideas?" Ash and Danny looked to each other, but both were drawing blank. "What if they're tryna trick us again?" she proposed, "There's three locks...what if it's just one-two-three?"

"Couldn't hurt." Ash figured.

Danny returned the keys to box '8', then he picked

up one each from boxes '1', '2' and '3'. He handed Zelda the '1' key, Ash the '3' key, and kept the '2' for himself. "On 'three' again…" Ash told them, "one…two…*three*." Each of them tried to turn their keys — but like before, they wouldn't budge.

They were wrong, but there was something even more worrying to contend with: while she was struggling with her key, Zelda had trouble holding on to it. "G-Guys…" she trembled, "my arm feels weak." She could see the worry on their faces: they all knew it would take at least two people to unlock the door — so if they lost one more, they would *really* be in trouble.

Danny rushed back to the table, and waited for the girls to call out new numbers.

"Three-six-nine!" Ash shouted to him.

Zelda thought for a moment: "Tesla?"

"Worth a shot."

He brought the keys over, and they repeated the process: they each put their keys in the locks and tried to turn them — once again, though, there was no movement. He put his face in his hands and rubbed his eyes. "This is *so* frustrating." he sighed, "Every second we're losing air, and we just hafta keep cycling through random numbers."

"Come on…" Ash encouraged them, "we can figure this out, just think."

"What about degrees?" Zelda suggested.

"What about them?" he questioned.

"Y'know, how all the angles in a square add up to three-hundred-and-sixty degrees?…And one-eighty in a triangle?"

"Alright…" Ash agreed, "let's try it." Danny got the necessary keys, and they tried again: wrong on '090°';

wrong on '180°'; wrong on '360°'; wrong on '720°'.

"Shit!" Zelda screamed, throwing her keys down in anger.

"Calm down..." Ash warned her, "we can't get worked up...just breathe."

"I can't take this!...I never thought I'd miss falling through the floor!" She leaned back against the wall, and Ash and Danny could see that she was breathing heavily.

"You're getting light-headed." Ash told her.

"Wait..." Danny noticed, "shouldn't I be the next one to feel it?"

"It's because of all that with Mav..." she said, "the slapping and everything...it musta burned up a lotta oxygen."

"He didn't know—"

"It's OK, I'm not blaming him...it's just the most likely explanation."

"Guys, stop..." Zelda mumbled, "let's keep going... what else can we try?"

"I guess there's a bunch." Ash replied, "There's Pi, twenty-two-over-seven...the first three digits of the golden ratio, one-point-six-one...nine-one-one...six-six-six...let's just try them all."

One by one, they went through every significant three-digit combination they could think of; but no matter how many they tried, they just couldn't get the keys to turn. Now things were getting even worse — Danny could feel *his* arm getting weak — they didn't have much time left to open the door.

By this point, Zelda was barely hanging on; it wouldn't be long until she was out like Mav and Sam. *Mav and Sam!* Danny rushed over to check on them. He knelt down to Mav first: he could hear a slow, drawn-out wheeze as his lungs gasped for air. Next, he put his hand under Sam's nose — still breathing, but for how much longer? Time was almost up: they had to get out of this room — *now*.

NINETEEN

Teddy woke up: it was hard to see in the dimly lit room, so he just stared at the ceiling, waiting for his eyes to come into focus. For a moment, he didn't remember where he was; the dreams of last night were still so vivid in his mind. Then he yawned — a long and lazy yawn. He stretched his arms and legs out as far as he could, creating an 'X' with his body — but his left leg bumped up against something. He turned his head, and saw a tangle of flowing blonde hair — now he remembered — it wasn't a dream, after all: it was real.

He gently pulled down on the sheets, and a shoulder peeked out from underneath. He straightened his head again; beaming ear-to-ear, as the memories of the previous night came flooding back into his mind. *How can things be so perfect?* he wondered, *How can she be so perfect?* He truly believed that in that moment, he was the happiest man on earth.

"Mmm..." he heard her moan; then the sound of the sheets ruffling. Emma, now awake, was slowly rolling over. He turned to his left, and saw those bright, crystal-blue eyes staring back at him. A smile formed on the corners of her mouth, which he couldn't help but replicate on his own — it was like her joy was contagious. "Hey..." she spoke, softly. He stared into her eyes, then they both leaned in and shared a kiss. He was in heaven; he could have stayed with her in this moment forever.

Beep! Beep! Beep! The alarm went off like a siren, jolting them both back to the real world — and in the real world, they had to go to work. They had spent most of the weekend together; and while the fairytale hadn't ended, it was definitely on pause — luckily, Emma had stopped at her place the day before and packed some clothes. Teddy told her to shower and get dressed, while he made breakfast: he went downstairs, to the kitchen, and pulled a box out of the cabinet. "'Add water and mix'…" he read, "how hard could that be?"

ΔΔΔ

He was just finishing up, when she descended the staircase: "Mmm, those look good." He smiled, with a sense of satisfaction: he had actually made real, edible food — in the kitchen, by himself. *So what if they're from a mix?* he thought, *This counts.* They sat down to eat, and he anxiously waited for her opinion. "They're delicious!" she cheered, hastily digging in for more. He exhaled his relief, then made a mental note to YouTube some cooking videos later on. "So, listen…" she said, between bites, "I was thinking about your problem…with the safe."

"Go on…"

"From what you told me…about the text, and the engraving…I think it probly belonged to someone who worked with him." Emma watched him; silently fidgeting with her ring, while trying to read his face.

Clang! Teddy dropped his fork on the plate: "Of course!…How could I've missed that?!" She smiled, and leaned back in her chair. "Maybe there's an old company directory around here?" he added, turning his head side-to-side.

"If there isn't, would it be hard to get one?"

"Umm, I dunno...but I'm sure we can figure it out."

"Yes..." she beamed, "I'm sure *we* can."

After that, they finished eating, then Teddy jumped in the shower. He wasn't in there very long; and when he exited the bathroom, he thought he heard Emma's voice speaking to him. "What was that?!" he called out — but there was no response. He walked to the top of the stairs, and tried again: "Are you talking to me?!"

"I hafta go..." he heard her say; she put her phone down, and looked up at him. "Oh, no, sorry, that was my neighbor...she said she hadn't seen me all weekend..." she giggled lightly, as she explained, "she's just being nosy, don't worry about it."

△△△

Teddy finished getting dressed, and they left for work. Throughout the subway ride, and the walks in-between, they talked about little things — jokes, and casual observations mostly — just things to pass the time. Once they got there, however, the office rumors were rampant.

Knock. Knock. It was Tony at the door: "Hey, bud!"

"Tony!" he exclaimed, "Come in, come in!" Tony entered the office, closing the door behind him: "Great party the other night!"

"You sure it was the *party* that was great?"

They both erupted with laughter — Teddy knew what he meant — he didn't actually do much that night but talk with Emma. Now, on Monday morning, the party — which was only three days earlier — seemed like ages ago. So much had happened since then, and he wasn't the same person he was before.

"Everyone's talking about you two..." Tony revealed, "and, did I hear right?...You showed up *together* this morning?"

"I'm not one to kiss and tell." he responded. He didn't have to tell — his face gave it away. Teddy had been on cloud nine since he walked in, and everyone knew why.

"It's cool, man, I'm happy for you...I hope it all works out." *So do I.* he thought.

"Anyway..." Tony continued, "just remember we have that lunch meeting at two."

"Oh, crap!...I completely forgot!"

"Yeah, I figured you had other things on your mind...don't worry about it, though, I got it handled... just make sure you're there."

"I will be!" he promised, "Thanks again, man, I really appreciate it."

"Cool..." Tony replied, as he stepped out the door, "see you then!"

Teddy sat for a while, reflecting on the past few days. *Wow, I could never have dreamed...*

ΔΔΔ

More time went by, and he got done what little work that he could; after Emma, and his mystery quest, there really wasn't much space left in his head for anything else. He checked his watch: it was one-fifty-five. *Almost time.*

Then, there was another knock on the door: "Just gimme a minute, Tony!...I'm almost ready!"

"Tony?" Emma joked, "Don't tell me you've found someone else?"

He rose to his feet to meet her, and they embraced each other with a long, passionate kiss. When it was over, he noticed that she'd left the door half-open: "You sure you wanna do this *here*?"

"Oh, let them talk...they're gonna do it anyway."

"I guess." he shrugged, then he leaned in and kissed her again.

When they finally let go of each other, Emma sat down and he continued gathering all the files and papers he needed for the meeting. "So, I was thinking..." she began, "maybe we could have lunch together?...Brainstorm some more about the 'secret project'?"

"I'd love to..." he told her, as he checked the time, "but I have a meeting in...I'm late!" He grabbed what he could, and ran for the door; then, he stopped suddenly, realizing he was running out on her: "Umm, how bout tonight?...My place again?"

"Oh, I can't tonight."

Instantly, he felt deflated; the thought of spending the night alone — something to which he'd become accustomed — now seemed like a daunting prospect: "Why, uh...why not?"

"I promised some friends we'd have a girls' night." she said, "We planned it weeks ago...I don't even wanna go, really, I—"

"It's OK..." he stopped her, "you don't hafta explain." He checked his watch again: "Well, I gotta go... just, uh...call me later?"

"Of course." she smiled, "Now, go!" She gestured with her hands for him to hurry, and he ran off to his meeting — he somehow managed to make it inside, just as things were getting started.

Luckily for him, Tony *did* have it under control. Teddy, who was usually the most prepared, most reliable person in the office, felt a little ashamed that he'd let this slip his mind. Actually, if he were being honest, he hadn't really done much 'work' at work, in the last week or so.

When the meeting ended, he went straight for Tony: "Thanks again, man, you saved me in there."

"It's cool, Ted, you've saved me plenty before."

"Still..." he went on, "I've been slipping lately...it won't happen again."

"Don't beat yourself up..." Tony patted him on the back, "we all have off days."

If you only knew.

ΔΔΔ

Later that night at home, Teddy decided to go through Miles' old work things again. He thought that if he could find a MilTech directory, then he might be able to match the initials 'DRZ' with an old colleague of his brother's. This time, though, he wouldn't go tearing through everything and have it scattered all over the floor — instead, he would be more methodical: open the box, open the container, search through, repack, put it away, move on to the next one.

He hadn't seen or heard from Emma in hours, but that didn't stop him from checking his phone every five minutes. "This is stupid..." he mumbled to himself, "you're being stupid." Feeling hungry, he got up and went downstairs. He walked into the kitchen and opened the fridge: "Of course it's empty!" He slammed the door shut, and picked up his keys — with all the excitement of the past several days, grocery shopping hadn't been high on his list of priorities.

As he drove, he thought about Emma — it had been so long since he'd had a real relationship. The years since the accident seemed like one giant blur: he was just twenty-two the other day, now he was forty — where did the time go? *What about Emma?* he wondered, *How's she still single?* She was beautiful, she was smart, she was funny, she was kind; yet in her early-thirties, she still hadn't found someone? *Maybe she did?...Maybe that was the person on the phone?* He quickly snapped himself out of it. "What's wrong with you?!" he yelled, "This girl actually *likes* you, and you're questioning it?!"

After he was done berating himself, he drove through a McDonald's and got a Big Mac and fries. He started to eat in the car; and by the time he got home, there was nothing left: "Oh, well." He threw out the empty bag as he stepped into the house; he knew he wouldn't be able to focus on anything else that night, so he took a shower and got into bed. *I'll figure it out tomorrow.*

△△△

Buzz. Buzz. He was half-asleep, when his phone started going off: he rolled over and picked it up off the nightstand — it was a text from Emma! As he opened the message, he saw the time: 2:36am. *What?...When did I fall asleep?* It read: 'Hey! I know it's late, but I might have a lead!'

He groggily typed a response: 'Really?! How?' Then he waited for her to reply — the seconds felt like years.

Buzz. "Finally!" he exclaimed: 'My friend's husband

used to work for MilTech!' He saw the three dots, indicating she was typing. *Buzz.* 'What years did your brother work there? He might have a directory!'

He wrote back: 'It was about 1997-2001. Anything in that range would help, but probably closer to the end would be best.' He waited again for her to respond — ten minutes went by; then twenty; then thirty. "Come on!" He couldn't stand it anymore — he had to send another text: 'Anything?' The three dots popped up again, but then they disappeared: "What the hell?!...OK, OK, just relax."

Buzz. 'Got it!' Teddy raised his fists, triumphantly. *Buzz.* '2000'.

'Thank you! Thank you! Thank you!' he replied; then one more: 'You're the best!'

Buzz. 'Don't forget it!' *Buzz.* 'See you tomorrow!'

'See you then!' he signed off.

He put the phone down and stared at the ceiling — the same ceiling he was looking at that morning, while Emma lay next to him: "What a girl!...I think I'm in love!"

TWENTY

"Come on!" Danny urged, "We hafta think!...Three digits, we can do this!" He went over to the wall, and examined the locks again. Zelda, now sitting with her back against it, had pulled her knees into her body — her head was down, and it was obvious that she couldn't hang on much longer. Danny looked at the keyholes — he knew there must be something they'd missed — and when he went to grab another torch, it hit him: "No!"

Ash was startled: "What is it?!"

"The torches!" he cried, "How could we be so dumb?!...They're burning up all the oxygen!" Her eyes shot open — even *she* hadn't realized it — they had to put them out!

They both picked up the torches, one by one, and crushed them into the floor: they stomped on the burning embers, eventually managing to put out all the fires except for one — seven torches were extinguished, but they still needed one for the light.

Danny looked down at Zelda: she was almost gone. "It's up to us!" he declared.

"Alright..." Ash resolved, "it must be another trick...look at the clue again...'tri-lock'?...It must be something with 'threes'."

"What about a sum?" he suggested, "Remember

what I said before, about the 'eights'?...It's like an infinity...maybe it's three numbers that add up to eight?"

"That's good..." she said, "let's try it."

"How should we start?"

"Let's do eight-zero-zero, then work from there." He picked up the keys, and brought them to her: together, they tried every variation of an '8' key with two '0' keys — but nothing worked. Danny was despondent, but Ash quickly moved on. "Seven, one and zero!" she called out. They picked up the new keys and tried again, using every possible arrangement; after those failed, they moved on to 'six-two-zero' and repeated the process.

Meanwhile, Zelda was totally gone: she was so fatigued that she had fallen over, onto her side. She was in a fetal position; barely conscious, with her back still touching the wall. "We hafta stop for a minute..." Danny insisted, "we need to check on the others."

"You check..." Ash told him, "I'll get more keys."

By now, he was feeling the effects too — he knew there must not be much oxygen left. As he wobbled his way over to the two boys, he felt light-headed, and the room started to spin.

He checked Mav first, then Sam. *Still breathing.* Next, he made his way back to Zelda; he knelt down and shook her gently: "Hey, you still with us?"

"Hmm..." she groaned; her eyes barely opened, and she struggled to lift her head off the floor.

"Don't worry..." he whispered, easing her back down, "we're gonna get outta here." He looked to his right — Ash had assembled more keys and was ready to go: "What's next?"

"Six-one-one." she replied. They went back to work, trying combination after combination — but each one failed; each one let them down.

"Aaah!" he screamed, "I can't do this!" He gasped for air: "I'm so weak...the room...the room is spinning..." She saw it on his face: his eyes were closing — he was going down!

"No!" she begged him, "Stay with me!"

"I...I...I..." He stumbled around in a circle, like a dog chasing its tail. She knew she had to get him back; she had to get his adrenaline going, somehow. Then his right knee buckled — he collapsed!

She caught him, just before he hit the floor — but he was losing consciousness — if he did, they were all doomed. Just then, a thought popped into her head — a crazy thought, yes, but she was desperate. She bent down, still holding two handfuls of his hoodie, and pulled him close to her — then she pressed her lips to his!

Danny's eyes shot open! His heart raced, and his palms began to sweat: he was no longer falling into the abyss — she did it!

Once she saw that he was awake, she pulled back and took a breath — his eyes were wide, and his mouth hung open. "How do you feel?" she asked him.

"G-Good..." he stuttered, trying his best to sound calm — inside him though, it was like the Fourth of July!

"OK..." she proceeded, composing herself as she stood, "*ahem*...let's finish this."

He put his hands on the floor, to push himself back up; but as he did, he caught a glimpse of the keyholes from a different angle: "Oh, my God!"

"What is it?!"

"A triangle!" he yelled.

"What?"

"It's a triangle!" He traced a line through the center

of each keyhole — there it was, right in front of them: *tri-lock* — *triangle*.

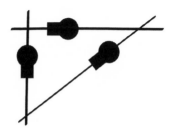

"You're right!" Ash exclaimed, "The numbers, they must each be a side!"

"But, what numbers?"

"If it's a right triangle..." she calculated, "then using Pythagoras' Theorem, the lowest numbers for each side would be—"

"Three, four and five!"

"Yes!...Let's get the keys!"

They ran to the table, and took a key from each box; then, they raced back to the wall and inserted them: '3' to the left, '4' in the middle, and '5' on the right. Ash held the first two, while Danny took the hypotenuse. "On 'three'..." she instructed, "one...two...three!" Together, they turned the keys — this time, there was no resistance. *Click! Click! Click! Click! Click!* The gears turned; the locks opened; then, finally, they heard a familiar sound — the wall grinding across the floor.

TWENTY-ONE

Inside the control room, both guards were on pins and needles. "Yes!...Yes!" the younger one cheered. They watched, in real time, as Ash and Danny opened the door. "They did it!" he shouted, leaping to his feet — he grabbed the jacket of his older colleague, and shook him back and forth.

"Settle down!" The older man pushed him off: "We're not supposed to root for them!"

"I know, I just—"

"We watch and report...that's it!"

"Yeah, sorry..." he agreed, trying to calm himself, "I know, you're right...but, wow!...That was intense, wasn't it?!"

"Listen, rookie, you'd better keep it together if you wanna stay in this job." He paused, gesturing for the younger man to sit down: "Besides, they have plenty worse than that coming their way."

The younger guard let out a heavy sigh: "Worse than *this*?" The older man nodded. "Damn...poor kids." He turned his chair back towards the monitors, still out of breath from his celebrations. "Should I call the Director?"

"Not yet." the older man replied, "Three of them are still out, on the floor...let's wait and see what happens before we tell him anything."

"Yeah, OK...then I'm gonna head outside for a quick smoke, if that's alright?"

"Sure, just don't take too long."

"Roger that!" The younger guard stepped out of the control room, and made his way through the corridor; when he exited the guardhouse, he pulled a cigarette from the pack in his pocket and lit it. *"Damn..."* he breathed, "that's good." He savored the feeling, as he exhaled a cloud of smoke.

He looked out, towards the main house, completely in awe of the imposing structure before him. This wasn't just some old, stone castle in the middle of nowhere; it was like a living, breathing entity unto itself. One giant machine, which lay hidden from the world—it could destroy you, or it could reveal your true nature. He marveled at the engineering of it all.

Equally impressive was the dense forest that surrounded it — it stretched for miles and miles in every direction. No one would ever find this place; unless, of course, they knew where to look. He did feel bad for the kids, though, but he also admired their courage. *They never once lost hope*, he thought, *I get why they were chosen.*

Just then, he was startled by the snap of a branch: "Hello?!" It came from nearby, in the woods. He took one last puff of his cigarette and flicked it away, then he walked over to the tree line to investigate.

He took out his flashlight and turned it on, pointing it in the direction of the noise: he moved the light around—to the trees, to the ground, all over—trying to detect any signs of movement. *Musta been a deer or something.* Then he switched the light off, and headed back to the guardhouse; the heavy, reinforced door closed behind him with a solid *thunk*.

Once he was back inside, the man in the woods lowered his gun and holstered it. He didn't need it — yet.

TWENTY-TWO

Seven carried the unconscious man back up to the twelfth floor. One by one he took the stairs, thinking it should probably be more difficult considering there was a grown man tossed over his shoulder. *Must be the adrenaline.* he figured, and didn't give it another thought. He was an assassin, after all; he had never been this close to a target, for this long. He was always in and out before anyone knew he was even there — so maybe he didn't know his full capabilities?

He had always prided himself on efficiency; but this time, they had come to him — on *his* turf — so he could take it slow. As he carried the man, he realized this would be the first victim he'd ever spoken to. Others had spoken to him, of course — well, begged, really — but he had never replied. It was his way of coping with it all; his way of keeping the distance.

Finally, he saw the sign with the '12' on it. He poked his head out, making sure the coast was clear — it was, so he brought the man inside his apartment and shut the door. He flopped him down, into a chair, and propped it up against the dining table; then, he opened a kitchen drawer and pulled out a shiny, silver roll of duct tape.

Waaaap...waaaap...waaaap. The sound of the unrolling tape, combined with the pressure on his wrists and ankles, seemed to be waking the man up. Seven didn't just need him awake, though, he needed him alert; so he went to the bathroom and took out a small packet of smelling salts from the medicine cabinet. When he returned, he could hear the man groaning; so he pulled a chair in to face him, and sat down.

Rip. He waved the open packet under the man's nose; and a few seconds later, he sprang back to life: "Wha?!...Huh?!" Seven leaned back, watching the man struggle and squirm in his chair — he was slowly coming to the realization of where he was, and more importantly, who he was with. Eventually, he stopped moving and just stared. His mouth hung open, and his glassy eyes grew wide; his hands were shaking, even while strapped down, as though electricity were pulsing through him.

Seven had never done the slow, drawn-out kill before — he always had to be quick. Maybe he would walk past someone in a crowd, stabbing them in a split second; or, use his expert marksmanship to shoot them from hundreds of yards away. But as he looked upon the scared, trembling, hopeless man in front of him, he realized he could take his time — he could extract everything he needed to know.

"You're probably used to being on this side of things..." he began, "well, that's OK, it's my first time too." He got up, and walked to the bedroom — the man in the chair could hear drawers opening and closing.

Then Seven returned: he laid out a lineup of knives, and his two guns on the table, before sitting back down. The man stared at those instruments of torture, all neatly aligned in a row. "I think we should begin..." Seven proposed, "don't you?" He pulled out a metal lighter, and began flicking it open and closed; the helpless man watched as an intense blue flame shot out of it like a laser, on and off, as if it were taunting him. "Let's get the obvious out of the way...you, and your...'friends'..." he gestured to the dead soldiers, "were sent here to kill me." He paused there, but the man didn't respond; so he flicked on the lighter and used the flame to brush his fingertips.

"Aaaaahhh!" the man screamed, reflexively trying to recoil his hand which was duct-taped in place.

Seven closed the lighter and spoke again: "So...you were saying?"

The man realized it was no use — he didn't have any options left — he had to cooperate, and hope that Seven would spare his life. "T-They sent us..." he trembled, "I-I'm just following orders." He hoped the assassin would understand.

"But, why *me*?"

The man shook his head; he looked around the room, desperately, as if there was someone else to whom he could plead his case: "Look...y-y'know how it is?... They don't tell us *why*...they just tell us."

"Hmm." Seven ripped off another piece of duct tape, and put it over the man's mouth. Sweat was now pouring down his face — he realized he had displeased the assassin with his answer. Seven stood up; he looked around the room and covered his mouth with his left hand — then with his right, he grabbed a knife off the table and buried it in the man's thigh!

"Uuuummmmhh!...Hmmmuuh!...Uuuummmmm!" The man tried to scream, but the tape stifled his attempts. The chair rocked and shook, as tears streamed down his face; his black pants began to glisten with blood, and he struggled to breathe through his now-blocked nose.

While the man was writhing in agony, Seven calmly walked to the kitchen and poured himself a glass of water: he drank it, then he washed the glass, dried it, and returned it neatly to its spot inside the cabinet.

When he was finished, he walked back over to the bound man and pulled the knife out of his leg, ripping his blood-soaked pants in the process. He flicked on the lighter; and using the searing blue flame, he cauterized the wound. The man tried his best to scream, but again, the tape prevented him doing so — all that Seven could hear were muffled hums and groans.

Once his hysteria had subsided, Seven ripped the tape from his mouth. The man, bloody and defeated, stared back at him with absolute terror. He knew now that there was no soft spot to which he could appeal; there was no chance of sympathy — this man had a coldness about him that was inhuman.

"Let's try this again..." Seven continued, "why do they want to kill me?"

"OK, OK..." the man surrendered, "all I know is, they said that you're a liability...and that we had to 'X' you." Seven could see the fear in his eyes — there was no doubt he was telling the truth. Did they know about his 'extracurricular' activities?

"I've always been a model soldier..." he asserted, "I've never asked questions...I've always got the job done." He paused for a moment, before finishing: "Why, all of a sudden, am I now a liability?"

The man went to speak, but hesitated. Seven felt that he would lie, so he picked up a gun off the table and rested it on his leg: "No!...Please!...I-I don't..." He was hyperventilating — he couldn't breathe, much less speak.

"Tell me what I want to know." Seven calmly instructed.

"Please!" the man begged again, "I—" Then he stopped; he went quiet, figuring it was now or never to make a deal: "If I tell you, y-you'll let me live?"

"Live?...You think you're bargaining for your life?" The man didn't speak; he just stared at Seven with tear-filled eyes. "You died the moment you walked through that door...but, if you give me what I want, you won't have to suffer through the short time you have left."

The man weighed his options: he thought if there was only something he could offer his captor, some reason to keep him alive, then it might just buy him enough time to escape. "Wait!" he remembered, "My phone!"

"Your phone?"

"Yes!" he exclaimed, "Back pocket, to my right!"

Seven stood up, and reached behind him; he took out the phone, then he pressed it against the man's thumb to unlock it: "What am I looking for?"

"The secure message system...look at the received from yesterday."

He found it: 'One of our agents has become a liability. He must be eliminated. Retrieve/destroy all data files in his possession. Highest priority for anything marked 'S.H.O.T.'.'

SHOT? There it was again. "What does SHOT mean?" Seven asked him.

"I-I don't know...I swear, they didn't tell me...all I know is, it's secret...only for the highest levels."

"The man I killed, the one with the flash drive... who was he?"

The bound man gulped down a lump in his throat: "He was a scientist...o-one of ours...he was trying to get information out."

"So, why did they think I'd look?"

"But—" the man started to answer, before quickly stopping himself.

"Go on." Seven assured him.

"But...you did." That pushed him into a rage! He kicked his chair over, and grabbed another knife — he was about to plunge it into the man's chest! "Wait!... There's more!"

"Speak!"

"OK! OK!...Someone alerted us!...Someone who was close to the scientist, and..."

"*And*?!"

"And, that's how we found out!...So, there's someone else...someone who knows about SHOT...I can help you find them!"

Seven didn't respond; he put the knife back down on the table, and picked up his chair — then he sat down, once again pointing the gun at the man's head. With his other hand, he picked up the phone and began scrolling through it — there was an address. He turned the screen around: "What's this place?"

"That's...umm..." the man racked his brain for the answer.

"Now!" Seven demanded.

"Someone who...they had something to do with it...I don't know, but I can help you!" He prayed that he had proven his worth.

"You have been a great help..." Seven admitted, as he eased back in his chair; the man sighed with relief, "but, your time has ended." He pulled the trigger! Another silent bullet shot out of the gun — it went through the man's forehead, snapping it backwards!

Seven stood up; he stared down at the address on the phone: "I think I'll have to pay you a visit."

TWENTY-THREE

Whoosh! Air rushed in, quickly filling the partial vacuum of the room; Danny felt it blowing past him, and he tried to inhale as much of it as he could — his lungs ached as they expanded, struggling to absorb every last drop of oxygen. The wall had slid away, to their right, creating a large opening that was roughly ten feet wide.

"We did it!" Ash cheered — she leapt up onto him, and he instinctively put his arms out to catch her. He was amazed at how light she felt; not that she should be heavy, but she almost seemed to be floating as he held her. Even when she let go, he didn't hear her feet touch down on the ground — it was like she was suspended from the ceiling by wires.

This wave of euphoria quickly faded, however, as they remembered they weren't alone — the others were still passed out, on the floor. "What should we do?" she asked him, "I don't think we should stay here, just in case it closes up again."

"But, we don't know what's out there." he countered, "If we move them like this, what if there's another trap?...We could be putting them in danger."

"I guess you're right..." she acknowledged, "we have air now, I suppose we can wait a little while longer." She paused, then turned towards the opening: "In the meantime, we should at least try to see what's out there."

"I-I don't think that's a good idea...what if it closes on us?"

"Don't worry, I'll just look from here." She moved to the opening and peered into it — she hoped that she'd be able to see something that would give an indication of what lay ahead: "It's really dark, I can't see anything... maybe I could just go in quickly?"

"No!" he objected, "We shouldn't split up." Danny walked over to look for himself: he was surprised to find that it wasn't the usual narrow corridor — this time, it seemed to be a large, open room. "Let's just wait." he said again.

"OK." she agreed, not wanting to push it further.

They went to Zelda — who still had her back against the lock-wall — and moved her out of the way. They laid her flat on the floor, like Sam and Mav; then, they sat down near the opening, and leaned back against the wall.

ΔΔΔ

A few minutes went by without any words — Danny was just trying to feel normal again — the adrenaline kick had worn off, and now he had a splitting headache. He tried taking a few deep breaths, figuring that would make it go away.

Ash, on the other hand, was busy plotting their next move: she thought about what trials might await them further on; and, with the others in such bad shape, would they be able to make it?

Danny was so focused on his breathing, that he hadn't realized they'd been sitting in total silence.

Should I speak? he wondered, *Does she want me to?* His mind went from calm and serene, to a beehive of worries. *What about the kiss?...Should I mention it?* More time passed, and he tried to muster his courage; but with each silent minute that went by, more and more doubt crept into his head.

Suddenly, as he was about to speak, they heard a noise: "Mmmm..." They jumped to their feet! "Uuummm..." It was Zelda — she was waking up!

"Zelda!" Ash exclaimed, "Relax!...Just breathe!"

"What...h-happened?"

"We solved it!"

They knelt down and helped her up: she couldn't yet stand, so they moved her to the wall and sat her against it. "Oh!" she cried, "My head is *pounding.*"

"So is mine..." Danny told her, "just take deep breaths, it helps." He was still a little wobbly himself, so he sat down next to her.

"I don't feel good..." she mumbled, "the room looks darker."

"That was us..." Ash revealed, "we put out most of the torches...there's only one left."

"What?...Why'd you do that?"

"They were burning up oxygen...that's why it ran out so fast."

"OK..." Zelda sighed, "I'll be alright, just gimme a minute."

"Take all the time you need..." Danny insisted, "we're not ready to move on yet." He pointed to the two boys, still lying motionless on the floor: "We hafta wait for them."

Zelda nodded, and closed her eyes; she sat up straight, trying her best to keep breathing — she knew this wasn't over, and she would need all her strength for whatever came next.

△△△

After a few more minutes, though, Danny got worried: Mav and Sam had been out for a while — long before the door opened — and they *still* hadn't woken up. He motioned to Ash: "We should check on them."

"OK." she replied, turning to Zelda, "You good?"

"Go...I'll be fine."

Ash and Danny walked across the room: he went straight for Mav, while she checked on Sam. As he crouched down and shook his friend, he could see Mav's face twitching into life. "Hey..." he prodded, "can you hear me?" He started to move: "Dude, wake up!" Mav moved his arms and bent his knees — finally, he sighed and opened his eyes. "Mav!" Danny yelled, "Are you OK?!"

He didn't reply right away; he turned to his left, and saw Sam lying next to him — also just coming to. "What happened?" he breathed, turning back to Danny.

"We figured it out!"

"Hmm...and, where are we?"

"Same room, but the door's open now."

"Mmm, OK." He lifted his head up, and looked around — he was trying to process everything that was happening.

"Just relax..." Danny eased him back down, "take your time, we'll move when you're ready." He looked over to Ash, who was helping Sam off the ground; then, he walked back to Zelda, and knelt down in front of her: "Feeling better?"

"Yeah, the breathing helps."

He nodded to her, and smiled; but as he was getting up, she grabbed his arm and held him back: "What is it?"

"I just..." she started, "I'm sorry...I've been giving you crap all night, and—"

"It's cool..." he assured her, "don't worry about it." Then he stood up, and grabbed the last remaining torch from its holder: he went back to the opening, being very careful not to cross the threshold, and held it out in front of him. He was hoping the light would show him something — *anything*. He thought that if he could get an idea of the next challenge, then maybe they could go in with a head start. It was no use, though, the dim yellow light wasn't strong enough to penetrate the inky blackness — so he returned the torch, and went back to the others.

ΔΔΔ

Eventually, Zelda was able to stand, then walk, and she joined Ash, Danny, and the other boys. Ash told them the story of what happened: that she and Danny had struggled with the combinations, and that he had figured out it was a triangle. She told them every detail, every little action they both took — except one.

Danny listened to her speak; he didn't interject at any point, but when she arrived at the part about the kiss, there was no mention of it — it was like it never happened. *Why wouldn't she tell them?...Does she not want them to know?* He decided there would be plenty of time to sulk later; now, though, Mav and Sam were able to stand, and they needed to move forward.

All five of them lined up by the opening: they looked around at one another, before stepping through.

They went on, slowly, being sure to stay close — then the door closed behind them. Their hearts raced; they waited in total darkness to see what would happen next. The seconds ticked away, but there was nothing.

Finally, they heard movement — more gears, and a light came in from the ceiling. It wasn't yellow light, but more white-and-blue — it was moonlight, and it was getting bigger. Then it flashed — it filled the room! They marveled: all around them were mirrors, strategically placed to reflect the light. The gears stopped: a staircase had descended from the ceiling and touched the floor — they were out.

TWENTY-FOUR

Teddy barely slept all night — there was just too much to be excited about. As if Emma wasn't perfect enough already, her help with the 'mystery quest' had been invaluable. He lay awake with his hands behind his head, staring at the ceiling. The room was starting to fill with light. Although he reveled in the good fortune that had come his way lately, in the back of his mind, there was still that lingering feeling of doubt. Good things rarely happened to him; and on some level, he was always waiting for the other shoe to drop.

But now, it was coming up to eight o'clock and he had to get to work. The route was the same — walks and subway rides — but when he finally made it, she wasn't there. His enthusiasm popped like a balloon.

He stepped into his office and closed the door behind him; he figured that while he waited for Emma to arrive, he could try to catch up on the work he'd been neglecting — so he sat down at his desk and got to it. Teddy wasn't the type to do things halfway — when he did something, he went all in. He tore through many days' worth of work in only a few hours: finishing reports, running analyses, sending emails, scheduling meetings, even planning ahead for the rest of the week — he was a machine.

△△△

Once he finally came up for air, it was already past one o'clock. *Where is she?* he wondered — he didn't understand why Emma hadn't come to see him as soon as she'd got in. He stood up and walked through the office, casually looking around to catch a glimpse of her — but she was nowhere to be found. *Very strange,* he thought, *she hasn't called or texted, either.* He walked back to his office and closed the door; then, he picked up the phone — it rang and rang, he wondered if she'd even answer.

"Hmm...hello?"

"Oh, uh...hey." he stuttered.

"Heeyy." Her voice had all of its usual cheeriness, but she didn't sound well.

"What happened to you today?...I was worried."

"I know..." she sighed, "I'm sorry...last night got a little crazy, and I wasn't exactly in the best shape this morning."

"It's OK..." he told her, "I just...wanted to make sure you're safe, that's all."

"I know, sorry...I am."

There was a long pause on the line. "So..." he continued, "I guess I'll see—"

"Oh, crap!...I'm such an idiot!"

"Huh?"

"The book!" she exclaimed, "I'm so sorry, you must think I'm a total flake."

"No, I—"

"I have it!...Why don't I come by tonight?...We can check it out together."

"Yeah, OK..." he agreed, "that sounds good."

"Great!...Text me later?"

"I will."

They said their goodbyes, and hung up. *Well, at least I know she's alright.* The rest of the day was much like the beginning; he burned through as much work as possible, so that he and Emma would be free to work on their 'secret project'.

△△△

Later that night, he was pacing anxiously around the living room. *You shouldn't be this nervous,* he told himself, *she's just a girl...and she likes you!*

Ding-dong! The doorbell snapped him out of it. "OK..." he whispered, "just be cool."

He opened the door, but it wasn't her: "I got a pizza for..."

"Yeah, it's for me...how much do I owe you?"

"It's, ahh...twelve-fifty."

"Here's twenty...keep the change."

"Thanks!"

He took the pizza inside and put it down on the table, then he resumed his nervous pacing. He didn't have to wait long, though, it was just about another ten minutes or so when the doorbell rang again: "OK, this is it." He took in a deep breath, and exhaled it slowly, as he opened the door. "Hey." he greeted her, trying his best to sound casual.

"Hey!" Emma threw her arms around him and hugged him tight. "Sorry about today..." she said again, "I don't usually drink that much, and...well, you know how it is."

"Don't worry..." he assured her, "it's fine." There

was a moment of silence, as he gazed into her eyes; but when he caught himself staring, he nervously pulled away: "Oh, uh...I got pizza...you hungry?"

"Starving!" she declared, "And...take a look at this!" She pulled the MilTech directory out of her bag, and handed it to Teddy: "I haven't looked through it yet...I thought we should do that together."

"Thanks..." he took the book from her, "but let's eat first."

He put it down on the coffee table, and they both dove into the pizza: while they ate, he listened intently as she filled him in on the night before. *Her friend's husband worked for MilTech?* he thought, *What're the odds?*

After dinner, he put away the leftovers and Emma helped him with the dishes. There was a brief moment in the kitchen, when he saw her from behind, that he couldn't help but think that they'd gone from 'hot new romance' to 'old married couple' in the blink of an eye — he loved it.

"So..." he started, picking up the book, "you ready to do this?"

"Yes!" she cheered, "I've *literally* been waiting all day."

He went upstairs and gathered everything he could from Miles' old job: his ID badge, letters, papers, even stationery and pens with the company logo — he didn't leave anything behind. When he returned to the living room, they spread it all out on the coffee table and sat down on the couch.

"Where should we begin?" she asked him.

"Well, we know the initials are 'DRZ'...I figure there can't be many people that have last names starting with 'Z'."

"How scientific of you." she joked.

"Hey!" he objected, "That's good reasoning...I'm like Sherlock Holmes!"

"OK, boss..." she giggled, "we'll do it your way."

He took out a yellow legal pad and put it down on the table: "We'll have to go through each page, line by line, and put anyone with a 'Z' name on the list."

"OK...do you wanna look through the names, or write them down?"

"I'll look...you go through the rest of this stuff, just in case there's something I missed."

"Alright."

He started on the first page, but there were no pictures or eye-catching graphics — instead, all he saw were five columns: 'Name', 'Department', 'Sub-Department', 'Building #', and 'Extension #'.

ΔΔΔ

Teddy went through the pages in painstaking detail — it took him almost two hours just to make it halfway through the book. When he looked up, he saw Emma's head hanging off to the side — she had passed out. He looked down at his watch: clearly, this wouldn't be a one-night task, so he leaned over and gently woke her. "Hey..." he whispered, "let's go to bed...we can pick this up tomorrow."

"Mmmhmm." she moaned in agreement. He helped her off the couch, and walked her upstairs to the bedroom; he gave her some clothes to sleep in, then he laid her down on the bed, covering her delicately with the sheets. After that, he went into the bathroom to brush his teeth.

He stared at himself in the mirror: it was only a few days earlier that he saw his reflection, and thought how old he looked — now, it seemed as though ten years had been taken off. *What a difference it makes to have someone.*

With all the stress and nerves of the day, he fell sound asleep the moment his head touched the pillow. That night, there was no anxiety or worries for either of them: Teddy and Emma slept peacefully, side by side — it was like they'd been doing it for years.

The next morning, he wasn't awoken by the shrill beeping of the alarm, nor by his own restless mind; instead, it was a soft hand subtly caressing his cheek. He opened his eyes, and saw Emma's smiling face right above him. "Good morning." she said, as she leaned down and kissed him on the forehead.

"Yes..." he beamed, "it is."

They lay in bed a little while longer, savoring this blissful moment in silence. Finally, Emma moved her head off his chest and sat up: "Why don't I make breakfast this time?...You can jump in the shower."

"Uh, sorry..." he stammered, "I don't actually have any food." His face began turning red at that admission: "But, we can pick something up on the way?"

"Hmm..." she mused, "that sounds OK...we'll need to get going pretty quick though, don't you think?"

"Yeah..." he shrugged, "I guess."

"Well then..." she flashed him a mischievous grin, "I'll just hafta join you for that shower." She grabbed him by the arm and yanked him out of bed!

ΔΔΔ

When they arrived at work, they were met by wide, prying eyes — so they made a beeline for Teddy's office and closed the door. Just as it shut, he grabbed her by the waist and pulled her close — then he kissed her.

"What was *that*?" she asked, breathlessly.

"You were right the other day..." he smirked, "let them talk." When he let go of her, he put his briefcase on the desk and took out the directory.

"You brought it with you?"

"Yeah..." he responded, "I got a lot done yesterday while you were out, so I figured I could keep going with this."

"How much did you get done?"

"Umm, basically everything I had for the week."

"Wow..." she marveled, "that's amazing."

"You weren't here...I had to keep busy, somehow."

That made her blush; she grabbed his lapels with both hands, and pulled him in for another kiss.

"Well..." she sighed, releasing her hold on him, "I have a lot to catch up on."

"OK, I'll let you know if I find anything."

"You better!" she teased, as she headed for the door.

Once she was gone, he sat down at his desk and picked up where he left off: he combed through the names, writing down anything with a 'Z' in front of it. As he reached the end of the book, he stared down at his list — ten names, but none of them matched. *What am I missing here?* He moved his eyes around the page: "I wonder... could it be a double-barreled name?" He flipped back to the beginning and started again; this time, searching for hyphenated last names that began with 'R'. The hours flew by, and he didn't take a break — except to have a quick lunch with Emma — he just dug in and ran through the entire book again, cover to cover.

Still no luck, though. He dropped the book on the desk and let out a heavy sigh; then, he leaned back in his chair and rubbed his eyes. "I give up!" he yelled, slamming his fists down on the table — it was time to go, anyway, and he'd had enough. He went to see if Emma was ready, but there was a project that needed finishing and she had to stay late; so they made a plan to meet later that night at his place, and he went home — alone, exhausted, and in a bad mood.

ΔΔΔ

Once he got inside, he threw his bag on the dining table and emptied his pockets: on his phone, he noticed a little red tag indicating there was a voice message. He put it on speaker and hit 'play' while he began making a long-overdue grocery list: "Hello, Mister Logan, I'm calling from Doctor Young's office...this is just a reminder of your appointment this Thursday at one o'clock...if you need to reschedule, please call and let us know...thank you." *Oh, crap, the dentist...I completely forgot.*

He finished the list and started for the door; but just as he was walking out, something clicked in his brain: "Wait...*that's* why I couldn't find it!...It's not 'DRZ', it's '*Doctor Z*'!"

TWENTY-FIVE

"Yes!" Mav cheered, "We did it!" Danny, Sam, and Zelda all joined in, but Ash was nowhere to be found. *Where is she?* Danny wondered. He saw her off to the side, looking at one of the mirrors: she wasn't celebrating like the rest of them — her expression was one of caution.

"Hey..." he approached her, "what's wrong?"

"This doesn't feel right." she whispered.

"Whaddya mean?"

"It feels like another trick."

The others were going up the stairs, so she left to follow them. Danny turned to go with her; but just as he did, he caught a glimpse of himself in the mirror: his short, brown hair was all a mess — he scrambled to fix it before she could see.

He stared at his reflection: his soft features made him look younger than he was, and although he hated to admit it, he still had a babyface. He looked closer, but couldn't quite make out his light-brown eyes — they looked worn and tired — he could see the toll this night had taken on him. When he looked away from the mirror, he realized he was alone; the others had all ascended the staircase, so he quickly ran to join them. At the top, he found them stopped in their tracks — Ash was right, they weren't out yet.

They stood on a large, rectangular rooftop terrace: in his estimation, it must have been thirty feet wide by sixty feet long. It was open on three sides, and there were no barricades or railings to prevent them from falling over — not even a raised ledge. The side that was blocked off — a shorter one — had a very high, smooth wall. Around them was a panoramic view: trees as far as the eye could see, and hills off in the distance. There were no lights — except for the moon, which was peeking out from behind the rain clouds; it reflected serenely off the still waters of a nearby lake. *Thunk! Clang!* They all whipped around! The opening of the staircase had sealed itself up, and was now flush with the floor.

"No!" Zelda panicked, "This can't be happening!" She was stumbling backwards, towards the edge, so Mav grabbed her and pulled her back in. Sam also wasn't looking good — he sat down on the floor, and put his head between his knees. They figured that since he thought they were out, he would find his cousin here waiting for him — it wasn't to be, though, the maze wasn't finished with them just yet.

Ash wasn't feeling the emotions of the others; she stayed calm, poised, and ready to tackle this new challenge. She cautiously approached the edge, and looked over the side — it was a straight drop to the ground. It was the same story on the other two open sides as well: there was no way for them to climb down. She told the others to look for themselves, thinking maybe they could find something she'd missed; Mav let go of Zelda and went to check, but he could only corroborate her findings.

"Maybe it's something with the wall?" Danny suggested. Ash agreed, and they went to check it out along with Mav. They realized right away that it was too high, and the stone too smooth, for them to climb; but just as they were stepping back from it, Ash's heel sunk about an inch into the floor — *click*. Suddenly, the entire face of the wall split in two and opened like a double door: the two pieces wrapped around the sides, revealing a flat, single-piece stone wall. On it, hung another screen with a handprint, which Mav didn't hesitate to unlock:

> In this test, you must look to the skies. Find the special object that opens the door — but be careful, each wrong answer will push you closer to the edge.

Below the screen, carved into the stone wall, was a crude model of the solar system.

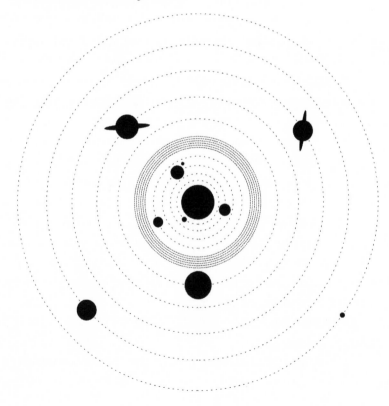

Mav, Ash, and Danny knelt down and stared at it, trying to decipher what it meant. Then, Sam and Zelda walked over: they read the clue and saw the model. "This is your field..." Ash said to her, "isn't it?" Zelda nodded in confirmation: "Any ideas?"

She got down on her knees, and felt the carving with her hands: "Well, to start off with, the positions of the planets are all wrong...so are the axes of Saturn and Uranus...and Jupiter and Neptune have rings, but they're not—"

"Forget all that..." Mav cut in, "how do we use this thing to open the door?"

She ran her fingertips around the 'planets' and the 'sun' — she noticed there were small gaps around the edges of each object: "These look like buttons...I think we hafta push them, and the 'special one' opens the door."

"Hold on..." Danny warned, "look at the clue...'each wrong answer will push you closer to the edge'."

"I was thinking the same thing." Mav acknowledged.

Sam looked puzzled: "What does it mean?"

"If we press the wrong buttons..." Danny explained, "the wall will move forward...that must be why there's no railings."

Ash stood up, and moved back, away from them: "So, let's think...we need to find the 'special one' to open the door...what about the sun?"

"I was thinking that..." Zelda revealed, "but it's too obvious."

"Maybe it's *so* obvious, they thought we wouldn't try it?"

"Listen..." Mav asserted, "we need to be careful on this one."

"That's funny coming from *you*." Ash remarked.

"Alright, just relax..." Danny cautioned, "we have time to figure this out."

"Yeah..." Zelda agreed, "besides, we could all use the fresh air." Ash and Mav both backed down. "The clouds look like they're blowing over..." she added, "once they do, we'll get a better view of the sky...we can probly figure it out then."

The other four agreed, and Danny sat down against the wall. Sam also took a seat, near the opposite side, and stared out at the lake — everyone knew what was on his mind, but no one dared bring it up. Zelda walked out, further than Sam, and looked up at the sky; she tried to find something that would give her the answer, or at least a hint. Mav followed behind her — he didn't want her to be alone after her mini panic attack.

While the others had walked off, Ash tried to examine the carving on the wall. She knew Zelda was right — they *did* need the fresh air — and although she'd never admit it, she wasn't looking forward to going back inside.

But Zelda soon came storming back, with Mav trailing close behind her. "He's insane!" she declared.

Danny stood up, and started over to them: "What'd you do now?"

"Nothing..." he replied, "I just made a slight suggestion, and she got all bent outta shape."

"*Slight suggestion*?...He wants to push a wrong button...on purpose!"

Ash rolled her eyes: "I knew it...he doesn't know what 'careful' means." By this point, Sam had taken notice of the commotion and come over to join them.

"Just hear me out…" Mav argued, "we don't know how many wrong answers we get, but I'm pretty sure it's not one—"

"Pretty sure?!" Zelda raved.

"Relax…" he continued, "anyway, if we see how far the wall comes forward, then we'll know what we're dealing with."

"What if it's two chances?" Ash objected, "Or three?…We'll be using up a try for nothing."

"Not really…" he countered, "we can try the sun… both you girls said that might be it, right?…So we either solve the puzzle, or cross it off the list." There was a brief silence, as everyone considered his proposal.

"It's actually not a bad idea." Danny admitted.

"Oh, my God!" Zelda screamed, "You too?!"

"It's a video game tactic." he told her, "When you're not sure about an obstacle, but have a few extra lives to spare, you can spend one or two trying new ways to get past it."

"Video games?" Ash questioned.

"No…well, yeah…" he stuttered, feeling slightly embarrassed, "it's just a strategy."

She weighed the idea in her head, before turning to Zelda: "I hate to say it, *but*…"

Zelda stared at her, bewildered — she couldn't believe Ash was agreeing to this madness. She then turned to Sam: "I guess you're on board with this too?"

"Why not give it a try?" he shrugged.

"Fine!" she yelled, "I'll be over *there*…have fun!" She walked as far away from the wall as she could, without getting too close to the edge.

"Maybe you guys should go with her…" Mav advised, "just in case."

Ash narrowed her eyes at him: "Push the button."

He waited for Sam and Danny to move her back a safe distance, then he stepped towards the carving and knelt before it: he slowly raised his hand and placed it on the 'sun' — he took a deep breath, then he pushed it.

The button went in, slightly; but when he released the pressure, it didn't pop back out. They waited in silence for a few seconds, then they heard something happening — it sounded like a violin being plucked — but there was still no movement. Mav was confused; he stood up, and turned around: "Maybe it's broken?" *Pow!* The wall shot forward!

TWENTY-SIX

Seven pushed his way through the cluster of bodies; it was almost eight-thirty, and the rush hour crowd were out in full force. There was no darkness to give him cover, so he approached the building in an easy, unthreatening manner. He walked inside and checked the walls for a map. *Third floor*, he read to himself, *Advanced Sciences*. He didn't go up, though, there were too many people; instead, he went back out to the street. He thought for a while about his next move; but every scenario, every angle he could think of, didn't get him what he wanted. He would have to wait until nightfall — only then, could he get inside without being seen.

It wasn't a disappointment, however, it gave him the whole day to plan; so he went to a private hotel downtown — one that he'd used for stakeouts and surveillance in the past. He walked up to the front desk, and got the key for his usual room: top floor, facing northeast. It offered the least obstructed view out, and, in a pinch, he could use the roof to escape — providing it ever came to that. It wasn't even ten o'clock yet, and already he'd survived an assassination attempt, killed three men, and discovered more about his mysterious employers than he had in the past several years.

He walked into the room and threw his bags on

the floor; then, he pulled the chair out from the desk, and began mapping out his strategy. The basics of it were simple: he would go back to the building, just before it was locked up for the night, and find somewhere to hide until no one else was around. If he had to kill a guard or two, so be it; but he wanted to avoid any trouble, just in case it limited his time — he would need as much of that as he could get. Next, he would locate the office of his target from the train; then he would go through everything, methodically and diligently: his books, his work, his contacts — Seven needed to find out *what* he knew and *who* he knew. He still had the address for the person of interest, but he didn't want to go there yet — not until he was armed with more information.

Once he'd finished planning, he packed away his things and stepped out to get some food. When he returned to the room, he swept it thoroughly — he had to assume they were on to him — then he set himself an alarm, and lay down on the bed. There would be no sleep tonight, so he had to get as much now as he could. He tossed and turned for a while — it may have been the adrenaline, or the anticipation that he felt — but eventually, he drifted off.

△△△

Beep! Beep! Beep! He rolled over and checked his phone. "Time to do this." he sighed. He stood up and stretched, as he stared out the window: the sun had almost gone, and it cast an ominous red glow on the surrounding buildings. He put on thin layers of black body armor, then he stuffed his gear into a backpack and set out.

As he walked through the crowd of people on the street, a strange thought popped into his head: he wondered how they would react, if they knew this normal looking guy, with a bag, casually slung over his shoulder, was actually a hardened killer. Even more, in that bag were guns, knives, night vision goggles, a gas mask, and a whole host of advanced gadgets, all designed to help him take lives. It was an interesting thought, but just something to pass the time; boredom was his greatest enemy now, as he figured getting to the truth of this matter would be a long, tedious process — but the fact that they wanted him dead told Seven they were afraid. *They're right to be scared*, he thought, *they know what's coming for them.*

He got to the building and slipped inside; then, he walked through the lobby, and past a door marked 'Maintenance'. From there, he found a storage room and picked the lock — now it was time to wait. He figured that while he did, he would take a closer look at the page he'd printed from the flash drive; so he pulled it from his pocket, then he reached into his bag and took out a flashlight. He stared at the table, but there was no way of knowing what it all meant — especially out of context.

2	M	65%	60%	63%	63%	65%
3	F	52%	53%	50%	78%	75%
4	M	63%	68%	65%	51%	53%
5	M	61%	60%	59%	71%	73%
6	F	73%	69%	67%	61%	55%
7	M	80%	75%	75%	65%	67%
8	M	52%	56%	59%	73%	72%
9	M	80%	79%	71%	63%	58%
10	F	63%	60%	62%	93%	95%

After a couple of hours had passed, and it seemed late enough, he pulled out his gear and got ready: bullet-proof vest, guns and knives on his waist, then the mask; finally, the goggles — the same goggles worn by the men who came to kill him.

He went to the service elevator and rode it up to the third floor: once there, he walked to each office and read the names on the doors. *301, no...302, no...303, no.* He kept going, slowly, all the while remaining vigilant for any signs of movement. *310, match.*

He picked the lock and went inside: it was dark, but he didn't turn on the light — that would only attract attention. Besides, he didn't need it: he turned on his night vision and went around to the desk — it was a mess! *Typical scientist.* He combed through the jumble of books and papers that covered it completely — he had to be careful, the entire pile seemed like it was held together only by friction.

This was a problem; he didn't want to linger, but the unorganized mass of objects made it impossible to be quick. Seven hated this — but he knew he had no choice.

Ten minutes went by, then twenty, then thirty; it made almost no difference — it was like he hadn't even started. He needed to find another way, so he opened the drawers and began sifting through them — they were worse! Nothing in there was together — it would take a whole team weeks just to organize this stuff, much less read through it all. He searched the bookcase, the shelves, the trashcan — nothing important; nothing with any relevance to him, or to 'SHOT'.

He was about to dive back into the desk, when he heard a noise that stopped him in his tracks — there was someone in the hallway. He moved away from it, and over to the door; he stood there, with his back against the wall, waiting to see if they would enter. The steps became louder, but they were slowing down rather than speeding up — whoever it was, they didn't seem like they should be here either.

The person in the hallway got to the door and stopped. *So, you are coming in.* Seven heard the key as it was slowly inserted into the lock: then, the knob turned — the door creaked open, concealing him behind it. He saw the person from behind: it was a man, with full, but partially grey hair, about 5'10". He walked to the window and closed the curtains; then, he made sure the shade was all the way down on the one to the hallway. Once he did that, he closed the door quietly and turned on the lights: "Oh, God!"

He saw Seven standing before him, dressed in full combat gear — his gun was out, and it was pointed straight at the man's head. He put his finger to his lips, and the man nodded, indicating he understood; then, Seven motioned for him to sit down.

There were two seats facing the desk, and the man

sat in the one further from the wall. Seven pulled the chain on the desk lamp to turn it on, then he flicked off the switch for the main lights. He walked around to the other side of the desk, and sat in the chair — the entire time, keeping the gun fixed on his new visitor.

"Hands on the table." he ordered.

The man did as instructed: "W-Who are you?"

"The better question is, who are *you*?"

"Doctor Gordon..." the man replied, "I work here."

"Hmm, I see...and what are you doing sneaking around in the dark?" He didn't answer; he just looked down. "You don't know?" Seven asked him, "Shame... well then, let me tell you what *I'm* doing here." The man raised his right hand, nervously — like a kid in school who had a question. "Ah ah ah..." Seven used the gun to motion downwards, "back on the table, please." His eerily calm voice was terrifying; it sounded both polite and sinister at the same time: "As I was saying...your friend here, is dead...I killed him yesterday."

"I-I know..." Dr. Gordon stuttered, "I was—" He stopped himself from speaking further.

"Go on..." Seven urged; he extended his arm out, moving the gun closer to the trembling man.

"Y-You work for 'them', right?"

"I do."

"Good..." Dr. Gordon said, faking a smile, "i-it's me...I'm the one who found out...I'm the one who *told* you."

"So..." Seven continued, now with a more serious tone, "you sold out your friend?...Your colleague?"

"Y-Yes...well, no...I mean, I—"

"It's yes, or it's no...and I'm leaning to the former."

"It's...it's just I...I didn't know they would—"

"Kill him?" Seven bluntly stated, "You didn't know they would kill him?...Is that what you're saying?"

"Y-Yes."

"What did you think they'd do?...Ground him?" The man opened his mouth to speak, but couldn't say the words—he just hung his head in shame. "Well, good news for you Doctor Gordon..." he looked up, and Seven could see the glimmer of hope in his eyes, "if you tell me what I want to know, I'll let you live...how does that sound?"

"Great!" he exclaimed, "It sounds great!"

"OK, then, what is SHOT?"

The doctor's face went pale; he didn't talk, so Seven fired a bullet into his arm: "Aaaahh!"

He stood up, and leaned over the table — he pressed the end of the silencer to the man's forehead: "Scream again, and you're dead." Tears filled his eyes, as he tried to suppress the pain—he nodded, then Seven removed the gun and sat down in his chair: "Now, tell me."

Dr. Gordon took a moment to compose himself, then he began: "It was many years ago, I-I wasn't here then...nobody talks about it...it was classified—"

"What *is* it?" Seven demanded.

"I don't know, really I don't!" Seven shook his head, and lifted the gun in the air: "Wait!...Here's what I do know...it was a small team...five, maybe six people... they worked on it for a few years—"

"Worked on *what*?!"

"I don't know what the project was!...It was highly classified, but I do know they buried it...t-they wanted to erase everything...make like it never happened."

"And this man..." Seven pointed to a picture of the dead scientist, "he was involved?"

"Yes, he's the last member of the team that's still

alive...or, was alive."

"Why did they want to kill him now?"

"Someone met with him...they had things, evidence...I overheard a conversation...they pay me to keep tabs on him, but they've never done anything before... they just wanted to know what he did at work, and if anyone came to see him...that's all, I'm not a bad guy."

"Who met with him?"

"I-I don't know who he was...check the address book, top-left drawer...I saw him write something down."

Seven opened the drawer and took out the book: he flipped through to the last page that had writing — there was a name, a phone number, and an address. "Interesting." he remarked. He took out the team leader's phone, and scrolled through to the address he saw earlier — they were the same. *I know where my next stop is.* "Well, Doctor Gordon, you've been most helpful." the man exhaled with relief, "Unfortunately, it now appears that we've reached the end of your story."

"What?!...No!...Y-You said you'd let me live!"

Seven narrowed his eyes; he looked genuinely puzzled: "But, doctor, I did let you live...I didn't say it would be forever." In one quick motion, he swung his arm up and pulled the trigger! Another bullet shot from the gun: it went through the man's forehead, leaving a large, red splatter on the walls and door behind him.

Seven put the address book in his bag, then he turned off the desk lamp and walked out the door — he had one more stop to make.

TWENTY-SEVEN

Mav flew through the air! He landed hard, face-down on the ground, then he slid across the floor until he stopped just short of the edge — right at Zelda's feet. The wall hadn't moved slowly, as they expected — instead, it sprang forward like it was shot from a cannon!

The others reached down, and helped him to his feet — he wobbled as he tried to stabilize himself, nearly falling back over. He was shaken; once again he'd played it fast and loose, and this time it nearly cost him his life. He couldn't hear anything but a high-pitched ringing in his ears — he was in shock!

As it died down, he could faintly make out Danny's voice speaking to him: "Mav!...Mav!...Are you OK?!"

"Huh?...What?"

"I said...are you OK?!"

"What happened?"

"You got hit pretty hard...your head is bleeding."

"We need to sit him down..." Ash insisted, "he could have a concussion."

Together with Sam, they walked him to the wall and sat him against it. Zelda followed behind them, sitting down between Mav and the edge — about eight feet to her right. "I'll stay with him..." she volunteered, "you guys keep watching the clouds."

The other three walked to the middle of the roof: the wall had come forward about a third of the way, leaving an area that was roughly forty feet long, by thirty feet wide. Ash looked over at Mav and Zelda, sitting by the wall; then, she turned back to the others: "I don't think any of us expected *that*."

Danny nodded: "It just goes to show, we can't take anything for granted."

"What now?" Sam posed — they looked to the sky, but the clouds were still too thick to see through.

"I guess we'll just hafta wait." Ash told them.

"In that case..." Danny motioned to the wall, "I'm gonna sit down too...I need a break."

"Mind if I join you?" she asked.

"What?!...Uh, no...i-if you want to?"

"Great!...Sam, what about you?"

"No, you guys go ahead...I'll be fine."

Ash and Danny walked over to the wall, and sat down — they were closer to the free end, than they were to Zelda and Mav, who seemed to be slowly recovering. Ash sat first, and Danny followed, positioning himself between her and the edge. Sam, meanwhile, sat on the floor with his back towards them: he pulled his knees in, and wrapped his arms around his legs. Danny watched him as he stared out at the lake — he could only guess at what was going through his mind. After everything they'd been through, surely he must know now that Katie was gone. Then it dawned on him: if it had been the other way around — if Katie had emerged from the final tunnel, instead of Mav — there's no way he'd give up hope.

"So..." Ash began, breaking his thought, "why haven't we ever spoken before?"

"Huh?!...W-Whaddya mean?"

"Well, we sit next to each other in class...but you never talk to me."

"I, uh...well..." he stuttered, "you...you've never spoken to me, either."

"That's true...but I don't go outta my way to avoid making eye contact." Danny's face turned red — he was found out! All those times when he'd wondered if she'd caught him staring — she had!

"No, I...that's not—"

"It's OK..." she assured him, "really, I get it...you're shy...I'm not exactly a social butterfly, myself."

Danny turned to her, making a point to look deeply into her eyes; he fought his natural inclination to look away, and really took in the depth and scope of her beauty. Ash's eyes were light-grey; they were big, with long, thick lashes. Her face was soft, and her full lips were a light, dusty shade of pink. Everything about her could be described as delicate, like a porcelain doll come to life; but her long, flowing dark hair added an element of steel to her otherwise feminine appearance. Here, now, in the pale light of the moon, she seemed to take on an otherworldly glow — he couldn't help but be mesmerized. She was ethereal; she was too perfect to be real.

"So..." she prompted, "tell me about yourself... other than play video games, and hang out with reckless people...what do you do?"

He chuckled: "That's about it, really...I dunno... I've never made friends easily...it's not that I don't like people, it's just...sometimes I can't relate, y'know?"

"I do."

"What about you?...You're super smart, you're just as brave as Mav, and you're—" He stopped himself from finishing the thought.

"What is it?...What were you gonna say?"

"It's nothing, I just...I was gonna say that...well, that you're beautiful." There was a pause — it was probably just a second or two, but to Danny, it felt like he'd be stuck in this silent limbo forever.

"Thank you." she finally spoke, "You're very sweet, you know that?" The weight of the world was lifted off him — then she looked away: "I don't think I've been very nice to you tonight."

"Whaddaya mean?...You've been great, it's just... it's been a lot to deal with."

"Well, in any case...I'm gonna be better, I promise." He didn't respond right away; he just savored this private moment between them, for a little while longer.

"So, your parents..." he went on, trying to keep the conversation alive, "they must be pretty smart...I mean, because you're so smart."

"Ahhh..." she sighed, "smart, yes, but not very affectionate...also like me." They both started giggling, but it soon evolved into full-blown laughter. Sam and Zelda peered over at them, but Ash and Danny didn't notice — they were lost in their own little world.

ΔΔΔ

"What're they laughing about?" Zelda wondered.

"Leave them alone..." Mav responded, "let my guy do his thing."

"What does that even mean?!...We have more important things to deal with, in case you haven't noticed."

"*Relax...*" he took her hand, "we're outside, everyone's feeling good...it's all gonna work out, you'll see."

ΔΔΔ

Back to Ash and Danny: he was just about done telling her his story. "I'm sorry..." she said, "about your parents."

"Thanks...it was a long time ago." She put her hand over his, and squeezed it gently; he smiled at her, then he continued: "Besides, I always have my dad's watch with me..." He pulled back his sleeve to show it to her, but he noticed something strange — the writing on his arm had disappeared. "Huh?...That's weird."

"What is?"

"In the room where I woke up, the clue was written on my arm...that's how I got out...now it's gone."

"We all had different puzzles..." she pointed out, "they musta designed them for each of us."

"But, who are 'they'?" he questioned, "That's what we still don't know."

"And we won't..." she replied, "not until we reach the end."

TWENTY-EIGHT

"Yes, sir...OK...will do, sir." *Click*. The younger guard hung up the phone.

"What'd they say?" his colleague asked.

"Just to keep watching." he replied.

"I can't believe it..." the older guard said, "they've reached the fourth level, and they're all still alive...I've never seen this before."

"You starting to believe yet?"

"Believe what?"

"That they could do it!" the younger man exclaimed, "That they could make it!" The older guard sat back in his chair: he swiveled side-to-side, as a grin slowly formed on his face. "You're coming around..." his partner insisted, "just admit it."

"Not yet..." he smirked, "not yet."

The older man got up, and went to the kitchen for some coffee. While the younger one was alone, he checked the monitor again: the kids had been stationed in place for a while. He tapped the screen, and it flashed briefly with static —then the older guard returned. "Hey, look at this..." he pointed out, "they haven't moved in a few minutes...whaddya think they're doing up there?"

"Don't worry about it..." the older man told him, "after what they've been through, they're probly just taking a breather."

The younger guard shrugged his shoulders, and turned his chair back around — he figured his older partner was right; after all, he had the experience. But unbeknownst to them, just outside the guardhouse, a small device had been placed on the main input line inside the junction box. That tiny, electronic clip had frozen the feeds for all their cameras — and the man from the woods had placed it there.

TWENTY-NINE

After a while, the conversation circled back to Ash. Danny wanted to know more about her — he wanted to know *everything* about her. "So, your parents..." he went on, "you didn't really talk about them before."

"Umm..."

"It's OK, you don't hafta tell me if you don't want to."

"No, it's not that..." she looked away, "it's...my family's very wealthy...I don't really tell people, because I don't want them to think I'm just some prissy rich girl."

"I would never—"

"I know, that's why I'm telling *you*." A wave of euphoria washed over his body: Ash trusted him — *him!* — with her most guarded secret. "Anyway..." she continued, "the truth is, I don't really see much of them... they're always traveling here or there, and, well...they're just too busy, I suppose." She paused there, to allow him to speak; but he didn't: "That's pretty much it, I'm afraid...I haven't heard from them all semester."

"Wow..." he uttered, "I'm sorry."

"It's fine, really...I'm used to it by now."

$$\Delta\Delta\Delta$$

At the other end of the wall, Zelda and Mav sat quietly: he had recovered from his injuries, when she suddenly realized they were still holding hands — so she pulled her arm away and punched him on the shoulder!

"Ow!...What's that for?!"

"Don't get any ideas!" she warned him.

He shook his head, and let out a slight chuckle: "You really don't like me, do you?"

"I know your type."

"Type?...What type is that?"

Zelda wound up — it was like she'd been waiting for this moment all night: "To start off with, you're incredibly vain...and you do stupid, reckless shit to prove how 'macho' you are, or whatever...you're the type of guy who measures his self-worth in romantic conquests, that's why you flirt with every girl you see...you just can't help it...and you don't have real relationships...you don't have platonic friendships, either...every female in your life exists in this ambiguous grey area between friend and lover, because you want the best of everything...you want the benefits of a girlfriend, without the responsibilities...that's probly cuz there's no one you've ever cared about, even half as much as you care about yourself."

His mouth hung open — he couldn't believe what she'd just said — Zelda shredded him, eviscerated him, destroyed his character in thirty seconds flat! "Wow...just...wow."

"Tell me it's not true." she challenged.

"I'd like to, but...that was about...I'd say, fifty percent of it."

"Which part was wrong?"

"Oh, no..." he conceded, "you're spot-on...but

that's not all I am...there's another side to me."

"*Really*?" She began looking all around them: "Where *is* this other guy?...Did we leave him behind, somewhere?"

"You'll see..." he smirked, "just give it time." She didn't respond with words; she just rolled her eyes, and leaned back against the wall.

ΔΔΔ

During all this, Sam kept staring out at the lake — he left the others in pairs, not wanting to disturb their private conversations. "I feel bad for him..." Ash confessed, "I can't imagine what he's going through."

"We're all going through it..." Danny told her, "I guess he's just dealing with it in his own way."

"But we're not missing anyone..." she countered, "half his mind is here, and the other half is somewhere else."

"Yeah, I know...that must be rough." He decided to change the subject to something less depressing: "So, what about this puzzle?...Any ideas?"

"Not really..." she sighed, "honestly, I'm hoping Zelda can solve it...I'm pretty drained."

"I was wrong about her..." he admitted, "earlier, I mean...you were right...I shouldn'ta jumped to conclusions."

"Don't worry about it..." she assured him, "this place will make us all crazy, if we aren't careful."

He stared into her eyes. *Should I bring up the kiss?* Then she turned away, and slipped her hand into his. Danny's heart raced; he was so nervous that he began to shake, uncontrollably. Her perfume still lingered in the air around her — that sugary-sweet scent that had hypnotized him back in the tunnel. With his free hand, he pulled down the zipper on his hoodie — even though it was cold, her lightest touch was causing him to burn up.

ΔΔΔ

Back at the other end, Mav was still reeling from Zelda's scathing rant. "Just so you know..." he began, "I think you're really smart, I think you're really funny... the fact that you're beautiful is just one of many reasons a guy would like you."

"Save the lines for someone who cares."

"You don't?"

"Does it look like I do?"

"Well, you did seem pretty upset when I fell through the floor."

"Ugh."

"Admit it, you were worried about me...just a little."

"Oh, *yes*..." she replied, "I don't want you to die, therefore I'm in love with you...am I *that* transparent?"

Mav put his hands up in surrender: "OK, OK, you don't like me...message received."

"Good..." she sat upright, "I'm glad you finally realize."

"But, admit it..." he said, touching her leg, "sitting here, it's dark, the moon is full...you're kinda feeling something, aren't you?" Her brow furrowed: she stared at him with her mouth half-open. "Hey, I'm sorry..." he pulled away, "I'm not tryna upset you or anything, honest—" She sprang to her feet! She ran forward, looking straight up at the sky!

"Look!" Danny pointed.

"What is it?!" Ash called out, "Did you find something?!"

Zelda turned around and shouted back to them: "It's the moon!"

THIRTY

Emma was stunned! She sat on the couch, looking up at Teddy who was standing before her: "Well?...Whaddaya think?"

"I...I can't...wow!" She couldn't speak; she was still trying to process it all.

"It gets better..." he continued, "I went through the list of 'Z' names again, and there's only one doctor."

"Who is it?"

He lay the yellow legal pad down on the table in front of her; then he got the MilTech directory, and placed them side by side. "Doctor Henry Zeller!" he exclaimed, slamming his finger down on the page.

"You did it!" she cheered — she leapt off the couch and into his arms!

"No..." he whispered, "*we* did it."

They opened a bottle of champagne to celebrate — then another — and by the next morning, Teddy's head was splitting open. *Idiot!...You're too old to drink that much!* He sat up in bed and rubbed his temples — he felt horrible. But when he looked over and saw Emma, sleeping peacefully beside him, he couldn't help but smile.

ΔΔΔ

Eventually, though, he had to wake her; and on their way to the office, they didn't exchange many words — neither one felt like talking, much less leaving the house. Luckily, he still didn't have much to do, so he decided to look Dr. Zeller up online.

"I don't believe it." he muttered to himself.

"Don't believe what?" Emma asked, closing the door behind her.

"Doctor Zeller..." he answered, "he still works there...look at this."

She walked around to his side of the desk, and looked at the screen: "This is great!...You gotta call him!"

Teddy picked up the phone and dialed the Mil-Tech main line: "Hello, yes, I'm calling for Doctor Henry Zeller...yes, I'll hold...thank you." He pressed the phone to his chest and gave her an update: "They're transferring me to his department." She flashed him a thumbs-up, as he put the receiver back to his ear: "Hi, I'm trying to reach Doctor Zeller, could you plea—" Emma watched, as he listened to the person on the line: "Umm, OK...no, it's fine, I understand...yes, I would...Teddy Logan, he knew my brother, Miles...yes, thank you..." He finished the call by giving them his phone number, then he hung up.

"*So?*" she prodded.

"He wasn't there..." Teddy leaned back and rubbed his eyes, "he's at some conference till tomorrow."

"What else did they say?"

"Well, I spoke to his secretary...she said he calls for his messages every now and then...hopefully, he'll call me later." He looked deflated: "I'll just hafta wait, I guess."

"Wrong...*we* hafta wait." She gave him a kiss, then went back to her desk.

"I hate waiting..." he mumbled.

△△△

Later that evening, Teddy was at home, staring at the safe. "Just a few simple numbers..." he spoke to it, "then I'll know what you're hiding." He sat there for hours, looking at the black cube; then, out of nowhere, he heard something buzzing. He opened his eyes and looked around: he was still on the couch, but flopped over, awkwardly. *Buzz. Buzz. Buzz.* There it was again. *My phone!... Where is it?!*

He jumped to his feet and tore through the cushions — they flew over his head, as he searched frantically. *Buzz. Buzz.* It was ringing again! "Where is this damn thing?!" He looked all around, turning his body in a circle: "Shit!" His foot kicked it under the couch! He dropped to the floor and stuck his hand underneath: he could *just* feel it with the tips of his fingers, but he couldn't quite get a grip on it. "Aaaahhh!" he screamed. He shoved his arm in — further than it should've gone — and grabbed the phone!

He pulled it out, and looked at the call history: there were seven missed calls, all from the same number. He pressed one of them to dial it back: "Hello?" The voice on the other end was disjointed: "Slow down, I can't hear you." It was Dr. Zeller! "Yes!...Thanks for returning my call...I dropped my phone, that's why I—" the doctor cut him off, "yes, I am...yes, he is...I mean, he was...well, that's why I'm—" The man seemed out of sorts: "OK... tomorrow's fine, should I come to your office?" He listened, as Dr. Zeller gave him instructions: "Sure, whatever works best for you...alright, I'll see you there at eight...thanks again!" He took the safe upstairs, and put it on the floor next to the dresser. Another sleep-deprived night followed; but in the morning, he went to meet Dr. Zeller for breakfast.

ΔΔΔ

When he got there, the doctor was already sitting down, waiting for him to arrive. He was shorter than Teddy expected: bald on top, with long, wiry grey hair around the sides of his head.

"Doctor Zeller..." Teddy greeted him, extending his right hand, "thank you so much for meeting me."

"Happy to do it..." he replied, "but please, call me Henry."

"Will do."

They sat down and ordered breakfast: Dr. Zeller had an egg white omelet with a side of toast, and coffee. Teddy had pancakes—ever since the other morning with Emma, he couldn't seem to shake the craving.

After the usual pleasantries had been exchanged, Teddy got down to business: "So, Henry...the reason I wanted to meet with you is...*ahem*...I found this small safe, under the floorboards in my bedroom, and, well...it had the letters 'DRZ' carved into the back."

Dr. Zeller sat back in his seat — he looked surprised. "Wow..." he remarked, "you must have done some digging, then."

"You have no idea."

"OK...well, yes, the safe was mine...I gave it to Miles to hold on to...I was...umm..." He looked nervous; his hands were shaking, and he was fidgeting with his cup.

"Is everything alright?" Teddy asked him.

"I..." he hesitated, "I don't want to get you involved too directly."

"Involved in what?" Dr. Zeller began to look around, anxiously — Teddy could see that he was getting very uncomfortable: "Listen, I don't want you to do anything you're not OK with..."

"No, it's not that, it's...it's just been a long time." He didn't respond; he waited for the doctor to speak again: "Miles worked on my team...he was the best, your brother...genius, in fact...we did great things together."

"I don't mean to pry, but you gave him that safe for a reason, didn't you?"

He nodded: "We both thought it best if it were hidden."

"OK, well, that was a long time ago...why don't you come by the house?...We can open it together."

"I—" he began, before quickly stopping himself.

Teddy knew something was wrong — he seemed reluctant to say what this was all about: "Or, you could give me the combination?...I could open it, then bring whatever's inside to you?"

Dr. Zeller stared out the window: "Miles was a good friend...I'm sorry about what happened...I've always thought that...maybe he...maybe *I* could've prevented it."

"It wasn't your fault..." Teddy assured him, "believe me, I spent years beating myself up over it...if only I had gone to see him that day, and not Stella...if I had done more to help ease the stress...there's a million things I've thought about since the accident, but that's all it was, an accident...these things happen, and there's nothing anyone could've done to prevent it."

"Maybe you're right..." the old man sighed, "OK,

yes...how's this evening?"

"It's great!...Perfect!...I'll text you the address!"

"No, no, I-I don't text." He pulled out a small book from his bag: "Write your address down here." Teddy did as instructed, and they made a plan to meet at eight o'clock that night; then, they finished breakfast, and went off to their respective jobs.

ΔΔΔ

Once Teddy got to work, he hurried to his office: Emma saw him, from across the room, and he discretely signaled her to follow. He opened the door and waited for her to walk in; as soon as she did, he closed it behind her, pulling the shade down on the window.

"What happened?!" she asked, excitedly, "What'd he say?!"

"It was weird, he was all over the place...really nervous and anxious."

"Yeah, but he's a scientist...what'd you expect?"

"Miles was a scientist..." he countered, "and he was nothing like that."

"You know what I mean...now, tell me!...What did he say?!" He leaned back against the wall, and crossed his arms. "What?!" she pleaded, "Come on!...Tell me!" He smiled, and she realized he was messing with her: "Tell me now, Teddy Logan!" She punched him on the arm, and they both started laughing.

"OK! OK!" he gave in, "He's coming over tonight... we're gonna open it!"

"Yay!" She launched herself forward and hugged him: "You hafta let me come, too!"

"I-I dunno...I wasn't joking about this guy being

weird."

"Please?" she begged, "Pleeease?"

"Uhh..."

"Oh, come on!...Don't forget who got you that book!"

"Fine..." he chuckled, "you can come."

"Yes! Yes! Yes!"

"Whoa..." he warned her, "settle down...we don't want people to think we're up to no good in here."

She wrapped her arms around his neck, and put her lips to his ear: "But I *am* up to no good in here." Then she pushed him up against the wall and kissed him deeply.

Teddy was caught off guard — he pulled away, and stared at her: she was smirking playfully, and biting her lower lip. *What the hell?* he thought — he grabbed her hips and drew her in for another.

When they finally emerged from the office, all eyes were on them. "Those two..." he heard someone say, "at it again, huh?"

"So...*ahem*...I'll, uh..." he stuttered, "we'll...I guess..."

"I'll see you later." she said, coolly; then she sauntered back to her desk and sat down.

THIRTY-ONE

Ash jumped to her feet and rushed to Zelda: "The moon?...Are you sure?"

"Look at it!" she replied, "Of all the things in the sky, what stands out to you?"

By this time, Mav, Danny, and Sam had joined the girls. Mav and Danny looked up, as Zelda instructed; but Sam faced the opposite way, back towards the wall. "I think she has it..." he said, "look at the carving again, Earth is the only planet with a moon...it's different from the rest."

"Exactly!" Zelda claimed, "The *moon* is the special one."

"Let's just think this over..." Ash cautioned, "this isn't like the other puzzles, we have time to get it right." She turned to Zelda, just in time to see her eyes roll.

"Yeah, I agree." Danny added, "I think she's probly right, but let's make sure...we only have two tries left."

"Fine!" Zelda pouted, "Do whatever you want!" She stomped back over to her spot on the floor, mumbling to herself along the way: "You wanted me to solve it, and I did, but, whatever..."

"Guys..." Mav tapped his hand on the wall, "she's right, just look at it."

"Yeah, I agree..." Danny repeated, "but there's no

harm in making sure."

"OK..." he shrugged, "take your time." He started over towards Zelda, leaving Ash and Danny to examine the model again.

"Come on..." Sam urged, "it's the moon, let's just try it...we need to get outta here."

Ash looked at Danny, before responding. "OK..." she sighed, "let's do it." Sam called to Mav and Zelda, who got up from the floor and walked back over to them. After what happened to Mav the first time, they didn't want to take any chances; so they counted off the distance between the wall and the far side edge, then, they made a calculated guess as to how far forward it would go if they were wrong. Danny, Ash, Zelda, and Sam all stood about thirty feet away from the wall: if it went forward twenty, like it did before, that would leave them halfway between the wall and the edge of the roof—not ideal, but about as safe as they could get.

Mav volunteered to press the button again; only this time, he would use the delay to move back a safe distance. He knelt down on one knee, in front of the 'solar system', and placed his finger on the 'moon' button: he paused to take in a breath, then he pushed it.

Just like before, it didn't pop out upon release; but after a few seconds, he heard something begin to wind up in the back. His eyes grew wide, as he jumped to his feet: "It's coming forward!" He ran to the others: they all locked arms, bracing themselves for the impending rush — but it never came. The wall began to slowly recede — they were right.

"Yes!" Zelda cheered, "Told ya!" The boys laughed with relief, and Ash happily congratulated her. The wall moved backwards; it eventually stopped, once it reached its original position.

"Hold on..." Danny spoke, putting an end to the celebrations, "something's wrong."

"What is it?" Ash asked him.

"It's back at the starting point, but there's no way out...we're still trapped up here."

"No, that can't be." She hurried off towards the wall, and the others quickly followed her: they checked all the seams and edges again, trying to find something that wasn't there before.

"What the hell?!" Mav raved, "We solved it!"

"Calm down..." she told him, "there must be something we're missing."

Zelda and Sam walked around the roof, trying to see if anything was different now, compared to before — maybe a stone in the floor had shifted, or a button or lever had appeared — by now, they'd learned not to take anything for granted. But when they rejoined the others, they had nothing to report.

"This doesn't make any sense..." Ash insisted, "if the puzzle is solved, then we should be able to move on."

"What if it's not solved?" Danny proposed.

"What're you talking about?" Zelda scoffed, "The wall moved back...it was the moon, we were right." He pointed to the wall, and the others turned to see what he was looking at: the screen was no longer black — another handprint had appeared.

They were stunned! Was there another puzzle to solve? Why would there be? It didn't add up. Ash wasn't going to wait in limbo for long, though, she stepped forward and placed her hand on the screen — it flashed, and the wall began to wind up again! "Run!" she cried. The others didn't need to be told twice — they all turned and darted in the opposite direction!

But when they stopped to look back, they saw that it hadn't sprung forward as they'd feared. "What the..." Mav uttered.

"It's going *back*?" Danny questioned, "*More*?"

"I think..." Ash started, "I think that's the way out!" The wall had moved backwards, revealing two holes in the floor — they looked around at one another, tentatively, before slowly approaching them.

"What *are* these?" Zelda wondered. Mav bent over, and tried to peer into the one on the left: "Can you see anything?"

"No..." he responded, "it's too dark."

"Wait!" Danny had an idea: he lay down flat on his stomach, then he stuck his hand into the right-side hole.

"Be careful!" Ash warned him.

"It's OK..." he assured her, as he looked up at Mav, "feel inside!"

Mav followed his lead: he lay on the floor, and reached his hand down, into the void. Zelda could see the surprise on his face: "What is it?...What'd you find?"

"It's smooth..." he answered, "*very* smooth."

Danny popped back up: "I think it's a slide!"

"A what?!" the others gasped.

"Yeah..." Mav confirmed, "that's what it feels like to me."

"Whaddaya mean 'a slide'?" Zelda puzzled.

"It's not a straight drop..." Danny explained, "it slopes down."

The girls got down on the floor, and felt for themselves: without any other possibilities, they had to assume he was right. "So, what should we do?" Ash prompted, "How do we know which one to go through?"

"Hey, guys..." Sam chimed in, "look at that." He pointed to the screen on the wall, which was now displaying new words:

It's time to take a leap of faith. Choose the next path that you will follow.

"What the hell does that mean?!" Mav exclaimed, "After everything we've been through, it's just dumb luck?!"

"Nothing so far has been about chance..." Ash remarked, "this has to be some kinda trick." All five of them examined the openings — they looked for a clue, or an indicator that could help them decide which one to choose. But with only the moonlight to guide them, they had a distinct disadvantage: each time the clouds rolled in, they lost what little light they had to work with.

"I give up!" Zelda yelled, "They're the same!" The others knew it too — they had to admit the obvious. There were no discernible differences between the two holes, except that the left-side opening slanted to the left, and the right-side opening slanted to the right — that was it, different directions were all they had to go on.

"Let's just take a minute and think about this." Ash suggested.

"Yeah..." Danny agreed, "good idea."

Mav, Zelda, and Sam drifted to the middle of the roof — they were arguing about which hole to choose. While this was going on, Ash and Danny went back to their spot by the wall; this time, however, they switched sides — Ash was on his left now, closer to the edge. He watched her as she closed her eyes: using her fingers, she brushed back her long, black hair. For a split second, he thought he glimpsed a small tattoo on the back of her neck — it looked to him like a tiny cross. He didn't want to be caught lingering, though, so he pulled his gaze away.

After about a minute or so, he turned back to her — but something wasn't right. Her eyes were wide, and her mouth hung open; he noticed that her lower lip seemed to be quivering — she looked terrified! He straightened his head, to see what she was staring at — then he saw — standing at the far edge of the roof was a man, dressed all in black.

THIRTY-TWO

Teddy checked his phone — still nothing: "Where could he be?!"

"Relax..." Emma told him, "he'll be here."

He sat on the edge of his seat, pressing his elbows into his knees, as his head hung low. Using his hands, he covered his ears, while his legs shook rapidly, up and down. Emma walked over and climbed on the couch: she sat behind him on the backrest, placing her legs either side of him; then, she pulled him towards her, and began massaging his neck and shoulders. Dr. Zeller was over an hour late — he didn't call, and he wasn't answering his phone. Teddy was worried; the man's erratic and paranoid behavior over breakfast may not have been unwarranted, after all.

Emma kept applying pressure to his knotted muscles, but they felt like they were made of stone: "You're too tense...just sit back and relax." He closed his eyes and inhaled deeply, as she kneaded his stiff, twisted shoulders. Every few minutes, she would move her hands to his temples, and rub circles around them with her fingers. Her magic touch, coupled with his deep breathing, seemed to be helping his physical ailments — but the anxiety, the black hole he felt in his stomach, that would only go away once the doctor arrived.

He tried to stand up, but she grabbed his shoulders and pulled him back down: "You're gonna give yourself a heart attack!" Her tone was much sterner this time, like a mother scolding her unruly child: "He's an old man, and he doesn't know how to use a cell phone...you said so, yourself." *She's probly right,* he thought, *I just need to loosen up.* He sat back, and relaxed his shoulders; Emma smiled, noticing the change in his posture, and began applying more pressure with her thumbs. "There, now..." she spoke, in a much softer voice, "isn't this better?"

Teddy exhaled, long and slow — he didn't realize how much air he'd been holding in. He knew she was right: worrying about the situation, going over countless possibilities and scenarios in his head, that would only make him crazy — so he did as instructed, he leaned back and emptied his thoughts. His mind was completely blank now: he felt peace, tranquility, a sense that everything was going to be alright.

Ding-dong! The doorbell! He leapt to his feet and rushed to answer it! He paused briefly to compose himself, then he opened the door. "Sorry..." Dr. Zeller said, "I know I'm late."

"No, i-it's fine..." he responded, "please, come in."

The doctor stepped inside, and looked around: "Oh, I didn't know you had company...perhaps this isn't the best time."

"No, no..." Teddy assured him, "this is Emma, my girlfriend...she's the one who helped me find you." Instantly, he realized what he'd done: they'd never talked about their relationship before, and now he'd just blurted it out. *Oh, God!* he panicked, *Girlfriend?!...What, are we in high school?!*

But Emma didn't miss a beat; she stood up, and

shook the doctor's hand: "Yes, I'm the girlfriend...pleased to meet you, Doctor Zeller."

"Oh, why, yes..." he stuttered, "likewise...but, uh...call me Henry, please."

She smiled: "Henry it is."

They all sat down at the dining table and talked for a while; Teddy and Dr. Zeller shared their stories of Miles, while Emma listened quietly, absorbing all she could. She felt like she was part of his world now: not just a visitor anymore, but someone with permanence, someone with meaning, someone who was on the inside — and definitely someone who was there to stay. The doctor refused everything he was offered, except for a glass of water that he sipped sparingly as they spoke.

"Well..." Teddy prompted, "let's get to the important stuff, shall we?" He asked Dr. Zeller to follow him upstairs, which he did, after gulping down the remaining contents of his glass. Emma trailed behind them: she knew the moment of truth had arrived — they would finally discover what mysteries lay hidden inside the black cube.

When they reached the top of the stairs, Teddy led them to the bedroom — there, still sitting next to the dresser, was the safe. Dr. Zeller stared at it like he'd just found a long-lost relative — they could see how emotional he was getting — he stumbled backwards, eventually finding a seat at the edge of the bed.

Emma moved closer to him: "Are you OK, Henry?" He didn't respond, or even acknowledge her, so she put a hand on his shoulder and tried again. "Henry..." she repeated, finally gaining his attention, "are you OK?"

"Oh, yes, sorry...it's just...I didn't think I would ever see this again...it's like it all happened yesterday."

When Dr. Zeller composed himself and stood up, Teddy and Emma moved aside, allowing him better access to the safe. He knelt down in front of it, and placed his right hand on the combination wheel — they could hear it spinning, as it cycled through the numbered sequence. Eventually, it stopped: the doctor pulled down on the handle and opened the door — he lingered for a while in front of it, blocking their view of the contents.

"Henry?" Teddy prodded.

Dr. Zeller slowly turned around: "Oh, I'm sorry... please, come look." Teddy and Emma looked at each other, before stepping forward: inside, they saw a stack of CDs, a few folded papers, and a small black box. "Here..." the doctor handed the box to Teddy, "this is for you."

He turned it over in his hands: "What is it?"

"I don't know, but it isn't mine...Miles must have put it in here."

"How do you know it was him?" Emma questioned.

"He's the only other person who had the combination."

"So, what're those?" Teddy gestured to the discs and papers.

Dr. Zeller hesitated, before answering; he realized that with Miles dead, he was the only one left who knew the secret. He had to tell them — if anything were to happen to him, at least someone would know the truth: "You two had better sit down...there's a lot you don't know." He began his story; starting from his career beginnings, his early work, and the possibilities that he envisioned. Then, he spoke about Miles: he told them Miles was different, unique, more special than his peers — most of all, he told them that Miles was a good man. Together, they began work on a top-secret program; it was an ambitious project, but one with the potential to change the world.

"So, what happened?" Teddy pressed, "Why didn't he ever talk about it?"

"Because, unfortunately...we succeeded." He continued on, but he didn't fill them in on all the details — frankly, they were finding it hard enough to follow the basics of what he was saying. Once he'd reached the end, though, he felt he had to tell Teddy what he had long suspected: that the accident which killed Miles and Stella wasn't an accident at all — he believed they had been murdered.

"No!" Teddy cried, "That's not true!...It can't be!"

"I haven't any proof..." he admitted, "but it's what I believe." Teddy was in shock — he couldn't believe what he'd just heard.

"Then why didn't they come after *you*?" Emma wondered, "You were working together, after all...why just him?"

"I've never been able to figure that out...maybe they thought I was too valuable, or that he was acting alone...I don't know...all I know is, from that day on, everything changed..." he held up the stack of CDs in his hand, "and I've been waiting for the last *eighteen years* to find these."

"What are they?" Teddy asked again.

"This is all of our work, everything we built together."

"Then, let's copy them or something...we hafta do right by my brother."

"It's not that easy..." the doctor sighed, "these are

encrypted files...they can only be opened on the secure network at MilTech, which means I'll have to take them in with me."

"That's a big stack to go through..." Emma pointed out, "aren't you worried they'll catch you?"

"It's a chance I'll have to take."

"Well then..." Teddy added, "if you're going through all that trouble, you'll need something a lot smaller on the way out." He opened the nightstand drawer: "Here, use this." Dr. Zeller extended his arm, and Teddy handed him a red flash drive.

THIRTY-THREE

"Look out!" Danny cried. He and Ash jumped to their feet, as the others all spun around. The man was dressed in black, head to toe, with a mask over his face: he wore blacked-out goggles, black gloves and boots, and some kind of breathing device over his mouth.

"What the hell is this?!" Mav yelled at him. The man didn't speak; he didn't make any movements — he just stood in place, staring at them.

Where'd he come from?!...How'd he get up here?! Danny's mind was in overdrive, as he tried desperately to figure out what was happening. The masked man stood perfectly still; he kept his back straight, and his clenched fists by his sides. The other three slowly backed up to the wall, but they were on the other side of the holes from Ash and Danny — Mav was closest to the edge, with Zelda next to him and Sam to her left.

"Who are you?!" Ash exclaimed — again, he didn't reply, so she took a deep breath and stepped forward.

"No!" Danny grabbed her wrist, "Don't!"

"It's OK..." she assured him, "maybe he's not with 'them'." When she moved again, his head ticked to the right, freezing her in her tracks. His movement was robotic — only his head had turned, the rest of him didn't budge. Now, his eyes were fixed on her.

"Step back!" Mav shouted, "Don't test this guy!" She didn't move forward, but she didn't go back, either. Then his head turned to the other side — he was now staring at Mav and Zelda. They could see that he was sizing them up, but they still didn't know what he wanted. Why hadn't he attacked them? Why didn't he offer to help? Was he part of the plan? Maybe he was involved with the new puzzle, somehow? Endless possibilities ran through their minds, as they struggled to determine his true motives.

Suddenly, he stepped forward: he walked menacingly to the middle of the rooftop and stared at the wall. Danny turned his head, trying to follow the path of his gaze. *Is he reading the screen?* Ash slowly turned around: she shook her head slightly, and shrugged her shoulders. *Even she can't figure this out.*

Now that the man was closer, they could see him more clearly. Mav looked him up and down: he didn't see any weapons, but his clothes weren't normal — they looked to be padded, like body armor. Even if he wasn't there to hurt them, he was certainly ready for a fight. "Hey!" he called out, adding aggression to his tone, "What's going on here?!" The man turned to him with his whole body, and came forward three paces — Mav wasn't going to be intimidated, so he also stepped out. There were still several feet between them, but they stared each other down like two gunfighters about to duel.

"Mav!" Danny warned, "Back off!"

He didn't listen; he just kept staring at the mysterious stranger. "Someone put us here..." he said, "we don't know why." The man stepped right up to him — they were now just inches apart. A bead of sweat ran down the side of his face, but his expression never changed — it was steely, it was purposeful, he wasn't backing down: "We're just trying to get outta here...I don't know what you're looking for, but maybe we can help each other."

Then the man spoke — his voice was distorted, synthesized, robotic: "No." Mav didn't have time to react — the man's left hand flashed upward and struck him in the chest! The sheer force of the hit lifted him in the air and sent him flying — he didn't touch down again, until he slammed into the stone wall!

"What the hell are you?!" Zelda shrieked. The man turned to her and began moving forward: Sam jumped in front of him and swung his fist, but the man simply leaned back and dodged the blow — then he grabbed Sam with both hands and flung him out of the way! Danny watched in awe as he hurtled through the air. *How is he that strong?!*

Ash realized that he now had a clear path to Zelda — she was standing in place, frozen with fear against the wall. "Zelda!" she screamed, "Down there!" She looked to Ash, who was pointing at the hole in the ground nearest to her. She had no clue where it led, or if she'd even survive; but as the masked man approached, she knew there was only one option — Zelda darted to her left, closed her eyes, and jumped in!

He lunged to grab her — but he missed! As she disappeared down the dark tunnel, Danny quickly turned to Ash: "We hafta follow her!"

She didn't know what to do about Zelda, but Mav was still on the ground and they needed to distract the man before he realized. "Hey!" she yelled, "Come try that with us!"

Danny's jaw dropped: "Are you crazy?!"

"Look at Mav, he's right on the edge!...We need to get this guy away from him!" Her plan worked: the masked man turned and started in their direction. He didn't rush, though — again, his movements were calm, calculated, almost machine-like. As he walked towards them, Danny could see Mav stirring in the background — he was getting up! The man drew closer, backing them into a corner — but out of nowhere, Sam flew in from behind and tackled him!

Mav and Danny rushed to help! Each one grabbed an arm, and Sam stayed on his back, pinning him to the ground; together, they tried to hold him in place, face-down on the floor. While Mav held his arm, he used his right elbow to jab the man's head: "That's for Zelda, asshole!"

"Mav!" Danny pleaded, "Cool it!" He didn't listen; he kept hitting the masked man until suddenly, he lost his grip — the man pushed up on the ground, launching Mav and Sam off his back and sending Danny tumbling towards the edge! Now free, he kicked out behind him — his foot hit Sam, blasting him across the floor! Danny had stopped rolling just as he was about to go over: he was on his stomach, with his right arm and leg dangling over the side. As he looked down and saw the drop, his heart skipped a beat. He rolled to his left: the man, now standing, grabbed him and pulled him up — he held Danny high in the air and tossed him to the middle of the roof!

As soon as he did, Mav punched him in the face! He put all his weight behind it, and the man staggered backwards, towards the edge. *This is it!* he thought, *I'll knock him over!* He pulled back his right hand, intending to finish off the masked assailant; but as he released it, the man blocked the strike — then he delivered a crushing blow to Mav's head! His body went limp; Danny watched, almost in slow motion, as his friend hung in the air — then he crashed to the ground! He was out cold!

While this skirmish was taking place, Ash kept moving around the terrace — she was trying to lure the man to the other side of the roof, in order to get herself and the boys onto the side with the holes. That way, they could follow Zelda; and if he were to come after them, they'd at least have the drop on him when he got out.

She had gotten around to the other side of the wall, and was inching her way towards the hole that Zelda went through. Danny knew he had to help her, so he decided to face the attacker by himself. "Yo!" he shouted, "Let's go again!" The masked man came at him, and he readied himself for the impact — but like before, Sam rushed in from behind!

This time, though, the man easily dodged him, and he went stumbling towards the edge! Danny could see Ash: she was almost there, but she had to help Sam — she ran as fast as she could, making it just in time to stop him falling over!

Danny now stood alone against this superhuman warrior. He stepped backwards, slowly, as the man came closer. He knew the ledge was coming up — he would have to get past him, somehow. He scanned the area around him, but there was nothing else in sight — so he stopped going back and charged forward at full speed! The man's reflexes were amazing; as soon as Danny was nearby, he grabbed him and tossed him over his shoulder. *Bam! Crash!* He landed hard, on his back, and slid across the floor.

The man turned to face the others: Sam came at him again, but he was easily subdued. Now, he squared up to Ash — she was the only one of them who hadn't tried to fight him. He approached her, slowly. He didn't seem to be breathing heavily — it was like he'd been toying with them all this time.

He kept moving towards her, and she backed all the way up to the wall — now, what was she to do? The boys were all down, and they weren't close enough to help, anyway. To make matters worse, she was on the wrong side! She needed to be on the *other* side of the roof to follow Zelda's path.

The man kept moving closer, and she knew her options were dwindling. She was right next to the second hole — the opposite one to Zelda's. She looked around, and realized she had no choice; so she stepped back, until she was right at the edge of it — then she jumped!

Danny lifted his head just in time to see her go: he knew now that the girls were separated — if one slide led to danger, there was a good chance that one of them was already lost. He saw the masked man staring into the black tunnels. *No, don't follow her!* Just when it seemed he would, Mav got up. "You're not following those girls!" he declared, "Over our dead bodies!"

The man turned his sights back to the boys, and started in their direction. Mav raised his fists, readying himself for the next attack: the man came up to him with his arms by his sides — Mav swung with his left, but it missed! Then he followed with a thunderous uppercut that landed square on the man's jaw! It rocked him backwards — he was knocked off his feet!

Danny and Sam rushed over when they saw him go down. As the man on the ground looked up, he saw all three boys in a line before him — he quickly spun around on his back and stuck his leg out, sweeping their feet from under them! Now, all four men were on the ground. The masked man drew his knees in, curled his back, and sprung himself into the air! He landed on his feet, and looked down at them, triumphantly.

The boys crawled backwards, never taking their eyes off him. Once they were a safe distance away, they slowly began to stand up. "Mav..." Danny wheezed, "we can't beat this guy."

"I know..." he admitted, "we hafta get him to the edge and knock him over, it's the only way."

"OK, great...how do we do that?"

"I...h-have a plan."

"That doesn't sound very convincing." Sam remarked.

"Well, it's somewhat of a plan, anyway."

The man drew closer to them — his pace still slow and deliberate — his head swiveled left to right, stopping at each of them momentarily. "OK..." Danny conceded, "what is it?"

"Sam and I break off to the sides...whoever he goes after leads him to the edge, then the other two come around from behind and push him over."

"Jeez!" Danny scoffed, "That's your plan?!"

"You have something better?"

"Ok..." Sam agreed, "let's do it!"

Sam and Mav split away, and for a moment it seemed to work. The man was confused: he stopped walking forward and began turning to each of them, unsure of which to pursue. *It's working!* Danny thought — then the man turned back to him. *Oh, no!* He moved forward with a quicker pace: "Uh, Mav?!...Do the plan now, Mav, do the plan now!" He came at Danny and pulled back his hand: he was right at the edge — one hit would knock him over!

Bam! Out of nowhere, Mav thundered a blow to the man's ribs! It knocked him off balance; and as he turned to retaliate, Danny got in a shot of his own — *pow!* — right to the side of the face! He was reeling now. Sam came over, pulled his knee up, and kicked him as hard as he could — the masked man slid across the floor, right to the edge of the roof! "This is it!" Mav told them, "We got him!"

Danny, Mav, and Sam all lined up in front of him. Mav swung his arm for the finishing blow; but before it could connect, the man kicked his left leg out — it caught Mav in the chest and sent him flying! Then he grabbed Sam by the neck, and threw him to the ground! Now, he was one-on-one with Danny, who started to backtrack. As the man followed him, there was only one thought left in his mind. *This is the end.*

But Sam wouldn't let it be — he jumped to his feet, and rushed the man at full speed! They collided, and both men went spinning towards the edge! Sam couldn't slow his momentum: they were moving too fast, and neither one could stop in time. Danny lunged forward to grab him, and for a split second their hands touched; but then something pulled him back — it was Mav! Danny looked on, helpless, as Sam tumbled over the edge: "Nooo!"

Mav held on to him tightly, as they collapsed to the floor: "He's gone, Danny!...He's gone!"

THIRTY-FOUR

Mav pulled Danny away from the ledge — they couldn't believe what just happened — Sam had pushed the masked attacker off the roof, but he had fallen over himself! Danny was in shock — he had Sam's hand for a moment there, he *had* it. Yes, he did hear someone get crushed, earlier that night; but there was still the glimmer of hope, raised by Zelda's doubts, that this could all be an elaborate hoax. Maybe, just maybe, there was a chance that when things got serious, someone would put an end to this sick game and set them free. But now he knew: there was no hope on the horizon, no saving grace — the only way they would survive would be to carry on. They could no longer look to the sky, for heroes that may never come — they had only themselves, and each other.

"We gotta keep moving..." Mav insisted; he knocked Danny on the shoulder, "let's go, the girls need us." He brought himself to his feet, then he reached down and offered a hand: "Come on, bro, they're all alone." Danny took it, and Mav helped him up; he didn't know how he was even standing, but somehow he managed to make it all the way over to the wall. His body was moving, but his mind wasn't there — it was like he was on autopilot. "They're split up..." Mav acknowledged, "aren't they?"

Danny nodded; he used his trembling hand to point to the hole on the right: "A-Ash went through this one." Mav patted him on the back, trying to calm his nerves. "And Zelda..." he continued, pointing to the left, "s-she went down there." They didn't know where each one led—let alone if they were safe—but they knew that wherever they went, the girls would be there, waiting.

Mav stared down at the two black holes. "We're gonna hafta split up..." he said, "it's the only way."

Danny already knew, though — going together would mean leaving one of the girls to make it on their own, and they couldn't allow that: "I'll follow Ash...you go after Zelda."

They both stepped forward to the edges of their respective tunnels. "Hey..." Mav extended his closed fist, "we'll find each other...before the end." Danny nodded, and touched it with his—then they jumped!

ΔΔΔ

Inside of the tunnel was smooth: there wasn't any type of coating, but the way Danny slid down—increasing speed the whole way—made it feel as though it were made of glass. The tunnel kept winding—left, right, left, right — all the while, he kept dropping further and further.

It was pitch-black inside; and he couldn't help but feel like Alice, falling through the rabbit hole to Wonderland. He kept going down, twisting and turning as the air rushed past him; after a while, the sound became deafening — it was like he'd stuck his head out of a moving car. But then, suddenly, as it seemed like this ride would never end—he shot out of the tunnel like a cannonball!

"Ow!" He crashed down on his back; this floor was no softer than the roof, and he could hear his own pain-filled voice as it echoed off the walls. The space around him was dark, and he was disoriented from the ride down — but he could hear something coming closer.

Soon, as his eyes were adjusting to the darkness, it became clear: "Hello?!"

"It's me!" he called out, "It's Danny!"

"Danny!" Ash exclaimed. As soon as she rounded the corner, she dropped to her knees and hugged him: "What happened?!...Where are the others?!"

She loosened her hold on him, and he eased himself up; his head was still spinning from the dizzying descent, so he tried to steady himself before he spoke: "M-Mav went through the other hole...to find Zelda."

"And Sam?...Did he follow him?" She almost choked on the words as they came out.

"No, we...we lost him."

She shut her eyes and swallowed hard: "OK...Mav and Zelda are still out there, and we need to find them." Once again, she willed herself to keep going. Of course, she was sad — she was gutted by the news of Sam — but she knew there'd be a time to grieve, and this wasn't it. They had to keep moving, or there'd be no one left to mourn him.

"So, where are we?" Danny asked her, "What's down here?"

"Come with me."

She led him around the corner, and through an archway; given the amount of time he was falling, he figured they must be deep inside the bowels of the castle — maybe even underneath it. As they walked, he couldn't shake the image of Sam, falling helplessly into the abyss

— the look of absolute terror in his eyes would forever be seared into Danny's memory. He knew that, now, he didn't need to get out of this place to save himself — not even to save the others — they had to find a way to avenge their fallen friend.

"Quickly..." she hurried him, "it's not far." They kept on walking; eventually, they rounded a sharp corner, and entered a very large, open room — it was huge, but there was nothing inside it. The ceiling was high, and the walls were lined with torches — they flooded the vast, empty space with a yellow-orange light.

"What is this place?" he wondered.

"Take a look at this." Ash directed his attention to the surrounding walls.

"Wow."

They were littered with strange, intricate carvings — not like anything they'd seen so far. There were shapes and swirls that seemed to be connected in some way, yet Danny couldn't find any obvious pattern. He and Ash moved to the left-side wall, so he could see them up-close: they were little dots and grooves that could've only been done by a laser.

"They're the same on that side too..." she told him, "an exact mirror."

"But, why?...What're they for?"

"Step back..." she instructed, "I'll show you." Ash quickly stuck her hand out, and pulled it back in — *shoo!* — an arrow shot from the wall on the opposite side!

"What was that?!" he panicked.

"That's what they're for..." she explained, "it's some kinda...motion-sensing field."

"Is there a way around it?"

"I don't think so." She pointed behind him, and

Danny turned around — on the wall, he saw an electronic screen with a handprint.

THIRTY-FIVE

Teddy and Emma sat on the couch in total silence: they couldn't believe what they were seeing on the news — Dr. Zeller had been murdered! He was found behind the Metropolitan Museum of Art, with multiple stab wounds to his chest.

"He was right..." Teddy muttered.

"Huh?"

"Henry..." he repeated, "he was right, they *were* after him!"

"What?!...No!...It could just be random, like a mugging or something."

"Come on, Emma, do you really believe that?!"

She didn't; she knew this was connected to the safe: "Then, what does that mean for us?"

"Oh, shit!" He realized they could also be in danger: "This is my fault!...I never shoulda gotten you involved!"

"You had no idea...besides, I begged you!" Whose fault it was; what they both should, or shouldn't have done; none of that mattered now — their only priority was staying safe. "Should we go to the police?"

"No!" he exclaimed, "If the doctor was right, then anyone that powerful would have the police bought and paid for."

"What about the FBI, or the media?...We could post it online!"

"No way!...We just need to lay low, and wait for this thing to blow over."

"You mean like Henry?...He did that for almost two decades, and look where that got him!"

Teddy stood up, and began pacing the room — he had gotten her into this mess, so now, it was his responsibility to get her out: "OK, new plan...you're packing your stuff and staying here with me."

"But this is where he came!...Wouldn't they be more likely to come here, than my apartment?"

"Yeah, but if we're at your apartment, we're five stories up with no way out." Emma weighed his proposition. "Look..." he continued, "the only thing that matters to me now is your safety...I won't let anything happen to you, I promise."

"OK..." she conceded, "let's head over there so I can pack a few things."

They set off in Teddy's car, but not a word was spoken between them. It dawned on him that Dr. Zeller must have been right about something else, too — Miles and Stella weren't killed by accident.

ΔΔΔ

When they arrived at the building, Emma told him to wait in the car while she ran in — but Teddy wasn't having it, he wasn't letting her out of his sight. He circled the block a few times, until he found a close-enough parking spot; then, they both walked inside, and went up the elevator to the fifth floor.

"Wait..." he stopped her, as she was pushing the

key into the lock, "maybe I should go in first." She hesitated for a moment, then stepped aside, allowing him access to the door. He opened it, slowly, as he reached his hand inside and turned on the lights — everything was exactly the way she left it.

"*See?*" she remarked. He wasn't convinced, though, so he had her wait by the door while he checked the other rooms; only once he knew the coast was clear, did he let her in.

"How many days should I pack for?" she asked.

"Indefinitely." he responded.

"Are you serious?"

"Well, pack for a week at least...you can always come back for more if you need to." She didn't want to argue — and after the news of Dr. Zeller, she *definitely* didn't want to be alone.

As soon as she'd finished packing, they hurried out the door; but as she was locking it, someone called out her name from behind them: "Emma!"

She turned around, to find her neighbor standing in the hallway: "Oh, hi Carol."

"You going somewhere?"

"Umm..."

"Vacation..." Teddy answered, "it was a surprise."

"Oh, wow!...You two are getting pretty serious, huh?"

"Well..." Emma smiled, nervously, "y'know..." They quickly wrapped up the conversation, and headed back down to the car.

"That was close." he whispered.

"Oh, no..." she assured him, "Carol's harmless... she's just nosy, that's all."

"Yeah, but if anyone comes asking where you

went, you don't want her saying anything that could lead them to us." She agreed with his logic; and on the return trip home, they were a bit more relaxed. The tension that they felt, from the initial shock of hearing the news, was starting to subside. "Don't worry..." he took her hand, "we're gonna be OK." His voice was calm and assured; it helped to put her at ease.

△△△

When they got back, Emma waited in the car while he checked the rooms again. "All clear!" he announced, as he emerged from the front door. He turned off the car, then he took her bags out of the trunk and brought them inside. Once they got in, she went upstairs to take a shower, leaving him alone in the living room to examine the black box from the safe. At first glance, it looked normal — but he couldn't figure out how to open it. There were four colored dots on one side, each with two small number wheels underneath. "It's an eight-digit combination..." he realized, "great, more secrets." He sat there, staring at the box and moving it around in his hands — he was so focused on it, that he didn't notice Emma walking down the stairs.

"Hey..." she sat down next to him, "you feeling any better?"

"Not really..." he sighed, "I just feel like bad things keep happening to anyone who gets close to me."

"It's not your fault..." she leaned over and kissed him on the forehead, "what happened to Henry was outta your control." Maybe she was right — maybe this *was* just what it appeared to be? He was so convinced that everything was part of some grand conspiracy, but did he see one because it existed, or because he was looking for it? Whatever had happened to Dr. Zeller, he tried to convince himself that they were in the clear. *No one came after me when Miles died, so why would they now?*

Teddy tried to put it out of his mind; he took a shower, then he and Emma went to bed. He didn't get much sleep, though; every creak, every howl of wind — they jolted him awake. By the next morning, his nerves were shot; but Emma simply rolled over, kissed him, and pulled him up. She walked him through his morning routine, and even got him to eat something — without her, he would have been completely lost.

ΔΔΔ

The rest of the day went by like a blur; they both kept checking the news, to see if there was any new information on the doctor's murder — but there was nothing else. They were stuck in this agonizing state of purgatory, with no way of knowing if they were in danger or not.

That night, they stopped for Chinese food on the way home; but neither one felt like eating, so they boxed it up and stuck it in the fridge when they got back. The next few hours went by without incident, and around ten-thirty, their stomachs began to growl. "Let's eat..." she said, "I'm starving."

"Yeah..." he admitted, "so am I."

They popped the containers in the microwave, then they spread them all out on the dining table; Emma mentioned that Chinese food always tastes better as leftovers, anyway — something that Teddy had long since known.

NICHOLAS HANNA

While they were eating, a strange thought popped into his head: "Hey, do you remember what Henry said? ...About him being too valuable for them to get rid of?"

"Yeah..." she replied, "that's why I'm not really stressing...if they needed him all this time, then why kill him now?"

"Well, what if the reason they kept him alive all these years...the reason he *was* so valuable...was because he's the only one who could recreate the project?"

"What?"

"Everything that was on those discs..." he explained, "all the work he did with Miles...what if *that's* what they were after?"

Clang! Emma dropped her fork on the plate — clearly, the thought hadn't crossed her mind. Was it their fault? Could they have helped deliver the very thing Miles died to protect? Did that also cause Dr. Zeller to become expendable?

Ding-dong! Teddy's head whipped around! His heart sank — and by the look on her face, he could tell that Emma felt the same: "It's past eleven...w-who would come here now?"

"Don't answer it." she warned.

"No, i-it's fine...killers don't use doorbells." He tried awkwardly to laugh it off, as he walked to the door; when he opened it, he saw a man standing there with his back turned: "C-Can I help you?"

"Oh, yes..." the man turned around, "I'm sorry to disturb you so late."

"Uh, that's OK...what's this about?"

"Are you..." he pulled out a small notebook and flipped through it, "Teddy Logan?"

"Yes...*gulp*...I am."

214

"Oh, good!...This is about Doctor Henry Zeller, I was wondering if I could ask you a few questions?"

"Uhh..."

"If you don't mind, that is...I'm guessing you've heard the news?"

He felt a black hole form in his stomach: "A-Are you...with the police?"

"Oh, no, we were coworkers...I'm just trying to figure some things out."

"Uh, OK...come in." He opened the door a little wider, and let the man inside; he took his jacket, then led him to the living room: "This is my girlfriend, Emma... Em, this is...umm...sorry, I-I didn't get your name..."

"Steve..." he told them, "and it's my fault, I should've introduced myself." He extended his hand, and Emma shook it, cautiously: "I'm very sorry again, about the time."

Teddy offered him some food, which he politely declined; then, they quickly cleared the table, and sat down in the living room: "So, what is it that we can help you with?"

Steve checked his phone before speaking, then he put it away: "To start, how did you know the doctor?"

"Umm...to be honest, we just met this week."

"Really?"

"Yeah, he worked alongside my late brother...but that was many years ago."

"What made you two connect now?"

"Well, I was going through some old boxes, and I found some things that belonged to him...I mainly reached out to return them."

"Ah, I see...that's understandable."

"You said you worked together?" Emma chimed

in.

"Yes..." Steve confirmed, "but only very briefly."

"Did you just join the company?"

"No, I've been there for a while, but I'm with a different department...they just recently put us together."

Teddy's initial reservations were starting to fade; the man seemed to be genuine, both in his words and his intentions: "Umm...like I said, I just met Henry a couple of times...I'm not sure how helpful I'll be."

"Oh, no..." Steve countered, "I think you'll be a *great* help." He rolled up the sleeves on his black sweater, revealing a tattoo on his left forearm — the number seven.

THIRTY-SIX

Mav flew out of the slide and crashed to the ground!

"Are you OK?!" Zelda rushed to his side: "What happened up there?!...Where are the others?!"

"Ohhh..." He rubbed the back of his head, as he slowly rose to his feet.

"What happened?!" she demanded, "Tell me!"

"Relax...we knocked that guy off the roof."

"*And...*" she pressed, "where are the others?!"

"Well, Ash was backed up...she couldn't get to this side, so she went down the other tunnel."

"Then what happened?!"

"Oh, uh, Danny went after her...and...I came to find you."

"What about Sam?!...Did he follow Danny?!"

"Umm...yeah, he did."

"OK..." she sighed, "I was out here alone, for so long...I was starting to think something happened to you guys."

"No, uh, it's all good." He decided to change the subject: "So, whaddowe have here?" He looked around, and saw that they were still outside — this time, however, they were on the ground, instead of an elevated terrace. Around them were high, manicured hedges on three sides — he could see rolls of razor wire jutting out from behind them. The fourth side of this rectangular pen was the building itself.

There were only two portals back in: the slide, which he'd just come through, and an open archway on the other side of a shallow pool. He didn't know what this place was, but he knew one thing for sure — it wasn't freedom.

"It's another challenge..." she explained, "I've been trying to figure it out."

"So, what is it?...What's the puzzle?"

Zelda directed him to the screen, and he read the clue; then, she showed him what it would entail: between them and the open doorway, was a shallow, rectangular pool — it ran from the edge of the castle to the fence, and there was no way to get around it, but to go across. It had circular, grey stepping stones, neatly aligned in rows; each stone was numbered from '1' to '5', but the rows were all arranged randomly, or so it appeared.

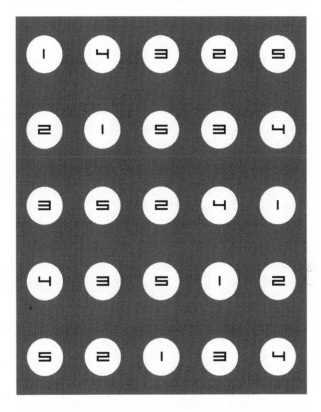

Mav turned back to the screen, and read the clue again:

To pass this test, you must unlock the golden code. Fail, and you will spiral to your doom.

"What does it mean?" he wondered.

"I dunno..." she confessed, "honestly, I was too worried about what was happening up *there*."

"Can't we just climb the fence?...Compared to what we've gone through so far, razor wire isn't that big a deal."

"No..." she broke off a branch from one of the bushes, "look at this." She ran the stick end along the fence — as she did, sparks shot off of it. "It's electrified..."

she said, "there's only one way out."

"OK...everything so far's been a trick, so I'm guessing if we step on the wrong stone, we'll fall in?"

"That's what I think." she agreed.

"But, what happens if we fall in?" He walked to the edge of the water and looked down: "Something's off here...it's gotta be like...three, maybe four feet deep... that's way too shallow to drown us."

"Well, you saw the fence, right?"

"You think it's electrified too?"

"It makes sense." she shrugged.

"OK, pass me that stick."

"Why?...What're you gonna do?"

"Don't worry, I'm just gonna splash it around a little."

Zelda picked up the branch and handed it to him: true to his word, he held the stick end, and put the side with the leaves into the pool. As he swished it back and forth, they could both hear zapping sounds in the water. He pulled the branch out and tossed it to the side — they were right about the consequence for failure, but what about success? How would they get across the stones safely?

"If you've got any ideas..." he offered, "now's the time."

"Hold on...look at that!" She stood at the left side of the pool and called him over.

"What is it?"

"Don't you see the pattern?...All down this side... five, four, three, two, one." She was right, the pattern was there.

"I dunno..." he argued, "that's just too easy."

"Like the *moon*?"

"OK, yeah...but still, this is so obvious...it's *literally* spelled out in front of us."

"Do you have anything better?" she asked.

"No..." he replied, "but there's no second chances with this one...if we're wrong, it's game over."

"OK..." she relented; she knew that he would make the first step, and she didn't want to push it if they weren't sure, "let's see what else we can find."

They both walked around the edge of the pool, looking at the stones from different angles; while Mav admitted her solution made sense, he also knew they couldn't afford to take risks. "What about that thing with the 'eights'?" he recalled, "Remember before, in the room with the tri-lock?...Didn't Ash say something about that?"

"Yeah, but it was wrong."

"Maybe, it was wrong *then*?"

"No..." she countered, "that wouldn't work here."

"Why not?"

"Look at the stones...even if you do three and five, then four and four, that still leaves an odd one at the end."

"Maybe...we hafta jump it from there?"

"Forget it...that's just stupid." She left him, still looking at the pool, and went back to read the clue again. *Golden code?...Now that could be something.*

"Come on..." Mav approached her, "you're supposed to be the smart one, aren't you?"

"Compared to *you* I am."

"Ha ha ha!...Now *there's* the girl I know!"

She tried to fight off a smile; but the more she resisted, the bigger it got. Eventually, she couldn't hold it in any longer — she began to laugh too.

Once they had both come back to their senses,

they returned to the edge of the pool and looked for more patterns. "I thought that it counted up..." he told her, "but the 'two' in the second row, and the 'three' in the third row, are on opposite sides."

"I don't think that's it...the clue said something about a 'golden code'...I think that means something."

"Well, what's the atomic number of gold?"

"Seventy-nine." she responded.

"And seven plus nine is sixteen...maybe the numbers add up to sixteen?"

"Hmm, now that sounds more like it."

Mav began counting with his finger: "One...five... two..."

"What is it?...Do you see something?"

"Straight down the middle..." he pointed, "add up the numbers."

Zelda followed his instructions: "Sixteen!"

THIRTY-SEVEN

Danny looked at Ash. "Go on." she assured him. He hesitantly placed his hand on the screen; and as the clue appeared, they both read it in silence:

Your task is to cross the field. You must find the vision to see what others cannot — then, look to the light.

"Great…" he sighed, "I dunno if I can handle any more."

"Don't give up…" she placed her hand on his shoulder, "we'll just take it slow, OK?"

"OK."

He stared into her eyes — but they seemed different, somehow. Up, on the roof, they were a pale shade of grey; but now, in the yellow glow of the firelight, they seemed to sparkle with flecks of green and gold.

"Let's figure this out…" she started, "'look to the light'?…That must mean something with the torches."

"Yeah…" he agreed, "or the torch-*holders,* like in the circle room."

"Hmm…that one pulled down like a lever, didn't it?"

Danny tried to remember; it seemed like ages since then: "If the torch-holders are levers, then what do they activate?"

Ash looked back to the screen. "'Your task is to cross the field'..." she read out loud, "it's the sensors!...It has to be!"

"What?...The sensors?"

"Yeah...each one must control a section of the motion field."

The lightbulb went on in his head: "You're right!... That's gotta be it!"

They moved closer to the left-side wall, and Ash pressed her head against it; she tried to get her eye as close to flush as possible, while she focused on the nearest torch-holder. She could see that it wasn't bolted to the wall — instead, it went *into* the wall: "We're right!... Take a look!"

Danny repeated the process and confirmed her findings. Now that they had that part figured out, he turned his attention to the second line of the clue. *You must find the vision,* he read to himself, *the vision...the vision...*

"I think..." he began, "I think we need to find something first."

"Find something?" she questioned, "Like what?"

"Look at the second line...'you must find the vision'..."

Ash finished the words: "...'to see what others cannot'."

"I'm thinking there's something in here that we hafta find."

"Like, something to help us see?"

"Exactly...something that will help us *see* the motion field."

"OK, well, that can't be too hard to find...there's not really much in here."

The two of them began their search: Danny had an idea that one of the bricks in the wall could be loose, and that they could slip it out to find the 'vision' device — whatever it was. They started on opposite sides of the room, and worked their way towards the middle. The wall went high, and whoever built this place couldn't have known how many would make it this far; so logically, it would have to be low enough for one person to reach on their own.

"Anything?" she asked him.

"No..." he responded, "not yet."

They checked every brick in the wall; from the floor, to as high as they could see. Danny even reached his hands up, and ran his fingers along the ones that he couldn't — he felt for symbols or shapes that might be carved into the faces. When that didn't work, he pushed on them, hoping to find at least one that was loose.

"Over here!" he shouted.

"What is it?!...Did you find something?!"

"I think so!...This brick, it's moving!"

Ash ran over and felt it for herself: "You're right!... Let's get it out!"

While the brick was loose, it wouldn't be easily moved — to start with, it was flush in the wall, and there was nothing for them to grab on to. They had to take turns reaching up, and rocking it side-to-side, trying to free it from the crumbling mortar — it wasn't easy, but even worse, it wasn't quick. He knew they didn't have much time to spend on this challenge; Mav and Zelda were out there, somewhere — and with that in mind, it was hard to focus on the task at hand. He didn't know where their tunnel had led — or if it was even safe — but after what happened to Sam, he realized now that the stakes were real.

"I think I'm getting it!" she exclaimed.

"You are?!"

"Yeah...ow!...Here, ah, take over...my arm's killing me."

They switched positions, and Danny managed to wedge the brick out far enough to grab it — then he pulled on it with his fingers, and popped it out of the wall: "Aaahh!"

"What is it?!" she cried.

"I'm fine!...I'm OK!...It's just dust or something, it fell in my eyes."

While he was recovering, Ash tried to look up into the space formerly occupied by the brick. "I can't see anything..." she said, "you'll hafta lift me."

"What?!...Oh, uh, OK."

He put his back against the wall, as she positioned herself in front of him; then, at her direction, he crouched down until his eyes were level with her waist: "Wrap your arms around me...now, push up with your legs." He did as instructed: once she was in the air, she could see clearly into the void. He heard her speaking, but he couldn't concentrate with her body pressed up against his face — even considering all that had happened that night, to Danny, this ranked up there with the most unlikely. *Bam!*

"What was that?!" he panicked.

"It's nothing." she replied.

"Didn't you hear that sound?!"

"Yeah, it was me...there's nothing up here...it was just a loose brick, that's all."

He put her down, and they went back to the drawing board — they knew there must be something that would help them see the field, otherwise, they would have to go through blind. "Let's just keep looking." he told her, "You were right before...we'll find a way."

Ash took a deep breath, before responding: "I know, it's just...nothing's been easy tonight." They resumed their search of the walls, meticulously going over each and every brick they could get their hands on. Fortunately, the room was very well lit: there were six torches on each side, making twelve in total — that also meant there were six parts to the motion field, providing Ash's theory was correct.

They kept moving inwards, until finally, they met in the middle — but they found nothing out of the ordinary; nothing that indicated they were on the right track. Ash sighed heavily and leaned back against the wall; she closed her eyes and tried to breathe — but then, her right foot slipped out from under her!

"Aaah!" she screamed, catching herself mid-slide.

"Are you OK?!"

"I'm fine!" she yelled, kicking her foot out in anger, "There's so much sand in here!"

Danny looked around: he noticed that there *was* something on the floor, so he knelt down to get a closer look. He picked it up, and rubbed it between his fingers; as he did, a slight grin slowly formed on his face: "I think I know what it's for." He stood up, and began spreading it around with his foot: he moved it into the corners, then across the base of the walls.

"What're you doing?" she wondered.

"I think I had it right...but it's not a loose brick in the wall, it's a loose tile in the floor."

"So, what's sand hafta do with it?"

"If there's a loose floor tile..." he explained, "the

sand will slip through the cracks around it."

She wasn't convinced, but she decided to help, anyway — until they had a better idea, this was all they had to go on. Between the two of them, they covered the entire area up to the edge of the motion field.

"Over here!" she called out.

He dashed across the room — in the corner, near the right-hand side, was a loose tile. Danny wedged it out of the floor: beneath it, they saw something wrapped in cloth — it was a pair of glasses! No earpieces, though, just two lenses inside a frame; he held them up to his eyes, and looked through: "Whoa."

THIRTY-EIGHT

Seven sat on the couch, listening to Emma and Teddy: he was a suspicious man by nature, and somehow he knew they were holding back. "I hope I'm not overstepping..." he began, "but Doctor Zeller was involved in...I guess you could call them 'special projects'...did he ever mention anything like that?"

"He, uh..." Teddy stuttered.

"It's OK..." Seven assured them, "really...after what happened, I'd be nervous too."

"It's not that..." he responded, "we just...we don't know much about his work."

"Look, I'm surprised you're even speaking to me... I certainly wouldn't do it."

"Really?" Emma questioned, "Are you not trustworthy?"

"Well, I sure think I am..." he chuckled, "but, you don't know me, and I don't know you...honestly, I'm just trying to figure out what happened."

"And..." she prodded, "what do *you* think happened?"

He cleared his throat, then adjusted the cushion behind his back: "I probly shouldn't be saying this, but...I believe Doctor Zeller was targeted by our organization."

"*Targeted?*" she feigned surprise, "Why?"

"You see, he was involved in some high-level experiments...top-secret stuff..." he paused, looking to the ground, "something happened recently...I don't know what it was, but for some reason...to them, anyway...he became more of a liability than an asset."

"Hmm..." Teddy nodded, "I see." He seemed to be buying into what 'Steve' was saying.

Emma, on the other hand, was far more skeptical: "How did you come to know all this?"

Seven had to fight off a smirk: "As I said, I can't blame you for not trusting me." As the conversation went on, Teddy and Emma listened to more stories from their guest — stories that were carefully crafted to lower their guard and gain their trust. This wasn't his first time, after all — he was a professional. "So, again..." he continued, "and I'm sorry to belabor the point...but did the doctor mention anything to you?...Any thoughts or worries that he might be in danger?"

Teddy looked to Emma: she was gesturing for him to keep quiet. He was conflicted, though; torn about whether or not to trust this man. What he was saying checked out, but did Teddy actually believe him? Or, was he just hoping for another ally in this fight? He must have decided and undecided a half-dozen times before he finally spoke: "Listen, Steve...I probly shouldn't say anything...and like I said, he didn't tell us much...but, Henry did have concerns."

"It's OK...believe me, I know, I'm having some of my own...that's why I'm here."

"Why don't you tell us what's going on..." Emma proposed, "then we'll see if we can help you."

She was smart, that much was certain — Seven realized he had underestimated these two. "I don't know if you're ready for this." he warned.

"Try us." she fired back.

"OK, here it goes…" he took a deep breath, "I believe that there's a conspiracy, at the highest levels of the company…I don't know what their plan is, or what they needed from Doctor Zeller, but…they had him murdered, and this morning they tried to do the same to me."

"What?!" they both yelled.

"No!" Teddy cried, "That can't be true!"

"I promise you, it is."

"What happened?"

"Three men with guns showed up at my apartment…luckily, I managed to get away." That statement was true — true enough to not be a lie, anyway.

"Wow!" Teddy exclaimed, "I can't believe it…I mean, I can…he was right!…All this time, they must've wanted something from him."

"Yes, exactly!…I believe that whatever it is you gave him, in some way, it was important to them…important enough to kill for."

"I…uh…"

"It's OK, I'm not blaming you…I mean, you probly had no idea what it was." Seven had chosen his words carefully — he now had them set up, right where he wanted them.

"Actually…" Teddy started, "Henry did—"

"He didn't say what it was about." Emma cut in, "So, you were telling us about your attack?…How exactly did you escape from three professional killers?"

"Professional killers?!" he balked, "I don't know anything about that…but, they had guns, and they broke into my apartment."

"*And…*" she pressed, "how did you escape?"

Teddy gave her a look; he tried to signal her to stop pushing: "It's...you don't—"

"No, it's fine..." Seven insisted, "and again, if I were in your shoes." Emma turned to Teddy and narrowed her eyes — she was clearly annoyed that they weren't on the same page. "I'd be glad to explain..." he went on, "I was out jogging, like I do every morning, and when I returned, I noticed that my front door was open...so I peeked inside, and that's when I saw them...after that, I just kinda snuck out."

"There..." Teddy remarked, returning her annoyed look, "that explains it."

Seven could see them starting to fracture; he decided that some time alone would be just what they needed to finish driving the wedge. "Do you mind if I use your bathroom?" he asked.

"Not at all..." Teddy replied, "it's upstairs, first door on the right."

"Thanks."

He stood up, and walked to the stairs: he paused briefly for a moment at the top, trying to listen in on their argument. But it was hard to hear, and he didn't want to waste the little time that he had; so he moved on, silently opening doors and drawers with the delicacy of a surgeon.

△△△

It had already been a few minutes, and he knew they'd get suspicious if he was gone too long; so he hurriedly looked around, and before rejoining them, he decided to make a quick pass through the master bedroom. Not a thorough search — he didn't have time for that —

just a light sweep.

He eased the door open, but didn't dare turn on the lights; besides, there was enough ambient light coming in through the windows to help him get a good feel for the room. *This doesn't add up,* he thought, *there's something they're not telling me.* He knew that too much time had already passed; surely, by now, they were starting to wonder where he was.

He turned to exit the room; but as he did, he noticed something on the dresser — there were a few pieces of old paper, bent and folded together, tucked underneath a picture frame. He picked them up and opened them: two of the three pages had the same type of technical data that he'd seen on the flash drive — but the last page, that one *really* looked familiar.

He reached into his back pocket and took out the data table he'd printed earlier — they were the same, except for two key differences. First, this page was typed, not written out by hand; and second, this one wasn't a partial — it was the full table.

NUMBER	TYPE	STRENGTH	SPEED	AGILITY	INTELLIGENCE	CREATIVITY
CONTROL	—	50%	50%	50%	50%	50%
2	M	65%	60%	63%	63%	65%
3	F	52%	53%	50%	78%	75%
4	M	63%	68%	65%	51%	53%
5	M	61%	60%	59%	71%	73%
6	F	73%	69%	67%	61%	55%
7	M	80%	75%	75%	65%	67%
8	M	52%	56%	59%	73%	72%
9	M	80%	79%	71%	63%	58%
10	F	63%	60%	62%	93%	95%

"These look like test results…" he whispered, "or, are they?" He didn't know exactly what he was looking at, but he did know that his hosts hadn't been honest. He felt the rage start to build inside him — *those* urges were coming back. He folded the papers and stuffed them in his pocket; then, he went to the bathroom, and picked up a small rag.

He stepped quietly down the stairs: once he reached the bottom, he could hear them still arguing in the living room — so he reached into his jacket, which was hung up by the door, and took out a small pouch. Inside, there was a glass bottle containing a clear liquid: he opened it, poured some out on the rag, then closed it again. He crept up behind Teddy without making a sound — and in one quick motion, smothered his face with the rag! Instantly, he was rendered unconscious.

Emma screamed! She leapt out of her chair and rushed up against the wall! "Please!" she begged, "Don't do this!"

"Relax…" he said, calmly, "you won't feel a thing." She made a desperate attempt for the door — but he grabbed her! She jabbed her elbows into his ribs, and stomped on his feet as hard as she could — but it was no use: he covered her mouth and nose with the rag. Then, she stopped moving; her body went limp.

THIRTY-NINE

"What is it?!" Ash wondered, "Whaddaya see?!"

"Here, take a look." Danny handed her the glasses; she held them to her eyes, and looked through to the motion field. What she saw left her stunned: a tangled mess of multi-colored lasers shot out from the walls in every direction — it was like a rainbow-colored spiderweb. "Whaddaya think?...How do we get through *that*?"

She lowered the glasses and stared out again: without them, all she saw was empty space — the lenses refracted the light, allowing them to see the laser beams. She then raised them back up, and noticed something she didn't the first time: "Hey, check this out." She handed them back to Danny, and he took a second look: "Do you see it?"

"Umm...I don't think so."

"The colors!" she pointed out, "They're separate!" The colored lines weren't all jumbled together as he'd first thought, it was just an optical illusion — they were actually separated into sections. The first section, closest to them, had green lasers; the next section had blue, then purple. The remaining three were red, orange, and yellow, in that order.

"You're right!" he realized, "They are!" Now, they both knew that they could navigate the field, one section at a time, using the colors to distinguish the near beams from the far. "But, wait..." he held up the glasses, "there's only one pair of these."

"Well, really..." she figured, "it only takes one of us to pull the levers."

"I guess." he agreed, "Maybe, we could take turns?"

"*Turns?*" she smirked, "How flexible are you?"

"Huh?...Umm, not very."

"That's what I thought." she said, "Don't sweat it, I'll go through."

"Oh, uh, well...how flexible are *you?*" Ash didn't reply, not with words anyway; she untied her boots and took them off. Next, she bent her knees, arched her back, and curved her arms behind her head — all the way until they touched the floor. She contorted her body into a crab-like position, and in so doing, created a perfect curve from her toes to her fingers — then, she kicked her feet up, and slowly flipped them over her head. Danny watched in awe, as they touched back down on the other side — the entire time, her hands didn't move. "Wow!" he marveled, standing bolt upright, "How did you..."

"Yoga." she shrugged.

It was decided then, Ash would make the trek through the field; but as she was getting herself ready, Danny found another problem: "Wait...no, this won't work."

"Whaddya mean?"

"The glasses...there's no way to keep them in place, without holding them."

"What?...No." She examined them a second time, but quickly realized he was right — without using her hands, they wouldn't stay on her face. "We've gotta be missing something..." she insisted, "maybe there's another loose tile?" They went about searching the room again, trying to see if there was anything else that was loose, or marked in some way — but there wasn't. "This just can't be right..." she muttered to herself.

"*Ahem*"

"What is it?...Did you find something?"

"Yeah...I mean, no...but, I think I figured it out."

"Then, how does it work?"

"Well, I think *I* hafta hold the glasses..." he explained, "and talk you through it."

"What?!" she balked, "So I hafta go in blind?!"

"Not blind..." he assured her, "I'll guide you." He could see the anxiety on her face; her breathing quickened, and she was fidgeting with her hands: "Trust me, I can do it...I won't let you down."

Ash considered his words carefully: she knew he was being sincere — she also knew that he couldn't get around the lasers like she could. "OK." she relented. It was more of a sigh, really, than an agreement; but, what choice did she have? She dropped her shoulders and slipped off her jacket; then, she brushed back her hair, and used a band on her wrist to tie it up neatly: "You ready?" Her voice was more certain now; more resolved to the task in front of her. Danny nodded, and she took one last look through the glasses — she was trying to find the best point from which to enter. Eventually, she settled on a spot near the middle, and positioned herself there.

"OK..." he began, "let's just take this slow."

"You don't need to tell *me*." she quipped.

She handed the glasses back to him, and he put them to his eyes: he moved around, examining the green section from different angles — the starting point she chose was a good one, and he could see a relatively clear path from there to the center. Another thing that worked in their favor, was the fact that the beams didn't move — they were static, meaning he could map out a basic route before she went in: "Which side should we go for?"

"Umm...maybe the left?"

He looked through the glasses again, and tried to visualize a trail to that side: "OK, I think we can make that work...do you want another look?"

"No..." she replied, removing her socks, "I trust you."

He moved behind her, and adjusted the lenses on his face; then, he began calling out instructions: "OK, just ease your right leg up, about halfway." Ash did as he said; once her leg was high enough, he continued: "That's good...now, push it forward, slowly." Again, she complied; her leg was now *inside* the motion field — and nothing happened. "You're doing great..." he told her, "now, gently lower it to the floor."

She inched her foot down; and as her toes touched the tile, she was finally able to release her breath: "That wasn't so bad."

"Don't worry, we're just getting started...you'll be dodging arrows in no time."

"Stop..." she giggled, "don't make me laugh."

He apologized, and continued his direction: "Alright, you need to crouch down...lower than that...a little more...OK, that's good." With her head in position, she ducked beneath the first beam — to her, she was dodging invisible wires; but to Danny, she was weaving her way through a multi-colored minefield: "Pull your left leg up to your chest, at a forty-five-degree angle."

Ash moved cautiously; once her leg was clear of

the beam, he told her it was safe to stand up. As she did, she exhaled—it was a long, slow breath that released her tension: "OK, now what?"

"Do you want a quick break?" he asked, "That was intense."

"No..." she responded, "let's keep moving."

He guided her through the green lasers, and she got herself to within a few feet of the left-side torch—but they encountered a new problem: the beams around it were more tightly packed than anticipated. He moved all around that side, trying to see a way for her to reach a hand through: "I dunno...this doesn't look good."

"What is it?"

"They're too bunched up in that corner...I think we might hafta try the other side."

"What?!...No way, I'm right here!"

"I can't see a way through...maybe, we could try it from another angle?"

"OK..." she consented, "that's fine." Easier said than done, however; the more she backtracked, the more it became obvious that there was no other path to the left. Eventually, she ended up back at her first position, near the center. "Ugh!" she scoffed, "We're going backwards!"

"I know, I know...actually, we're pretty much in the middle now...let's just try the other side."

Ash was annoyed — she hated the feeling of not being in control — but she had to give in. She realized that while she was in the laser field, she would have to go along with whatever he said.

"Duck down and to the left..." he instructed, "good, now, slowly move your left leg up, about a foot... a little higher...OK, now push forward, and down to the floor." She squatted and crawled through the tangled web of invisible lines, twisting and turning her body into unfathomable positions. Danny was amazed — he didn't know it was possible for a human being to move like that: "You're almost there...stop!"

"What?!"

"Pull your left hand in...towards your body." She followed his directions; only once she was clear of the danger, did he reveal what it was: "I swear, your finger musta *just* missed that line." They got back to work, and he guided her underneath the first torch — finally, the moment of truth had arrived. Ash got her hand on the wrought iron piece, and pulled it down: there was an audible *hum*, and the green laser beams vanished. "Yes!" he cheered, "It worked!" He ran to her, and she met him with open arms.

"Wow!" she exclaimed, "I can't believe we just did that!...I couldn't see anything!"

"I know, that was crazy!"

But their euphoria quickly faded: they remembered that they had only made it through the first section, and there were still five more to go. "Well..." she proceeded, "on to the next one?"

"Don't you need a breather?"

"Yeah, I do...but I just wanna get out."

She lined up at the edge of the blue section, and Danny once again guided her in. Now that she had practice, she moved through it with ease — she made it all the way to the right-side torch-holder and pulled it down. He watched, in real time, as the blue lines disappeared. They repeated the process for the purple section, but that one seemed more difficult than the first two — even so, she emerged unscathed.

"I think they're getting harder..." he observed, "the lines seemed closer together in that one."

"Yeah..." she confirmed, "they were."

They were halfway through now: halfway to the end of the challenge, and halfway closer to finding Mav and Zelda — or at least, that's what they hoped. Ash moved in front of the red section, and Danny could almost see through to the end. Now that the cool colors had gone, the rest of the motion field seemed like it was on fire. The tangled mess of red, orange, and yellow lines triggered something inside him: his heart began beating faster, and the sweat on his hands made it difficult for him to keep a firm hold on the glasses.

The spaces between the lines were definitely shrinking as they advanced. Ash couldn't seem to find a good starting point, so Danny decided that dead center would be best; he guided her past the first few lines, and she found a spot in the middle where she could stand up. "OK..." he encouraged her, "you're doing great." But they were now faced with a dilemma: left or right? He decided 'left', and verbalized to her what she had to do: "...now move your arm up...arch your back some more..." Even she was finding this difficult: her body was twisted sideways, into a half-bridge shape. Then, as she tried to slide her right leg forward — it slipped!

FORTY

"So..." Mav turned to Zelda, "whaddowe do?"

"I dunno..." she replied, "they could both be right."

He stretched his arms out behind him, and let out a heavy groan; as he did, he noticed that she was biting her lip, and her eyes were darting around nervously. Although he would be the one to make the first step, Zelda had just as much to lose if they were wrong: she would still be trapped, she would still have to solve the puzzle, and she would probably have to get through the rest of the maze on her own.

They stood at the edge of the pool and gazed down at the stones, still unsure of which to choose; Mav knew they couldn't take long to decide, however, Ash and Danny were still out there — and so was Sam, as far as Zelda knew.

"I just don't know..." she sighed, "let's take a minute, and think about this."

"Nah...I'm done waiting." He walked over to the bushes and started looking under them; next, he moved to the wall with the screen, and felt around it with his hands.

"What're you doing?" He didn't respond, so she walked over to him and tried again: "Hey, what's going on?"

"I'm sick of playing by their rules..." he said, "so I'm not gonna do it anymore." His actions were confusing her: he was walking all around the gravelly area, on their side of the pool, checking everything within reach — he was clearly trying to find something, but she couldn't figure out what it was.

"OK..." she conceded, "just tell me what you're looking for, and I'll help you."

"I dunno."

"You don't know what you're looking for?"

"Just something big..." he told her, "something heavy."

"Heavy?...For what?"

Mav paused his frantic searching, and looked her in the eyes: "The way I see it, we have two choices, and we don't know which to go with, right?"

"Right..."

"So, let's just throw something on one of the stones and see what happens...if it holds, we know it's right...if not, we go with the second option."

"Hmm, that's actually not bad..." she admitted, "I'm surprised I didn't think of it."

"Don't worry..." he smirked, "somebody's gotta be the smart one."

Zelda smiled and shook her head, as she turned away; then, she went to the remaining bushes, and checked under them for heavy rocks — but there weren't any. Next, she pulled on the roots, to see if she could find a loose one — still no luck. "It's no use..." she remarked, "good idea, but they musta thought of it too...there's nothing around here that's heavy enough."

"Oh, yes there is." He walked back over to the

electronic screen — once again, he ran his fingers around the edges. He found a small gap, near the top-right-hand corner, and pulled it out. "Aah!" he cried, as his fingers jammed behind it.

"What happened?!"

"Nothing, *ah*, I'm good." He wedged his hand further inward, until there was a *crack!* Then a *snap!* "Grraaah!" He used all the strength he could muster, and ripped it off the wall!

"What the..."

The screen was wide and heavy — it blocked his forward view. "Help me!" he shouted.

"What?!...I can't lift *that!*"

"No, you need to guide me!" Zelda ran over and touched his hand: she carefully led him to the edge of the water, and he set it down on the ground. "OK..." he panted, "well...that wasn't so hard, was it?"

"You'd better know what you're doing..." she warned him, "you've just lost our clue."

"I'm sure you'll remember it...now, which one do we try?"

She examined the grid again, and pointed: "The 'five' in the first row." Mav hoisted the screen back up, and steadied himself at the edge of the pool; at the same time, Zelda moved around behind him, and held onto his jacket — just in case he lost his balance. He took a deep breath, and tried to visualize the distance in his mind — he still couldn't see anything — then he heaved it up, and let go!

It seemed to hang in the air, momentarily, before crashing down on the '5' stone. *Zaaap! Zap! Zaaap! Zap! Zaaap!* Instantly, it sunk into the water: "Well, I guess that rules out the left side." He moved in front of the middle column; then, without any warning—he stepped out!

"No!" she screamed — but he was alright — he was standing firmly on top of the '1' stone. He stuck his arms out to the side and closed his eyes, savoring his moment of triumph.

When Zelda's nerves had calmed down, he went to take the next step — to the '5' in the second row — but before he could, she called out to stop him: "Wait!"

"What is it?"

"We were wrong!" she yelled, "It's *not* sixteen!"

"Whaddaya mean?...I'm standing on the first stone."

"Yeah, that one was right, but sixteen isn't the answer." She pointed to the column on the far-right side: "Four, two, one, four, five...that line equals sixteen, too."

He added them in his head, then he looked down to the '5' in front of him: "Maybe I could stick my foot out?...Try to get some pressure on it?"

"Don't you dare!" she snapped, "Just come back!"

He looked at her, then back to the stone; he shifted his weight onto his left leg, then stuck his right foot out in front of him. As he eased his toe down, it seemed to be holding: "Hey, I—" Then it sank! It threw him off balance, and he wobbled on one leg — he was tipping over! At the very last moment, he pushed up with his standing leg as hard as he could — he flew backwards through the air, landing face-up, right at the edge of the pool! His legs were hanging over the side, but he managed to keep them out of the water.

Zelda dropped to her knees: like before, he reached his hand out to her — but she swatted it away! Then she began raining down open-handed slaps onto his face: "What the hell is wrong with you?!"

"Stop!" he begged, "I'm fine!"

"Good!...Now I'm gonna kill you!"

When he finally managed to get her off, they both stood up and surveyed the pool again: they knew that the starting point was the '1' in the first row, and that the '5' in the second row, directly in front of it, wasn't the next step.

"I guess..." he started, "it was never gonna be as easy as a straight line."

"Yeah..." she agreed, "I *wish* we could read the clue again."

"OK, OK...that was my fault, I admit it."

"Do you remember the last line?" she asked.

"No..." he responded, "what was it?"

"It said something like...'don't spiral to your doom'."

"There's no spirals here...just fall in and get shocked."

"Exactly!...In math, the golden spiral is related to the Fibonacci numbers."

"So?" he questioned, "How does that help us?"

"Fibonacci numbers follow a sequence..." she explained, "where each number is the sum of the two that came before it."

"Yeah, but...wait!" He finally realized what she was saying: "So if we start at 'one'..."

"The next number in the sequence..." she finished, "would be 'one' again!"

He liked her theory — and if he had to put his life on the line, based on the word of someone else, she'd be near the top of the list. "Alright!" he exclaimed, "Let's do it!" He walked to the edge of the pool, and stepped back onto the '1' stone; his leg wouldn't be able to reach the '1' in the second row, so he'd just have to go for it: "Here goes nothing."

Zelda didn't look — she couldn't bear to watch if they were wrong. She stood frozen in place at the edge of the pool, squeezing her eyes shut; but after a while, she realized she didn't hear anything. She opened them to find him standing with his arms above his head — in the *second* row. "Yes!" she cheered, "We did it!"

"Come on!" he called to her, "Follow behind me!" She hopped on the first stone, as Mav moved to the '2' in the third row — it worked again! Then he jumped to the '3' in the fourth row, to the '5' in the fifth row, and finally, to the other side!

She followed the path; once she'd made it safely across, he grabbed her in a tight embrace — she hugged him too.

FORTY-ONE

Ash's leg slid through the beam — *shoo!* — an arrow shot from the right-side wall! She threw herself back to dodge it and it flew past, just grazing her right shoulder.

"Are you OK?!" Danny shouted.

"I'm fine!" Her back was now laying flat on the floor.

"Your arm!" he called out, "It's bleeding!"

"I'm OK!" she repeated, "Just get me outta here!"

He held the glasses up to his eyes: she was in a tight spot — her leg was just an inch or two below the red line. "This is gonna be tricky..." he warned, "we'll hafta go slow."

"Fine by me!"

He guided her, cautiously, as she pulled her leg underneath the beam. Now, the hard part: she had to twist her ankle almost ninety-degrees, and wedge her foot under the laser. "Careful..." he instructed, "easy... just a little further...keep going...you're clear!" He talked her back to her feet, and they continued on their path to the wall — she was almost there, when he realized he'd painted her into a corner.

"Come on..." she hurried him, "what's taking so long?"

"Uhh, just gimme a sec...this one's really tight." He

examined her position from different angles, trying to find the best way to get her through: "OK, I think I got it...move your left hand up, kinda in a diagonal." Ash followed his directions: "Now, hold your arm in place...just like that."

"You sure you know what you're doing?" she asked him.

"Trust me..." he responded, "I got this." She held her arm in the air, stuck in this awkward position for what seemed like eternity; finally, though, he found the next move: "Keep your arm like that and just *slide* it forward." She did as he said, but blood was now running down her arm; it pooled in the crease of her elbow, and the makings of a first drop hovered dangerously, just above another beam. "A little closer..." he urged, "closer...closer...got it!" She pulled down on the lever and the red lines vanished. He threw his hands in the air to celebrate, but Ash didn't join him — she collapsed against the wall and slid to the floor: "Are you alright?!"

He rushed to her side! "Yeah, I'm good..." she assured him, "just lemme breathe."

He examined the gash on her shoulder: it wasn't deep, but it was long — and bleeding quite heavily. "We need to tie this off." he insisted. She nodded, and he began looking around for a makeshift tourniquet — there was nothing, however, but bricks and sand; so she ripped off the bottom of her tank top and handed it to him. The thin strip of white fabric wasn't wide — just about two inches or so — but Danny wrapped it around and around; he made sure to keep it tight, as he covered the wound completely. After that, he helped her to her feet, and they looked through the glasses again.

By now, he'd also worked out the other purpose

of the colors: while they were used to differentiate the sections, the order was deliberately arranged to confuse the navigator — green then blue, blue then purple, purple then red — and with the increasing density of each field, he sometimes didn't know if he was looking at a beam in the current section, or the one that came after. No matter, though, they now had two more.

Ash stepped forward, until she was at the cusp of the orange grid; she turned her head around and signaled to him that she was in place. "Remember..." he said, "they're getting harder."

"I know..." she acknowledged, "I can handle it." He guided her in past the first few lines, but she ended up crouched down, uncomfortably, below a three-way cross. There, she waited for him to find a clear path: "Whenever you're ready."

"Umm..."

"I don't need 'umms'." she told him.

"OK, OK...let's go right...move your left leg up, then over, about a foot." He carefully steered her again, and she was nearing the wall on the right side: "Just a little more...that's it...almost there..." Ash was close — she could almost touch it — but she now stood, awkwardly, with her hand just inches from the torch. Danny moved around, trying to see a way for her to reach it; another problem that he hadn't anticipated, however, was the color — the beams around the torch were getting lost in the light.

"What's the holdup?" she inquired, clearly annoyed at how much time he was taking.

"Uhh...almost have it." She was tired of waiting, and figured she could be quick; so she launched her hand forward — through the beams — and grabbed the handle!

In one quick motion, she threw herself to the floor, pulling the iron piece down with her! *Shoo! Shoo!* Two arrows flashed past! "No!" he cried — but it didn't matter — the field was shut down!

He wanted to scream at her; he wanted to tell her how stupid that was — but he didn't say anything. He just watched as she stood up, and got in position for the last section. "Let's go." she ordered.

Danny complied — but this, the final section of yellow-colored lasers, was by far the most difficult. To start with, it easily had the most beams; and the residual yellow glow they emitted seemed to get lost in the light of the torches. "This isn't gonna be quick..." he informed her, "so don't do anything crazy." She was no longer the only one who was annoyed.

"Fine..." she pouted, "let's just do this."

"OK...there's a long, horizontal line right at the front...you'll hafta duck low to get under it." She did as directed, managing to wedge herself past the threshold: "You're doing great...now, a little to the left...not that far...good, you're OK...just take it slow." She ducked and weaved, bent and twisted, and finally, after much more time than it took her before — she made it to the wall and shut off the motion field!

"Yes!" he yelled, "We did it!" Ash grabbed him and hugged him tight; but they didn't linger in their embrace for long — even though they'd passed the test, they weren't out of the maze yet. They had to keep moving; they had to find the others.

ΔΔΔ

There was an opening in the wall, directly in front

of them, so they went through it — just like the other corridors, this one was dark, tight, and narrow. They meandered through, being very careful not to lose each other — it was pitch-black inside; not a speck of light could be found anywhere. "Where do you think this leads?" he whispered, "You don't think that was the end, do you?" His mind went back to the other tunnel on the roof—the one Zelda and Mav had gone down.

"No..." she replied, "it can't be."

Eventually, they saw something up ahead — it wasn't firelight, but they could see, so something had to be lighting the space. When they got there, they saw what it was: a small, circular intersection of three passageways — they had come through one, so that left two more to choose from. The light came in through a high, open roof; it was crossed with iron bars, but the light from the moon was able to shine in.

Ash stepped forward and stared into the forked tunnels: "Well, whaddaya think?"

"Umm, I dunno..." he shrugged, "it's a fifty-fifty chance either way."

"Judging by what we've been through..." she guessed, "I'd say they're equally bad." They weren't stuck in their decision for long, however, because from one of the corridors came a noise: "Did you hear that?!"

"Yeah!" he confirmed, "It sounds like voices!"

They waited breathlessly to see what would happen next — then, they heard footsteps. The sounds were steadily getting louder, as they drew closer...closer... closer...it was Mav and Zelda!

FORTY-TWO

Teddy cringed; his sinuses were burning, and his head felt like it would explode. He heard a voice, but couldn't quite make out the words. As he struggled to bring his eyes into focus, he realized that his hands were bound together behind his back; his feet, too — he was tied to a chair. There was duct tape over his mouth, which prevented him from speaking. All at once, it came back to him. He looked over, and saw 'Steve' standing in front of Emma — she was also tied up, and he was waving something under her nose.

When they were both awake, their captor sat down on the couch: he stared into their eyes, shifting his gaze from one to the other, every few seconds. Once he was satisfied that they were fully alert, he leaned over and removed the tape from Teddy's mouth. Then he did the same to Emma — she screamed as it was ripped off. The man he had welcomed into his home, the man he had trusted, now sat before him holding a pistol in his right hand: "Let's try this again, shall we?"

Teddy turned to Emma — he wanted desperately to tell her she was right. It was his fault; he didn't listen, and this was the outcome: "W-What do you want?"

"The truth." Seven calmly replied.

"But, we told you—"

"Lies!" he charged, slamming his gun down on the coffee table, "You told me lies!" They could see the rage burning inside him: "Tell me now!...What do you know of Zeller's work?!"

Teddy and Emma looked at each other again: before, their goal was to protect the secret — but now, the only thing that mattered was getting out of here alive. "Who...who are you?" he asked.

Seven pointed the gun at his head: "I ask the questions...you answer them...understand?"

"Y-Yes..." he trembled, "I just...don't you work for 'them'?"

Seven sighed, and leaned back on the couch: "I understand your confusion...you're wondering if I killed him, aren't you?" They both nodded: "Well, let me put your minds at ease...I did." They were stunned by the callousness of his admission. "My name isn't Steve, either..." he confessed, pointing to the tattoo on his arm, "it's Seven." He turned the gun to Emma, then he continued: "Now that we're all properly acquainted...tell me what you know."

"Alright..." Teddy gave in, "I'll tell you everything...but, please, just let her go."

"No!" she objected, "I won't leave you!"

"A very noble gesture..." Seven stated, "OK, if you tell me the truth...and I mean everything...then, I'll let her go."

Teddy agreed: "Henry was a biogeneticist...he and my brother, they worked on genetic engineering projects."

"What kinds of projects?"

"He said they were...I dunno, it's all technical stuff, I-I didn't really understand."

"*Try*." Seven coaxed, pointing the gun back at him.

"They weren't anything bad!" Emma exclaimed, "He said they started out to help people...the blind, the handicapped...they wanted to cure diseases, too, like cancer...they wanted to save lives!...That's what he said! ...That's what he told us!"

"Then why did 'they' want him dead?"

"I don't know!" she yelled, "You're the one who killed him!"

Seven paused at that; he lowered the gun, and tried to think for a moment. *Genetic engineering?...Sure, they probly started out with good intentions.* "OK..." he pressed, "what else?"

"He said..." Teddy went on, "he said that their bosses, or the people higher up...they wanted to use their research for some kind of...military program...or, wait... he didn't use the word military, but—"

"What did he say?...The *exact* word."

"He said...uhh..." Teddy tried to remember, "he said...soldier."

Soldier? Seven was a soldier — that's what they called him: "What do you mean?...They cured soldiers?"

"No, not cured...more like...enhanced."

Seven reached behind his back, and pulled out the crumpled papers; his eyes went down the numbers in the far-left column—there it was: '7'.

NUMBER	TYPE	STRENGTH	SPEED	AGILITY	INTELLIGENCE	CREATIVITY
CONTROL	–	50%	50%	50%	50%	50%
2	M	65%	60%	63%	63%	65%
3	F	52%	53%	50%	78%	75%
4	M	63%	68%	65%	51%	53%
5	M	61%	60%	59%	71%	73%
6	F	73%	69%	67%	61%	55%
7	M	80%	75%	75%	65%	67%
8	M	52%	56%	59%	73%	72%
9	M	80%	79%	71%	63%	58%
10	F	63%	60%	62%	93%	95%

His gaze then shifted to the tattoo on his arm: could this be what happened to him? Is that why he feels the need to kill? *They must've done this to me...they must've experimented on me.* His emotions were going off the charts now — he was barely in control. He looked back up at them, realizing there must be more to this story: "Keep going!"

Teddy looked over at Emma, and swallowed hard: "That's it...MilTech found out they were planning to go public...that's why they killed my brother."

"MilTech?...Is that who you think is behind this?" They stared at him blankly: "You do know that MilTech is just a shell, don't you?" They had no response: "Oh, wow...you two really are in over your heads."

"Please..." Teddy begged, "that's all he told us."

Seven was trying to decide whether or not to believe them. "We're telling you the truth!" Emma pleaded, "Just let us go!" He didn't respond — he just kept staring at his tattooed arm.

Teddy felt helpless; he hoped that at least Emma would be set free, but then — Seven stood up and pointed the gun at her: "What're you doing?!...You said you'd let her go!"

"I am letting her go...she'll suffer no longer in this world." *Click.*

FORTY-THREE

"Mav!" Danny called out.

"Danny!" he shouted back, "Is that you?!"

"Yeah, it's me!"

Mav and Zelda raced towards his voice: as they came into the light, Zelda launched herself forward — she grabbed Ash and Danny and hugged them both. They reciprocated without saying a word — they understood.

When she finally let go, she inquired about Sam; she looked all around, trying to locate him. Ash and Danny exchanged puzzled glances; then they looked at Mav, who they realized hadn't told her.

"Hello?" she pressed, "Where is he?...Did he go down one of these tunnels?"

"Sam, uh..." Danny stuttered, "he...he didn't—"

"He wasn't with us." Ash replied — she, too, had realized that a distraught Zelda would be the last thing they'd need.

"So..." Mav changed the subject, "what's this place all about?"

"We dunno..." Danny shrugged, "we just got here."

"But..." Ash added, "we know where we're going." They had come through one tunnel, Mav and Zelda had come through another — that left one more.

"Well, what're we waiting for?" Mav headed into

the third passageway; it was much tighter than the ones they'd just come through, so they had to walk single file. Ash went behind him followed by Zelda, with Danny at the back; like before, there was no light, so they had to use the walls to guide them. They felt cold — much colder than the others — and wet, too, like the inside of a refrigerator.

Danny alternated his hands from the left wall to the right, but there wasn't much space between them. He figured they'd know where the tunnel ended, when they either saw a light, or, the space got wider. Eventually, it did, and he was able to stretch both arms all the way out — but he couldn't feel anything around him.

"What's going on?" Zelda whispered, "Are you guys still there?"

"We're here..." Ash told her, "I think we're in another room."

"Danny?" Mav prompted, "You with us?"

"Yeah..." he responded, "did you find the walls?"

"Not yet...let's feel around."

They carefully moved away from each other, making sure to keep their hands out in front — they were trying to grasp, or feel something that would give an indication of where they were. The air felt heavy, like it was on the cusp of becoming liquid.

Suddenly, there was a noise! It was like stones grinding again, but this time it was accompanied by a mechanical *buzz* and *hum.* They all stumbled back together — it was instinctive, rather than a conscious act.

Then the noise abruptly ended, and a light appeared — another screen! Mav stepped forward and used his hand to unlock it — this was a puzzle; another challenge:

No more tricks. No more riddles. For your final task, you must find a way to leave this room. Locate the correct hatch and freedom is yours. One mistake will not divide you, but be warned — too many and you will drown.

"That's pretty straightforward." he remarked.

"Yeah..." Zelda agreed, "and it says it's the last one."

"'Too many and you will drown'..." Danny read, "you don't think..."

"I do..." Ash answered, "look." With the light from the screen, they could finally see the space around them. All over the walls were circular, numbered hatches — each one was sealed in place with a T-handle, which could be used to open it.

"So..." Zelda figured, "we hafta open the right hatch to escape, but for each wrong one, we'll get flooded?"

"That's what it seems like." Ash confirmed.

"Well then..." she turned to Mav, "we need to take our time...that means no rash decisions."

"Why'd you look at *me* when you said that?"

Danny, meanwhile, was busy exploring the room: he noticed that the hatches weren't all the same. Some were large, some were small — some were even on the ceiling! He realized that the water could come at them from any one of five different sides; the only parts of the room without a hatch, were the floor, and the strip of wall that sealed the passageway. *That must've been what we heard.*

"Check this out!" Mav exclaimed. They joined him in the corner, and he showed them what he'd found: "Hatch number one...it's right here, and it's tiny."

"So?" Ash questioned, "We can't fit through *that*."

"Yeah, obvi...but it's like, the size of a golf ball... let's pop it open...that way, we can see how fast the water comes in." Zelda was about to erupt, but he preempted her: "I know, I know...dumb risks...but, they've worked so far."

"OK." Ash said, catching Danny and Zelda off guard.

"What?!" she balked, "Are you serious?!"

"He's right...they've worked so far."

"Danny..." Zelda implored, "you think this is a bad idea, don't you?"

He did, but what could he say? Did he have it in him to go against his best friend *and* his crush? "I... umm..."

"Thank you!...Even *he's* not sold!"

"Come on, Dan, you know I wouldn't do this unless I thought it was safe."

"I, uh...I guess."

That was all the consent he needed — Mav grabbed the handle, turned it, and unlocked the '1' hatch!

FORTY-FOUR

"Something's up..." the younger guard banged on the monitors, "they haven't moved in way too long."

"Yeah, this isn't normal..." the older one admitted, "go outside to the box and reset the signal."

"How do I do that?"

"Just pull the lever down, then back up...after that, press and hold the red button for ten seconds."

"OK, I'm on it!"

He stepped outside and walked to the junction box: "What?...Why is this open?" He did as his colleague instructed; first, he pushed the small lever down, then quickly pulled it up again — but the space was tight, and his hand fit awkwardly: "Ow!" Next, he pressed down on the red button and counted to ten. *One...two...three...*

When the time was up, he let go and turned to walk back inside; but just as he did, he stepped on something: "Huh?...What's this?" He picked up the small device, and looked at it closely: it was a grey, plastic clip, with a red blinking dot. He assumed it must have broken off when he pulled the lever, but he couldn't see where it fit inside the box. He figured his partner would know, though, so he took it with him.

"Hey..." he started, as he entered the control room, "does this—"

"Get in here!"

"What is it?!...Did the feed come back?!"

"Yes!...They're in the last room!"

"Oh, crap!" He dropped the device on the table — forgetting all about it — then he picked up the phone and dialed frantically: "Hello?!...I need the Director, right away!" He was panicking now — he knew they were in *big* trouble: "Yes, sir...I'm sorry, sir...w-we had some technical issues, and—...they're in the last room...I know, sir, I'm sorry, it was out of our control...I—...I will...yes, sir!" As the line went dead, he turned to the other guard: his face was pale — he was terrified!

"What did he say?!"

"He's pissed!...Oh, God, we're gonna get it!"

"Relax, stay calm...let's go through the arrival protocol."

"Yeah, OK."

"If we have everything ready, they'll probly forget about this."

They grabbed what they needed and rushed to the main house. The guard station was left unattended now, but that didn't matter — they had to make sure everything was perfect before the others arrived.

In their rush of activity, they didn't notice that one person was missing from the group. If they had looked up, even once before they ran out, they would have seen a monitor, off to the left — they would have seen a body, lying face-up on the ground. Just one body, though, not two.

FORTY-FIVE

There was nothing—Teddy couldn't hear a sound. It all happened in slow motion: the trigger was pulled, and her head dropped. He was screaming; he was fighting to get free. The wires that bound him cut through his skin, soaking his hands in blood.

Seven stood, emotionless, watching him writhe in desperate agony. They were two sides of the same coin — one had no feeling, the other felt too much. Teddy's senses were coming back to him: he felt the searing pain in his arms, and his face was drenched with tears. Then sounds, all around him — they flooded his chaotic mind. He wasn't thinking clearly; he wasn't thinking. His screams filled the room, as they tore at his vocal cords: in the time it took for Seven to pull that trigger, his entire world had come to an end.

"It's OK..." the assassin calmly spoke, "you won't be apart for long." He pointed the gun at Teddy's head, and steadied his hand: he would put him out of his misery — it was mercy, he was doing the right thing. But then, he felt something buzzing—it was a phone; not his, but the one he took from the man in his apartment. He lowered the gun and reached into his pocket: there was an alert — a meeting! *This could be interesting,* he thought, *I may need this one for later.* He walked around behind

Teddy — and in one swift motion, smashed the gun into his head! For the second time that night, he was out cold.

Seven didn't have time to waste; it would take him over two hours just to get there, so he had to be quick. He wrapped Emma in blankets, and put her in the backseat of the car; then, he removed Teddy from the chair, retied him, and taped over his mouth. He locked him in the trunk — that way, if he woke up, he wouldn't be a problem. The last thing he did, before setting off, was pick up the backpack with his gear — he'd stashed it behind the garbage cans earlier that night, before he rang the doorbell. Now, fully prepared, he set off to end things.

ΔΔΔ

He had to leave the city and drive upstate. It was late — so late it was becoming early — but the highway still had more cars than he anticipated. Once he got off, though, onto the twisting, winding backroads, he was able to make up the time. The only lights around were those of his headlamps, and the stars overhead — whenever they weren't blocked by rainclouds. The road was wet; it had obviously been raining quite heavily before, and he was very pleased with Teddy's choice of car. *If nothing else, he's good for something.* The phone said he was almost there, but he couldn't see anything up ahead — there was nothing on the GPS, either.

Just a few miles to go, and there was a clearing in the trees: he glimpsed something as he drove past, so he turned around and went back to see what it was. An old, abandoned house — more like a cottage, really — he went inside and looked around.

He recognized immediately what had happened.

Fire damage. It wasn't recent; this place must have been deserted long ago. It did provide one benefit, however — he cleared out a space in the rubble, and placed Emma's body there. He covered her up crudely, with stones and dirt and pieces of old wood — this wasn't a burial, just a place to hide her so she wouldn't be easily found. After that, he got back in the car and kept driving.

ΔΔΔ

As far as the maps knew, he wasn't even on the road anymore — he was driving through trees. But he was almost there: less than a mile away. He slowed his pace, and pulled over to the side of the road; there was a gap in the tree line, so he drove into it, concealing the car. He took out his bag, and put on his body armor; then, he loaded his guns, and put them in his utility belt along with the knives — the rest of the journey would be on foot.

As he slowly made his way through the dense forest, he was sure to keep an eye out for boobytraps. With the night vision, he was able to see clearly, and he knew they'd have sensors or tripwires around the compound — he was right, but instead of disabling them, he went around. He didn't want them to know he was coming, and a security device going down would only raise suspicion.

Up ahead, he saw an end to the trees: it was just open land at first, but as he approached, he saw a building — a castle. There was a long, gravel driveway — it wrapped into a circular path, just in front of the main door. He lingered for a while, admiring the sheer magnitude of it all, but something was odd — there were still no lights. He took off his goggles and looked around — nothing. *Maybe they're not here yet?...No, someone must be.*

He looked back, towards the gate, and noticed a smaller, more modern building — it wasn't a house; more like a utility structure. He decided to get a better look; but as he approached, he saw someone walk out — it was a man, lighting a cigarette. Seven inched forward, being very careful to watch his step; he hid behind a large tree, but as he tried to peek out from the side, he stepped on a branch — *crack!* He could've kicked himself for being so careless! The man came closer, and Seven took out his gun: he didn't want to kill him, though — not yet, anyway.

Luckily, the man threw his cigarette to the ground and went back inside. Seven relaxed; but he waited there for a long while, to make sure no one else was around — then, he moved out from behind the trees. He walked slowly around the building, realizing what it was: a security post — a place where they could monitor any nearby activity. He located the junction box and took out a signal scrambler: he clipped it to the main feed wire, freezing all camera inputs to the surveillance system — now, without them watching, he could roam freely.

He took his time, walking the entire circumference of the grounds — but he found no other people; no signs of movement. He was about to go back to the car, to make sure Teddy was still contained, when he saw something — high up, on a large, flat section of the roof: there were people moving.

FORTY-SIX

Mav opened the hatch: nothing happened — no water came in. Maybe they were wrong?

"Alright..." Danny posed, "now what?"

"That couldn't be the answer..." Ash insisted, "could it?"

"No..." Zelda argued, "how could it be?"

Mav crouched down, and tried to peek inside. "Do you see anything?" Danny asked him.

"No..." he replied, "it's empty."

"I have an idea!" Zelda announced, "Maybe it's only the *even*-numbered valves that have water, and the odd numbers let it back out?"

"Hmm..." Ash mused, "you might have something there."

Mav stood up, and looked around the room: "Should we try one more?" They all agreed, and Danny found another small, odd-numbered hatch: number '19' — it was just slightly larger in diameter than number '1'. Like before, Mav grabbed the T-handle and pulled it open — the result was the same: nothing.

"OK, then..." Zelda noted, "at least we're getting somewhere." After that, they opened two more: numbers '7' and '23'. Both were about the same size as the others, and just as safe. What they needed now was to find a hatch wide enough for them to fit through — one that would lead them out of this final challenge, and hopefully, to whoever was behind all this.

While the others were looking for large, odd-numbered hatches, Ash stood in front of the screen, reading the clue again: "'One mistake will not divide you'...'one mistake will not divide you'..." She kept repeating that line over and over again.

Danny noticed her standing alone, mumbling to herself: "Hey, you OK?"

"Look at this..." she pointed out, "does this line sound odd to you?"

He examined the text, but didn't see anything out of the ordinary: "You know they word things funny...it's probly nothing."

Just then, Mav called to them — hatch number '9' looked to be the most likely candidate. It was wide enough for them to *just* squeeze through, and it was also the right height — close to the ground. Logically, it seemed like the best choice.

"But, why use the word 'divide'?" she wondered, drawing his attention back to the screen, "They coulda said 'one mistake will not be the end'...or, 'one mistake will not cost you'...but they didn't."

"Yeah..." he agreed, "but we already know the odd numbers are safe, so it's fine."

"I guess." she shrugged. But then, she was hit with a sudden realization — she quickly turned to Mav, who was opening the '9' hatch: "Stop!"

It was too late — the water rushed in!

FORTY-SEVEN

Seven opened his eyes — how long was he out? He didn't know, but he couldn't believe he was still alive. As he started to move, he realized he had landed in the bushes: other than a few scrapes and scratches, he was unharmed. The body armor must have helped, but to survive a fall of that magnitude? It was amazing — it bordered on miraculous.

He winced and groaned as he slowly stood up; he still had his goggles on, so he could see perfectly despite the darkness that surrounded him. Once he made it to his feet, he stretched his arms and legs out, making sure nothing was broken: right in front of him, plastered on the ground, was one of the kids from the roof — the tall, lanky one with the green jacket. He hadn't been so lucky — he'd missed the bushes and landed face-up on the concrete path.

Seven stared for a while at his broken, mangled body; but then he moved on — he had a mission, and those kids were just a minor distraction. The first thing he had to do was locate his utility belt — it had gotten caught on a jagged stone, about halfway up the wall, and he was forced to unhook it. "Come on…come on…" he scanned the area around him, "where is it?"

Eventually, he found it: when it dropped, he assumed it had fallen to the ground — but it hadn't; it was dangling from a jutting piece of rock, about thirty feet up. He climbed the wall, cursing under his breath the whole way. He'd almost reached it, but he had to lean out — it was just beyond his grasp. He eased himself further off the side; and, with the tips of his fingers, he managed to pull it in. He got it free of the rock; then, he swung it outward and let go.

As he was making his way back down, he noticed something off in the distance. At this height, he was about level with the trees, and he could see streaks of yellow and red lights coming closer. He knew what it meant — 'they' were almost here.

He hurried down from the wall, grabbed his belt, and began making his way back to the car; once he'd reached the trees, however, he crouched down and watched the procession. The gate opened, and four black Range Rovers drove in: they went past him and around the circular driveway, stopping just in front of the castle. He looked on, as several people stepped out of the cars and went inside.

These were the people who had the answers. These were the people who tried to kill him. These were the people who would *pay*.

FORTY-EIGHT

Mav and Zelda were knocked off their feet! They slid across the floor, crashing into Ash and Danny! The water was coming in too fast for the small, open valves to let it out — if they didn't act quick, they wouldn't last more than a few minutes!

"They tricked us!" Zelda cried.

"No!" Ash exclaimed, "It wasn't odd numbers, it was *prime* numbers!"

"Prime?!" Danny questioned, "Are you sure?!"

"That's what the line meant...one mistake won't 'divide' you!" They were so eager to get out, that they hadn't thought it through: prime numbers can only be divided by themselves, and the number 'one'.

The water was coming in harder now — they had even less time than they thought. The room was filling up, and they still had no idea which hatch led to safety. "Everyone!" Mav yelled, "Find a prime hatch and open it!" Their feet weren't touching the floor anymore — they were swimming!

It was hard to see anything, especially under-water, so they had to feel the numbers with their hands. Danny held his breath and dove down. *Three...no, it's thirty-three...not that one!* He kept going, rejecting one after the other. Soon, though, he had to come up for air;

and as he did, he heard Ash's voice: "I got one!...Number seven!"

"How big is it?!" Mav asked her.

"Not very, but it's something!...Keep looking!"

He took another breath, and went under again. He cycled through possibilities at a rapid pace, but he couldn't keep track of them all — he found himself wasting time, going back to hatches he'd already checked. Darkness, panic, and being submerged, was hardly the recipe for efficiency. Luckily, while he was floundering, Mav managed to open the '3' and '11' hatches — they, too, weren't very big, but they helped to slow the rise of the water. "This is useless!" Danny shouted, "All the prime hatches are too small!"

"That's it!" Ash realized, "There's gotta be only one that's big enough!" Yes, of course, that must be it! Of all the prime-numbered hatches, they should only be able to fit through one!

This was a much more effective way to search: the big hatches were few and far between, and not only were there less of them, but their size and spacing made it easy to keep track of the wrong ones. The water was rising quickly, though — there were only a few feet left before it reached the ceiling. They each took a wall, and Danny hurried through his checks. *Six, no!...Ten, no!...Twelve, no!* His panic was at the redline: this was it — they had to get out now!

Then, it hit him. *The ceiling!* With the water level this high, they were finally able to check it. He swam upward, and saw that there were only three big hatches. *Fifteen, no, come on!...Twenty-two, no!...One more, that has to be it!* He went over and felt it. *Two?!...No, that can't...wait, two's a prime number!* He twisted the handle and pulled it open — air! He found the way out! He stuck his head up and took a breath, then he went back for the others.

First, he found Zelda, and pointed her to safety; Mav was close by, so he sent him through next. *Where's Ash?!* He looked everywhere, but he couldn't find her. *There she is!* Her jacket was caught on something! A T-handle was stuck in her pocket, so he wedged it out; he put his feet against the wall and grabbed her waist — then he pushed off! He pulled her with him through the water: when they were below the open hatch, he shoved her straight up — Mav grabbed her and pulled her out. When Danny emerged, he saw her hunched over on her hands and knees — she was coughing, but she was alright.

FORTY-NINE

Danny climbed out of the hole, and tried to dry himself off. He was ringing the water from his hoodie, when Ash approached and wrapped her arms around him.

"Thank you." she whispered.

"It was nothing..." he blushed, "you'd have done the same for me."

"Yeah, but still...thanks."

They all got as dry as they could: the last challenge was over now, and it was time for answers. There was only one way for them to go — through an opening in the wall, which led to a wide corridor. They went on, cautiously, as their shoes squished and bubbled with every step; their damp clothes seemed to magnify the cold, and the sounds of their chattering teeth echoed off the walls.

After a few minutes of walking, they saw a light — this was the end. Mav stuck his arms out, stopping them just before they rounded the final corner: "Whatever happens, we stick together...agreed?" The others nodded; then, they all stepped forward.

The room they entered was huge, with very high ceilings. Columns of moonlight shone in through tall, narrow windows, and hundreds of yellow flickering candles formed illuminated pools all around them. There were still small pockets of shadows, however, scattered sporadically throughout; but a large chandelier in the center kept them mostly confined to the outer edges. The windows were flanked by long, heavy curtains, which were tied in place against the walls. Below the chandelier were two tables, arranged in a 'T' shape. The short side had five empty chairs — seemingly one for each of them, plus Sam. At the long table sat six people: two men on the right side, with a woman between them; a man and woman on the left side, with one empty chair — and finally, at the head of the table was their professor, Mr. Bell.

"Well done!" He rose to his feet and applauded, as they entered the room, with the other five quickly joining him. "Please..." he gestured, "sit down." They moved slowly towards the empty seats, trying as best they could to absorb this bizarre scene. "Towels are on the chairs..." he told them, "and your personal items are in boxes over there."

Zelda took the seat on the far-right, and Ash sat next to her; Danny followed, sitting down in the middle chair, while Mav went to retrieve the boxes: "Here you go, Dan." He handed them off as he sat down — Danny took his, then he passed the rest to Ash and Zelda.

"I'm sure you all have many questions..." Mr. Bell acknowledged, "believe me, I know, I went through this experience myself."

"*Experience?*" Mav scoffed, "What the hell did you do to us?!" He slammed his fists down, startling the people at the long table.

"Now, now..." Mr. Bell calmed them, "it's OK... after what they've been through, this is to be expected."

"Mister Bell..." Danny started, "what is this?...

Why are we here?"

"It was a test, Danny...an initiation, of sorts...and you passed, you did brilliantly!"

"A test for what, though?"

"We are all members of a special group..." he explained, "known simply as 'The Order'."

"Is that the secret club?" Zelda asked him.

"Not a club...a *society*, of exceptional individuals."

"And, what does this secret society do?" she inquired.

"In short...everything."

There was a long pause, as they tried to process his words; then, Danny spoke again: "So, the infinity symbol...that's your sign?"

"Correct...The Order *has* always been, and *will* always be...The Order is infinite." He saw that he'd piqued their curiosity, so he went on: "The world as you know it is an illusion...I know it may seem like things are random or chaotic, but everything is actually a deliberate orchestration."

"What?" Mav balked, "No way."

"It's the truth..." the lady on the right insisted, "technology, finance, energy, governments...we control them all."

"OK..." Ash chimed in, "supposing all this is true, what's it have to do with us?"

"Everything." Mr. Bell claimed, "*You* are our future."

"Future?" Danny puzzled.

"I told you, our group is one of exceptional people...only the truly exceptional could have made it through the maze."

"And..." Zelda followed up, "how many *have* made

it through?"

"You're the first to do it in almost thirty years." he revealed. Then he turned to Danny, looking him square in the eyes: "In fact, the last time anyone made it out was your parents' group."

"My parents?...They were involved in this?"

"They were two of our brightest young minds." he beamed, "They met here...they sat right where you are now." He couldn't believe it — were his parents really members of this group? The trials he'd just gone through; the close calls and near misses — is that how they met?

"So, what's the purpose?" Ash challenged, "What does 'The Order' do?"

One of the men on the right spoke up: "We exist to serve humanity...to help the world...to do for people what they can't do themselves."

"You mean you control them..." Zelda sniped, "you manipulate them."

"Look at your phones..." Mr. Bell urged, "who do you think developed the technology?...The Internet?... All the things you can't live without?...*Electricity*?...Who do you think was behind it all?" They didn't respond: "The Order goes back centuries...our methods may have changed over the years, but our mission has always been the same...we do what is necessary to advance civilization, no matter the cost."

"Lemme get this straight..." Mav asserted, "you kidnap people...you put them in life-threatening situations...and whoever makes it out, you offer them jobs?"

"That would be the layman's way of looking at it." the man on the left replied.

"Then, where are the others?" Zelda wondered, "The ones who *didn't* make it?"

Mr. Bell looked to his colleagues, before responding: "Unfortunately, there will always be losses on the road to greatness."

"What does that mean?...They're dead?!" He hesitated for a moment; then nodded lightly, confirming her fears: "What about their families?!...How can you justify this?!" He explained that the following day, there would be a news report about a building that caught fire, killing all inside; the ones who didn't survive the trials would be listed among the casualties. "Wait..." she suddenly realized, "where's Sam?...There's an extra chair...did he get out?"

"We thought he was with you..." the professor said, "but the guards discovered his body just before you arrived...it seems he fell from the roof."

She snapped around to Mav: "You lied to me!"

"It was that man!" Danny yelled, "Sam tackled him, and they fell over together!"

"Man?" Mr. Bell questioned, "What man?"

"There was a man on the roof..." Ash informed them, "he attacked us."

"There...there wasn't anyone else..." he stuttered, "just two guards, who monitored your progress...but no one was inside the maze."

"Yes there was!" she charged.

Mr. Bell looked around at his colleagues, but they could offer no explanation: "What kind of man was he?"

"The bad kind." Seven answered. He stepped into the light, holding his gun out in front of him. With his free hand, he grabbed an empty seat and pulled it out; then, he reached behind one of the curtains, and dragged someone towards it. They were bound and gagged — he shoved them down into the chair.

Instantly, Danny leapt to his feet: "Uncle Teddy!"

FIFTY

Danny was petrified — why was his uncle here? Why was he tied up, with duct tape over his mouth?! Mav put a hand on his shoulder, and slowly eased him back down; as he looked up, he realized why — the assassin's gun was pointed at his head.

"What do you want?" Mav asked him.

"This doesn't concern you..." he replied, "just keep quiet, and stay out of my way...I'll let you go when I'm done."

"Mmm...hmmm...mmm!" Teddy tried to warn them, but the tape muffled his attempts.

"Shut up!" Seven smashed an elbow to the back of his head! He then turned to the people at the long table: "Do you know who I am?" They glanced around at each other, but no one responded, so he casually raised his gun and pulled the trigger — the silent bullet hit one of the men on the right side, killing him instantly. The others recoiled in horror, as he fell to the floor: "Let's try again... do you know who I am?"

"Yes." the professor spoke up, "I do."

"Very good." Seven moved closer to him, and noticed that his right hand was under the table: "I'm afraid you're wasting your time...the guards are dead." As Mr. Bell slowly moved his trembling hand back on top, he looked around at his colleagues, who seemed more frightened than the kids. They had just been through hell, after all — why would coming face-to-face with the Devil shock them? "S...H...O...T." he slowly spelled out, "What does it mean?"

"Shot?" Danny answered.

Seven looked back and showed him the gun: "Speak again, and you're dead." He returned to Mr. Bell, pushing the end of the silencer to his temple: "*Now*."

"OK, OK...what do you want to know?"

"What is it?...What does SHOT mean?...What did they do to me?"

"Do to you?"

"Yes!...The experiments, tell me everything."

"They...they didn't do anything *to* you..."

"I'm not in the mood for games..." he threatened, "you have five seconds to tell me the truth...four...three..."

"Wait!...OK...S.H.O.T....it stands for Synthetic Human Operations Team."

"Synthetic human?...What is that?"

"It was a secret project that a few of our scientists worked on...it was a long time ago."

"What was the purpose?"

"In the beginning, they were trying to find cures for—"

"That's enough." the lady on the left objected.

Seven swung his arm to her and pulled the trigger — *thud* — she fell out of her chair, and hit the floor. His eyes never moved from the professor — he didn't blink once: "You were saying?"

Mr. Bell looked around at his three remaining colleagues — they were crippled with fear — he had no choice, but to cooperate: "I was...uh..."

"Synthetic human program..." Seven reminded him, "keep going."

He swallowed hard: "Right, well...it started out as genetic engineering, trying to cure diseases at the molecular level...but what they found was that they weren't just able to change bad cells, they could change good ones, too."

"Change them how?"

"Make them stronger, make them better...more resilient."

"What does that have to do with *me*?" Seven jammed the gun further into the man's head.

"I'm getting to that!"

"Get to it fast."

"As the project advanced, they were able to grow new cells...then tissue...eventually, they realized they could create an entire *human being* from scratch."

"What?!...You're saying I'm some sort of...Frankenstein monster?"

"Synthetic human..." Mr. Bell repeated, "or 'Models' as we called them...you have blood, organs, nerves...you're made of the same things we are, just with some...improvements."

"Improvements?...What does that mean?"

"You're genetically enhanced to be better than the average person...you have abilities we could never hope to possess." His eyes then moved to the assassin's tattoo: "You're *Model Seven.*"

ΔΔΔ

While all this was going on, Teddy tried to signal

Danny with his eyes — he was gesturing for them to get out. Seven had agreed to let Emma go, too, and he knew how much that promise was worth.

"What's Teddy tryna say?" Mav whispered.

"I dunno, but we can't leave him here."

ΔΔΔ

Suddenly, the assassin erupted with rage! He slammed the table, then smashed the gun into Mr. Bell's head! "Wait!...Stop!...There's more!" Blood was now splattered on his face.

"Speak!" Seven yelled.

"We can help you!...That rage you feel, it's how they made you...it's how they *designed* you...we can help you be free."

"What are you saying?...I can't control my actions?!"

"No, of course you can!...But the anger, the desire for death and destruction...they made you this way...to feel no empathy, no pain...you were created to be the perfect killing machine."

"Because that's what *you* wanted!" Seven charged, "You made us this way, because you needed soldiers!"

"U-Us?" the professor stammered, "You know about the others?"

Seven took the papers out of his pocket, and threw them on the table: "Open them."

Mr. Bell did as instructed. "They're not all like this..." he said, looking down at the data table, "they're not all like...you."

"What does that mean?"

"You were made to be a soldier...others were too,

but not all...some had a different purpose."

Seven looked at his arm: "So others were given happiness, while I was fated for despair...who are you to play God?"

"It wasn't me..." the professor pleaded, "I wasn't involved."

Seven turned the gun to the man on the left, and fired — another dead: "Who was?"

"T-They're all gone now...the Director is the only one—"

"Aren't *you* the Director?"

"No, I'm not!...No one sees him!"

"Where is he?"

"I don't know, I swear!...None of us do!"

He paused for a moment, then asked again: "Who *else* was involved?"

"There's none left..." Mr. Bell insisted, "Henry Zeller was the last one...his partner, Miles Logan, was... removed, many years ago."

"You killed my father?!" Danny screamed.

"Your father?" Seven uttered, "It was your father who made me this way?"

Teddy knew what would happen next — he leapt up and over the table, just as the trigger was pulled. "No!" Danny cried. It was too late — the bullet hit him!

Mr. Bell and the others saw their opening — they grabbed Seven, and tried to wrestle the gun away from him! He kicked one of the men off, then shot him in the stomach; next, he grabbed the woman by the throat, and began choking her.

Danny reached over and ripped the tape from Teddy's mouth: "I'm gonna get you out!...You're gonna be OK!"

"It's t-too late." he coughed. He was panting heavily, and blood poured from his open chest: "Go…now."

"No!…I won't leave you!" Danny grabbed his uncle, as tears streamed down his face.

"Black box…" Teddy choked out, "i-in the living room…now, go!"

Seven tossed aside the woman's lifeless body like a rag doll — he was now one-on-one with the professor. Ash and Zelda bolted for the door, while Mav grabbed Danny and pulled him away.

"Go…" Teddy wheezed.

Once he saw that Danny was safely out, he closed his eyes: his head fell back, and rolled to the side. The last thing he saw were streaks of sunshine, falling on a tangled mess of blond hair — then, the light consumed him; he was gone.

FIFTY-ONE

"Hurry up!" Zelda screamed. Mav pulled Danny along, but it was like dragging an anchor. There were four black SUVs in the line, and the girls ran to the first one — Ash got in the front passenger seat, while Zelda hopped in the back. When the boys caught up, Mav shoved Danny in next to her; he then moved to the driver's side door, but he was in for a shock — a dead body fell out! Clearly, Seven didn't lie about killing the guards.

Ash checked the mirror, and saw the assassin step out the front door: "He's coming!" Mav jumped in and started the car: he mashed the throttle, and the Range Rover twitched and squirmed on the loose gravel driveway. Seven watched, unfazed, as they sped away — he knew they wouldn't get far. He turned and ran to the trees, headed straight for Teddy's Subaru.

"Something's wrong!" Mav exclaimed.

"What is it?!" Ash asked him.

"The car...it's all over the place!"

He tried his best to keep it on the road, but the rear tires had been slashed — even *he* couldn't keep it pointing straight! When they made it through the gate, the pavement was still slick from the earlier rain; the tires were shredded — and as the metal rims touched the asphalt, the car snapped around! The back end swung off the road, and the wheels dug into the wet soil: the four of them looked on, helpless, as the world around them tipped sideways. Bits of broken glass scattered everywhere, as sparks shot across the driver's side — the car flipped over! It was skidding down the road!

When it finally ground to a halt, Mav was the first to speak: "Is…is everyone alright?"

"Yeah…" Ash answered, "I think so."

"Me too." Zelda added.

"Danny?"

"Yeah, *ah*, I'm good."

They crawled to the back of the car, and exited through the rear hatch. Now what? Seven was coming, and they were stranded again.

"Let's move…" Mav insisted, "we're sitting ducks out here."

They followed him further down the road; they thought about taking refuge in the forest, but being so close to the castle, they didn't want to risk falling into another trap. Still, they hugged the tree line, ready to take cover at a moment's notice.

Then, Ash saw something up ahead: "What's that?"

"What?" Mav questioned, "I don't see anything."

"I do!" Zelda confirmed. It was a house — a small house — just ahead. They approached it, cautiously, moving around it in a circle: it looked abandoned, so they decided to go in. The cottage was barely standing; the wooden beams and pillars were charred black, and parts of the roof had collapsed.

"This place sticks out…" Danny warned them, "he'll come in here for sure."

"Good…" Mav declared, "at least we'll be ready for

him."

"What?!" Zelda balked, "We can't beat that guy... didn't you hear what they said?...He's some kinda...super soldier!"

"Look..." Mav explained, "we can either wait for him to catch us, or set a trap for him here."

There was a brief silence, then Ash agreed: "OK, what'd you have in mind?" Mav pointed out that one of the main support pillars was breaking, near the back-left corner. At the top, it had a five-way joint that connected the roof beams to the walls: if they could somehow get him into that corner, then knock out the post, it would cause that section of the roof to come crashing down on top of him. It was a good plan, but a risky one.

"What the hell?" Danny shrugged, "Let's do it." Zelda was the last one on board; but once she was, they got to work moving stones and pieces of wood — they had to get everything ready: *fast*.

Then she screamed! She was standing at the other side of the room, staring down at a pile of rubble.

"What is it?!" Ash cried.

"There's a dead body here!"

They ran over, and moved the debris: it was a woman, rolled-up in blankets. Mav reached down and touched her hand: "She's still warm."

"Wait..." Danny noticed, "these blankets, they're from my house."

Mav stood up, and brushed off his hands: "That's where he got Teddy...she musta been there too." Just then, a car pulled up outside. "Quick!" he ordered, "Get in position!"

They each took their hiding places, and waited on pins and needles. Seven didn't kick down the door, or smash it in — instead, he gently opened the handle and stepped inside. "Hiding in a little stone house?" he taunted them, "What does that make me?...The Wolf?" They didn't reply; they didn't make a sound, as he slowly moved through the cottage. The light from the car came in at his back — to Danny, crouched down behind two wooden barrels, it looked as though the Grim Reaper had just arrived: "Come out, come out, wherever you are..."

Then, as he stepped over an 'X' on the floor — Mav let go! He fell from the ceiling, landing right on top of him: "Now!" The others jumped out from the shadows: Zelda grabbed the gun, and Ash took the knives from his belt. Danny rushed to help Mav; but, before he could get there — Seven pushed up off the floor, sending him crashing into the wall! Now on his feet, he grabbed Danny and rammed him into the post — it cracked, but it didn't break!

Next, he turned to Zelda — she had the gun pointed at his chest. "Do it..." he told her, "kill me." Her nerves were out of control: her hands trembled violently, as her eyes filled with tears — she couldn't shoot him even if she wanted to!

With one swat of his hand, he knocked her down — the gun went flying across the floor! It was Seven and Ash now, and her nerves were far steadier. He faked to the right, but she didn't flinch; then he faked left — again, she was unmoved. He relaxed his shoulders and stood upright: "You're not afraid, are you?"

"No." she replied. He could tell she wasn't lying — the steel in her eyes backed her up.

"Neither am I!" Mav yelled. Seven turned to his right, and stared down the barrel of the gun — Mav squeezed the trigger! Again! Again! Three shots! The first hit him in the left shoulder, the second in the chest, and the third in his right hip — he was rocked! As he stumbled backwards, Danny got up and kicked him from behind: he fell forward, into the back-left corner of the room — he was right where they wanted him!

He began to stand up, so Mav rushed in and threw his fist — it caught Seven in the face and he went hurtling to the floor! "Now!" Danny shouted. Mav aimed the gun at the pillar, and emptied the clip — it was on the verge of failing, but it wasn't quite there yet.

Seven was starting to get up again, so Mav spun around and hit the post with a roundhouse kick — it broke, but the roof didn't collapse! He was on his feet now; he wiped the blood from his side, and looked up at them: "Is that it?"

"No..." Ash said, "this is!" She held onto Mav's shoulders and swung herself around — her right foot smashed the damaged post, breaking it completely! The beams collapsed, taking parts of the walls and roof down with them — he was buried!

They all held their breath, waiting anxiously for signs of movement — but there weren't any. "Come on..." Mav sighed, "let's go."

FIFTY-TWO

Mav, Danny, Zelda, and Ash walked out together. Teddy's car was still running, so they opened the doors and got inside. Mav drove, with Zelda in the passenger seat; Danny got in behind, and Ash sat next to him. This night had changed them: they could never go back to who they were before — those people were gone forever.

As they drove down the winding backroads, a light began to creep in from the east. The sun was rising: it came in through the trees, and stung their weary eyes. That's what happens when you're in the dark too long — you forget that it's not forever.

They kept driving onwards in total silence. What was there to say? Danny turned to his left, and stared out at the trees as they went by; then he looked to the right, just ahead of him: Zelda's head hung to one side — she had passed out. He knew they could all use the rest, but how could he sleep after what happened?

Ash, on the other hand, was wide awake: she stared out the right-side window, relishing the warm sunlight as it kissed her face. He didn't know what she was thinking; but for the first time since he saw her that night — standing alone, in the large circle room — he didn't care. Teddy was dead; his uncle, the man who raised him, the only family he'd ever known. What were they to do now? Where were they to go? They couldn't go back to school, it wasn't safe anymore — but, where was?

These weren't questions that could be answered quickly; so he checked with Mav, who assured him he was fine to keep driving, then he sighed and shifted his body. He leaned his head against the glass, and closed his eyes; but just as he did, he felt something touch his hand — he looked up, and saw Ash staring back at him. She bit down on her lower lip, as little blue streaks dripped from her eyes. She didn't speak; there was nothing to say.

FIFTY-THREE

Sunlight poured in through the holes in the roof and walls. Miniature dust storms raged and swirled all around. There was a calmness, though; an unsettling quiet that hung in the air. Suddenly, a twitch from the rubble — then nothing; there was no one around to hear it, anyway. Then another one, louder this time — the pile shifted!

He rose from the ashes: the assassin, the soldier, the *Model*. He walked through the front door, and into the light. He examined his body: no broken bones. His shoulder and hip wounds weren't bleeding, either — they were *healing*.

There was a long, thin knife on the ground — he picked it up, and plunged it into his chest! He didn't wince; he didn't make a sound. He found the bullet and wedged it out, then he held it up to the light. When he looked down again, he saw that the hole was closing — he smiled.

End of Vol. I